Dear Mystery Lover,

Doug Allyn is a nine-time Edgar nominee. That's right, nine nominations! He is considered the master of the mystery short story and last year he took the Edgar home. I'm very pleased to introduce *Icewater Mansions*, his first DEAD LETTER mystery, and a truly inspired one at that.

Michelle Mitchell is a single mother with a very interesting way of making a living. She's been a deep-water welder stationed in the Gulf of Mexico, but when news of her father's death in Michigan surfaces, she returns to her hometown to settle his affairs. What she discovers makes her put her deep-water talents to the test in the icy waters of Lake Huron.

Icewater Mansions is tightly knit and full of spellbinding investigation. Doug is so skilled at bringing the underwater world to life, that you'll be taking deep breaths hours after you've finished the read.

Doug's next Michelle Mitchell mystery, *Black Water*, is now available in hardcover from St. Martin's Press.

Keep your eye out for DEAD LETTER—and build yourself a library of paperback mysteries to die for.

Yours in crime,

Shawn Coyne
Senior Editor
St. Martin's DEAD LETTER Paperback Mysteries

Other Titles from St. Martin's Dead Letter Mysteries

ICEWATER MANSIONS

MANSIONS

DOUG ALLYN

St. Martin's Paperbacks

ICEWATER MANSIONS

Copyright © 1995 by Doug Allyn.

All rights reserved. No part of this book may be used or reproduced in any manner whatsoever without written permission except in the case of brief quotations embodied in critical articles or reviews. For information address St. Martin's Press, 175 Fifth Avenue, New York, N.Y. 10010.

Library of Congress Catalog Card Number: 94-47204

ISBN: 0-312-95764-5

Printed in the United States of America

St. Martin's Press hardcover edition/March 1995
St. Martin's Paperbacks edition/March 1996

10 9 8 7 6 5 4 3 2 1

SPECIAL THANKS TO:

Gordon Lightfoot, for his lyrics,
Jim Allyn, for his inspiration,
and Bill Atkins, for his expertise.

CHAPTER 1

A WINTER'S DAY IN PURGATORY. I was brooding in a smoky lakefront saloon, listening to Willie Nelson moan "Blue Eyes Crying" from a jukebox that somebody'd kicked half to death. The roughnecks down the bar looked even sorrier than Willie sounded, gloomy losers in seedy clothes, muttering about the Pistons-Bulls game on the TV, reading their futures in the bottom of a glass.

Two hardcase young studs in leather jackets were shooting pool in the corner, eight ball, dollar a point. The frost-rimmed window behind them rattled with every gust of wind off Thunder Bay.

I'd hate to think I blended in, but I probably did. A woman drinking alone, still wearing the scruffy jeans and parka I'd thrown on for the long flight home, no makeup, not even lipstick. My hair hadn't seen a comb all day and my mood was a perfect match for the bar's ambience. Surly. Sad. Down in the dumps.

The bartender was a semihunk by local standards, black hair pulled back into a taut ponytail, white shirt open at the throat, a gold Jerusalem cross resting on smooth copper skin. Ojibway blood perhaps, or Cree. The ponytail made him look like a gangster from a *Miami Vice* rerun, which was appropriate, since he was pocketing half the cash that came over the counter.

The only other female in the room was the waitress. I'm tall for a woman, nearly five nine in stockings, but she was much taller, a redheaded amazon in a black Detroit Pistons T-shirt, camo fatigue pants. And combat boots. She could've passed for

1

Jack Palance's sister, wide mouth, muscular arms, large red-knuckled hands. One of the pool shooters patted her casually on the bottom as she passed. She gave him a tight grin and a friendly elbow to the ribs that nearly folded him in half. Good for her. He didn't touch her again.

"You ain't made much of a dent in your beer, babe," the bartender said, startling me out of my blues. "Anything wrong with it?"

"Actually, there is. The lipstick smear on the glass isn't my shade. Could I have a clean glass? Please."

"No problem, hon." He picked up my stein, his eyes locked on mine, then slowly licked it clean with tip of his tongue. "How's that? Better?" he asked, sliding the mug back in my general direction, slopping suds on the bar.

I eyed the foam a moment, flushing, feeling the misery of the last few days simmering, coming to a boil. "You know," I said carefully, "I've been in some deadbeat saloons in my life, but you've got to be the rock-bottom worst bartender I've ever seen. You're not even a good thief."

"What?"

"You heard me. If you're going to steal, sport, don't do it in front of the customers. It's a lot safer to pilfer the till after you close up."

"Look, lady, if you don't like how I run this place, don't let the door hit you in the ass on your way out."

"You're half-right," I said, easing up off my stool. "I don't like the way you run this place. But I'm not the one who's leaving. You are. But before you go, maybe you'd better empty your pockets on the bar."

"You're out of your tree; I ain't emptyin' squat. What are you, some kinda law or somethin'?"

"Worse," I said. "Unfortunately for both of us, I'm the new owner. Michelle Mitchell. Does the name ring a bell?"

"So what if it does?" he said, not giving an inch. "I never seen you before, and you can't just walk in here and—"

"Give it up, Carney," the waitress said. "It's her. Shan

showed me her picture once, and even if he hadn't, she looks enough like him to be his sister."

"Daughter, actually," I said. "As in prodigal."

"I don't give a damn if you're his mother," the bartender growled. "I don't hafta take no crap off you or anybody else. Hey guys, I got me a live one here lookin' for action. Anybody feel like a little fun?"

A couple of rowdies stood up, brightening at the prospect of a scuffle, sharks tasting blood in the water. One of the pool players sauntered toward me, leering, carrying his pool cue.

"Now everybody just cool out," the waitress said, intercepting the pool shooter. "Nobody wants a hassle."

"Especially not over this place," I said, backing away from the bar, moving cautiously around the pool table to keep it between me and the kid with the stick. "I used to wait tables here back in high school. Anybody remember me?"

No response. Only blank stares and the bartender's leer. Chivalry might not be dead around here, but it was in deep trouble. And so was I.

"Never did like it in here," I continued. The kid with the stick reversed his field, blocking the path to the door.

"Why not?" the bartender said. "Too good for it?"

"Nope," I said. "I liked the job fine, just hated being inside. It's always dark as a bat cave in here. The lake and the harbor are less than fifty yards away, but you'd never know it. No view."

I picked up an empty bar stool, hefted it carefully to check its balance. The kid with the pool cue froze, eyeing me warily. Everyone was. "No view," I repeated. "And no ventilation." I took a deep breath, then wheeled and pitched the stool through the front window, exploding it out into the parking lot.

The February wind howled in like a rabid Rottweiler, snapping at the curtains, spraying snow around like foam flecks.

"Gentlemen," I said, picking up a cue stick from the rack, "the Crow's Nest is officially under new management. And as of now, we're closed for remodeling. Drive safe, now, hear?"

"Hey! Wait a minute!" the bartender yelled, outraged, but he was overruled by the swirling windblast and the plummeting room temperature. His customers knew a lost cause when it blew in. They were already gulping their drinks, shrugging into their coats, and heading for the door. I thought the kid with the pool cue might be trouble, but the waitress said something to him and he grinned and tossed his stick on the table.

"Mr. Carney," I said, still holding the cue stick, "I want your keys and the money in your pockets on the bar and then I want you gone. Any problem with that?"

"Look, lady, I know we ain't off to a good start here—"

"We haven't started at all," I said. "We've finished."

"But damn it, I wasn't stealin', exactly. I figured I'd be buyin' you out anyway, so—"

"Maybe you will," I said. "But not today. So I want your keys. And the cash. Please."

"Ah hell," he said bitterly, tossing a wad of crumpled bills on the counter. "Workin' for Shan was bad enough. He was nuts, too, but at least he didn't wreck the place. The damn keys are on the desk in the office. But you ain't seen the last of me, lady. You comin', Red?"

"I don't know," the waitress said, eyeing me frankly. "How about it, Miss Mitchell? Am I fired, too?"

"That depends," I said. "At the moment, I think this place needs a cleaning lady a lot more than a waitress."

"I know which end of a broom is up," Red said, "but I don't do windows. Or at least not quite the way you do."

"Ordinarily, I use Windex like everybody else," I said, looking over the damage. "I'm, um, not quite sure what happened there. I've had kind of a rough week."

"I imagine you have." Red nodded. "Still, you did okay. I usually have a helluva time clearin' the room at closing."

"Speaking of closing, we'd better do something about this draft," I said. "And maybe you could rustle up that broom you mentioned?"

～ Small northern Michigan towns have their pluses, even in the dead of winter. I called Huron Harbor Hardware and Glass and a wizened little gnome in grubby coveralls showed up within the hour: Leonard Misiak. He remembered me and offered his condolences, for the death of my father and my trashed window.

He took his time measuring the frame, clucking over the shattered glass. I frankly expected a song and dance, especially after I said I wanted the new window triple the size of the old one. But when he'd finished his calculations, he said if I'd settle for a unit an inch or so smaller than the triple-size I'd mentioned, he could have an oversized bay window installed by quitting time the next day, and with luck, the insurance should cover most of it. Try finding service like that in Dallas or Detroit.

The local law was only slightly less prompt. I was taping a temporary cardboard patch over the window frame when a sheriff's department black-and-white rolled into the parking lot. Two officers climbed out. I vaguely recalled the taller one from the old days, Charlie Bauer. Remembered his size more than anything else. He stood six six, probably weighed three hundred plus, and looked as big as a building in his bulky brown uniform. He'd gone a bit jowly, soft around the middle, but he was still impressive, square-faced, gray-eyed, steel gray brush cut.

His partner was only slightly smaller, an iron-pumper from the look of him, broad shoulders, narrow waist, his eyes hidden behind mirrored aviator shades. His brown hair was tightly permed, artfully combed to camouflage a rising forehead. Charlie strolled up to the window, eyed the bar stool and the broken glass all over the ground, then picked up the stool one-handed and carried it in with him. His partner trailed him in like a surly shadow.

"What's going on here?" Charlie said, parking the stool beside the door.

5

"Spring cleaning," I said. "A little early."

"The place can definitely use it," his partner said, glancing around, scowling behind his sunglasses. "Always was a pig-pen."

"Thank you," I said. "Can I offer you gentlemen anything? Before you leave?"

"No thanks," Charlie said. "Not on duty. You're Michelle, right? Shannon Mitchell's daughter?"

"Guilty as charged," I said, offering my hand. He hesitated but accepted it. Grudgingly, I thought.

"Didn't see you at Shan's funeral," he said.

"I've been working down on the Texas Gulf. Mail to the rigs gets delayed sometimes."

"You were workin' on an oil rig?" the deputy said. "Doing what? Cookin'?"

"No, marine construction, actually. Deep-water welding, laying pipe, whatever."

"They hire women for work like that?"

"They don't hire women at all, or men, either, for that matter. They just hire qualified divers who can handle the job. Strange place, Texas. They even elected a lady governor."

"That's their problem."

"Put a cork in it, Jackowski," Charlie said evenly, without turning. "Anybody fill you in on what happened to your dad, Miss Mitchell?"

"Not really," I said. "His attorney, Mr. Cohen, said he was killed in an auto accident."

"Not in the wreck, exactly," Bauer said. "He'd been drinking, ran his pickup off the road a few miles from his house. Apparently got confused in the dark, wandered off into the swamp instead of back to the road. And, um, hypothermia finished him."

"Froze to death," Jackowski put in.

"I know what hypothermia is," I said, swallowing. "You two should have been medics, Charlie. You've got a wonderful bed-side manner."

"Sorry, I never was very good at . . . breakin' bad news."
Bauer shrugged. "And as I recall, you and your dad didn't exactly part friends."

"That was a long time ago," I said.

"Was it? See; that's one of the problems with gettin' older. Nothing seems very long ago. Anyway, love can last a lifetime. Sometimes grudges do, too."

"If it'll ease your mind, there was nothing much left between my father and me, love, hate, or otherwise."

"There was blood," Bauer said. "There was at least that. He left you everything he had."

"Nobody asked him to."

"Most things you inherit come without asking. You two were of a size, you and Shan. You favor him a bit, too, same dark eyes, dark hair. And judging from that broken window there, could be you inherited his temper, too. Too bad. He could be mean, your old man. I was kind of hoping he took it with him. You gonna be staying in town long?"

"I honestly don't know," I said.

"Well, if you stay on, I'd just as soon not have to pick up any more furniture outta your parking lot. We understand each other, Miss Mitchell?"

"Absolutely," I said.

"Good. I knew Shan a lotta years. To be honest, I always expected he'd cash in early, get blown away by a jealous husband or a girlfriend or maybe go divin' out in Lake Huron a time too many. It bothers me some, the way he died. He was banged up in the crash, but he was an old-time hardguy, your father. I've seen him get up off the deck after takin' a punch that would've put most men in traction, then proceed to whip three badasses half his age without breakin' a sweat. He'd been drinkin' that night; blood alcohol was point oh-four. But he drank most nights, and I never saw him so trashed he couldn't crawl out of a ditch."

"What are you saying, Sheriff Bauer? Is there any doubt that it was an accident?"

"No, ma'am, none I'm aware of. You know any reason why there should be?"

"No. But I've been away a long time."

"So you have. Maybe it just bothers me that there was no class to it. Shan was no saint, but by God, he had style. I'm gonna miss him. He deserved to go out better."

"Doesn't everyone?" I asked.

"Maybe they do at that." He nodded, taking a last look around. "Well, I'll leave you ladies to your labors. They've got your dad's pickup over in the county impound lot. Got a few dents, but it's drivable. You owe the county a sixty-buck fee for towing and storage. And for what it's worth, I'm sorry about your father, Miss Mitchell."

"You needn't be on my account," I said evenly. "As you said, we didn't exactly part friends."

CHAPTER 2

"CHARLIE'S NOT A BAD GUY," Red said after Bauer left. "Comes across a little rough sometimes, has to, I guess, but his heart is basic teddy bear."

"Teddy or grizzly?" I said.

"Teddy." She smiled. "His deputy, Jackowski, is more the grisly type. An iron-pumper with the brain of a newt. You have to watch him; he figures all that steroid-laced beef makes him irresistible to the fair sex."

"When it comes to sex, I never play fair. I learned to cope with rough trade on the oil platforms. You don't meet many liberal-arts majors out on the Gulf. What's your name?"

"Marylou Klements," she said, offering her hand. "Everybody calls me Red." Her handclasp was dry and firm. It lingered perhaps a moment too long and our eyes met. "You're straight, aren't you?" she said, releasing my hand. I nodded.

"Thought so. No offense, but from the way you're dressed, I wondered, you know?" She shrugged. "I'm not straight. Is that a problem for you?"

"Not unless it keeps you from swinging a mop," I said. "And for what it's worth, I thought you were the best-looking person in the place."

"Damn faint praise," she said dryly, "but I'll take it. Look, if you've got things to do, papers to sign or whatever, I can take care of this on my own."

"No thanks. I handled most of the details over the phone or by mail and the rest can wait. I've been cooped up in offices and airplanes for the last two days. I need to *do* something. And Jackowski was right—this place is a pigpen."

"Your dad never worried much about mops, and Carney let it slide after Shan died. Figured to drive your price down."

"I see. Well, as they say in Texas, if you gotta kiss a frog, don't look at it too long. Let's shovel this joint out."

Red fetched mops and buckets while I finished taping cardboard over the broken window; then we began a frontal assault on umpty-years of grime, grunge, and nicotine. We worked like charwomen scrubbing down the walls, the long, scarred oaken bar, the heavy oak captain's tables and chairs.

Mostly, we worked in silence. If Red had questions, she kept them to herself, which suited me just fine. I was in no mood to talk, or even think, and the work kept me from doing either. Despite the tough-kid front I'd shown Charlie Bauer, I wasn't unmoved by my father's death. No one could be. Perhaps there wasn't love between us anymore, or even much of a connection, but there was . . . unfinished business. At least that. A parting with no good-byes, no chance to say what we needed to say to each other—whatever that might have been. I shrugged off the thought.

"Have you worked here long?" I asked Red.

"Almost three years. I paint. And sail. Came up here on a girlfriend's sloop. Liked the light, liked the people, decided to stay on awhile."

"What do you paint?"

"Ships and trees and lovers. None of them recognizable as such, which is one reason I also wait tables. But I like the work, too. You meet interesting people. Like you, for instance. By the way, what do I call you? Ms. Mitchell, ma'am, seems a bit formal for somebody who throws chairs through saloon windows. Do you prefer Michelle? Or maybe boss lady?"

"Mitch," I said. "People call me Mitch."

"Not particularly feminine."

"Just remember to enunciate the M. How did you get along with my dad?"

"Well enough that I'm very sorry about what happened. And I think you are, too."

I glanced up at her. Her eyes were pale blue, almost gray. Honest eyes. "Yeah." I nodded. "I *am* sorry. Maybe I've been working out on the Gulf too long. You learn to keep your guard up around strangers. And sometimes friends."

"I know the feeling." She nodded. "I thought it was just me. That's your son's picture in your dad's office, right?"

"What picture?"

"The newspaper clipping—nine-year-old saves pal from drowning! It ran in the local paper a few months ago and Shan had it blown up and framed. Proud as a peacock about it. Good-looking boy. Did you bring him with you?"

"No," I said coolly, "he's in school. A boarding school, actually."

"Mmmm." Red nodded, recognizing the "end of subject" tone in my voice. "Well, probably wouldn't be the best time to come home, anyway."

"This isn't his home," I said. "He's never lived here. And I'm not sure it's mine anymore, either. You missed a corner of the bar there."

"I'm saving it for contrast," she said cheerfully. "Like a before-and-after shot? Damn, if I'd known how good this place looked underneath the mung, I'd have taken a serious shot at it a long time ago."

She was right. The carpeting was stained beyond redemption, should have been replaced long since. But minus the grime of years, the knotty-pine walls glowed with a honey-golden patina that you couldn't buy new at any price. Which was fortunate. I had my severance pay from Exxon, so I wasn't broke, but I wasn't exactly Ivana Trump, either.

Around nine, we ran out of Spic and Span and I ran out of gas, a combination of lost sleep and the backbreaking labor generally referred to as "woman's work." We agreed to hit it hard again at ten the next morning. I locked up the building, climbed into my rented red Ford Escort, and drove. . . .

Not home. To my father's house. It had never been home to me. I never knew my mother; she died bringing me into the world. I was raised in Detroit by my grandmother, a terrific lady who slid irretrievably into the shadows of Alzheimer's disease while I was still in grade school. It finally took her when I was thirteen, and I went to live with the stranger who was my father.

I knew him, of course. I'd been spending summers with him for years, or more accurately, working for him. He kept a few small motorboats at his cottage in those days and rented them to fishermen or scuba divers. I rustled gear and swamped out the boats, hung out on the beach, and generally had a wonderful time. The summer that I moved in with him, he taught me to scuba dive in Lake Huron. He was a hard teacher, impatient, unrelenting, exactly the kind of instructor I needed to learn that particular craft. There's no margin for error in deep water, no charity, no forgiveness. Fatal mistakes are the only kind there are.

I was a willing pupil, though, took to the water like an otter. I would've walked through fire for him in those days. He taught me the trade I've followed ever since and opened up a whole world for me. And it wasn't all work. We had good times that first summer, some of the best I've ever had. But a year later, he sank his savings into a waterfront bar with a bait and tackle shop attached. He stocked the shop with diving gear and re-named it the Crow's Nest. But soon he was spending more and more time in the bar. And everything changed—for the worse.

The drive out to the cottage was grim business, twelve miles along an icy, twisting track of a back road. I hadn't driven in serious snow for years, and I'd forgotten how tricky handling a car on ice could be. I was exhausted from the flight and the long day. But even half-asleep, I instinctively slowed the car as I approached the Silver Creek Bridge.

The shallow snowdrifts along the right-hand side of the road had been gouged and rutted by a number of vehicles. Snow had fallen since, but not enough to erase the scars. I eased the little Escort over to the narrow shoulder and stopped.

In the headlamp glare, the trampled snowdrifts and the frozen swamp beyond loomed in stark contrast, an inky study in black and white. The ice was jumbled and broken a few meters from the bank, but smooth as a millpond farther out.

This was the place where it happened. The marks were there, but I think I would have sensed it anyway, felt it, like a whisper of wind in the dark.

He apparently veered off the road twenty meters or so from the bridge, plunged over the bank and into the swamp. But not very far. And not very hard. The mud would have softened the impact, and Sheriff Bauer'd said the truck wasn't badly damaged. Why here? The road was relatively straight, no reason to swerve. And why hadn't he simply crawled back to the bank instead of wandering off into the swamp? Drunk? Or dazed by the crash? Or both?

It seemed such a senseless way to die. But then, my father'd never worried much about what seemed rational to other people. He'd always lived on his own terms. He apparently died the same way. A cold, hard way. For a hard man. Bauer was right—he was no saint, my father, but he deserved better than this.

I haven't been inside a church in years, but I said a small prayer there in the darkness beside the road—for my father, and for my son and me. And then I drove on.

—— The house looked older and lonelier than I remembered, a quaint fieldstone and clapboard beachfront cottage built in the lumber-baron days of the 1880s. The original owner must have cherished his privacy. He built on the tip of Ponemah Point, a fingerling peninsula that juts out into the vastness of Lake Huron from the southern shore of Thunder Bay.

I'd forgotten how isolated the place is, a dozen miles from town, its nearest neighbor more than a mile away across the point. The cottage looked eyeless and abandoned, lonely as a gull in winter. I parked in the yard, grabbed my duffel bag out of the trunk, and was hounded to the porch by the wind whining out of the dark pines that ringed the yard like sentries.

I unlocked the door, stepped in, and promptly stumbled over a chain saw in the darkened entryway and barked my shin. Damn! The house was as cold as a witch's kiss and no more friendly. I hit the light switch. Nothing happened. No electricity. There never had been any power or phone lines this far out on the point, but I'd hoped in the ten years since I'd been here, Shan might have had a line run out. No such luck. I hoped to God the generator had fuel.

I dropped my bag in the living room, found a match and lit the LP gas stove, cranked it to maximum heat, and huddled in front of it for a few moments, thawing out. Better. At least I wouldn't freeze. Now, as to the electricity . . .

I zipped my parka up under my chin, then trotted back outside to the generator shed. The fuel tank was full, and after a couple of healthy yanks on the starter cord, it settled down to a near-silent hum. A string of yard lamps glowed to life, lighting my way back to the house.

The milk in the refrigerator was frozen solid, but otherwise the place seemed habitable. I heated a tin of beef stew on the stove, brewed up a cup of coffee, and took stock.

The cottage was as clean and Spartan as a YWCA: two bedrooms, a kitchen, living room, and bath, lacquered knotty-pine walls, hardwood floors. Handmade oaken furniture with brown canvas cushions, probably as old as the house. Backwoods country chic. The only decorative furnishings were a half dozen magnificent pieces of ship's "jewelry," antique gear scavenged from wrecks on the bottom of Lake Huron. The Great Lakes waters are littered with shipwrecks, six thousand or more, from the first ship that ever sailed them, *The Griffin,* to the *Edmund Fitzgerald.* You can go to prison nowadays for possessing deepwater antiques, but that never mattered much to my father. He figured the artifacts belonged to the people who risked their necks to bring them up. I could fault his logic but not his taste. He had a wonderful walnut helm wheel over the small brick fireplace, a couple of beautifully tarnished brass running lamps, and an elaborate brass and maple ship's compass in one corner, with a rifle leaning against it.

I recognized the gun; it was my grandfather's old '94 Winchester 30-30, a standard deer rifle in northern Michigan. I picked it up, looked it over, remembering late-autumn afternoons, my father running me through drills with this rifle: Shoulder, focus, squeeze. Never waste a shot, treat every gun as if it's loaded, and . . . But this gun felt like it actually *was* loaded.

I racked the action and ejected a live round, then six more, which surprised me considerably. Guns are as common as saltshakers in North Country homes, but not loaded. Never loaded. Frowning, I put the rifle carefully back in the rack where it belonged, picked up the ejected rounds, and replaced them in the open cartridge box that was sitting atop the compass.

Except for the Winchester, the gun rack was empty. There should have been two more guns. I found one of them, my father's army .45 automatic, in a holster hanging behind the front door. It was also loaded, a full clip and a round in the chamber. His shotgun seemed to be missing, assuming he still had it after all these years. I wandered through the house looking for it, and found something almost as odd as the loaded weapons.

Negligees. Two of them. And a woman's embroidered silk robe in the bedroom closet. My father liked the ladies well enough, appreciated them the way some people love art, or music, or classic cars. He always had women around him, a long series of interchangeable strays, usually summer boating people he met in the Nest. Occasionally, he'd take one seriously enough that I'd bother to learn her first name, but none of them had lasted very long. And he almost never brought them out here. Said he liked waking up in his own place . . . alone. The *alone* was something he stressed a lot, the years I lived with him.

Apparently, he'd mellowed. Well, why not? It had been ten years since I'd seen him. And now I never would again. I thought I might feel something, coming back here after all this time, a connection, a shiver of mortality, something. But I didn't. Last living relative or not, I had damn few memories of Shannon Mitchell, most of them bad. And I'd crossed a lot of bridges since.

The bedrooms would be chilly until morning, so I unrolled my sleeping bag on the sofa near the little stove. But sleep wouldn't come. Too many images: the lawyer's office, the hassle in the Crow's Nest, Sheriff Bauer . . . and the guns—loaded, out here in the middle of nowhere. Maybe it was the creaking of the cottage in the night wind, or maybe paranoia is hereditary, but I got up, took the .45 and its holster from behind the door, and placed it on the floor beside the sofa, near at hand. I'm often a restless sleeper and I expected to toss all night. Instead, I promptly fell into the sleep of the just, deep and dreamless.

Until someone turned on the lights, or at least that was my first impression. I blinked into dazed awareness, trying to focus, to remember where I was, what was happening. The ship's clock on the bookcase showed a little after two. And yet the room was suffused with a silvery glow, bright shafts of light bleeding around the edges of the drapes. Someone was spotlighting the house from the beach. Sharply awake now, I rolled off the sofa, slid the .45 out of its holster, then pressed myself against the wall beside the living room window and cautiously lifted a corner of the drapes.

Ice. My God. Thunder Bay was a crystalline, glimmering ice field that stretched unbroken to the horizon, and probably five hundred miles north to the Canadian shore. There was no spotlight out there, only the moon, three-quarters full, beaming through scudding snow clouds, refracted by a billion prisms, setting Lady Huron aglisten in a cloak of shattered diamonds.

I swept the drapes open and stared out into the glittering dark, stunned, absolutely mesmerized. Ten years of diving in tropic seas, Florida, the Caribbean, the Texas Gulf, I'd almost forgotten how the dead hand of winter transmuted the Great Lakes into thousands of square miles of jumbled ivory floes and fields, as lifeless and magnificent as the valleys of the moon.

I must've stood watching most of an hour. Eventually, I started to wobble as exaustion overtook me. But still I didn't go back to bed. I snuggled down in an easy chair instead, facing the bay ice with my sleeping bag wrapped around me, unwilling to give up the beauty of the night, even to sleep. I dozed, woke, marveled, and dozed again. And once, I saw something moving out there, something large and dark and serpentine, miles offshore. And I knew I must be dreaming—nothing could live out there—and yet I saw it and could even mark its progress past a twisted ice pillar that thrust skyward like crossed fingers. A while later, the moon went down, yet the Lady continued to luminesce with a spectral phosphorescence of her own, candleglow from emerald chandeliers in the halls of her icewater mansions.

CHAPTER 3

DAWN NEVER CAME. I woke a bit after seven to a heavily overcast sky and a storm drifting down over the lake from Canada, snow devils dancing and swirling ahead of it like gossamer ballerinas.

Let it come. The stove was warm, the cottage snug, and I didn't have to be anywhere for a few hours. I brewed up an exquisite pot of coffee, toasted a couple of English muffins, sprinkled them with a dash of cinnamon, then carried the lot into the living room.

Nestled in the easy chair, I munched breakfast, looking out over the bay while the local AM radio station murmured Huron Harbor news in the background, farm-market reports, births, a Chamber of Commerce meeting. And for the first time in . . . a very long time, I felt at ease. As lonely and isolated as it was, this cottage was as close to a home as I've ever known. Home. An alien concept for me the past few years.

I was still trying to define the feeling when I heard the faint whine of an approaching car lurching along the track. I peered through the frosty glass of the kitchen door. A white Cadillac had pulled up beside my rented Ford Escort. A small blond woman in a chic white trench coat and snow boots climbed out and strode briskly up the steps, carrying a briefcase. I opened the door before she knocked.

"Good morning," she said briskly. "I'm sorry to bother you so early, Miss Mitchell. Your attorney, Mr. Cohen, told me you were staying out here. I'm Karen Stepaniak, with Century Realty?"

"Realty?" I echoed, frowning. "Oh, right. Mr. Cohen mentioned something about the Nest being for sale. What can I do for you?"

"I wonder if you could spare me a few minutes? I realize you've only just arrived and that my timing is terrible, but we do have a purchase offer and I thought you should know about it."

"I suppose I should," I said. "Come in. I'm having coffee. Would you care for some?"

"No thank you; I really can't stay," she said, glancing around warily. She was probably fortyish but wore it very well, a pretty heart-shaped face, hazel eyes, trim figure. She seemed competent and collected. And just a tad uneasy.

"The offer is pretty straightforward. A hundred and forty thousand for this cottage and the Crow's Nest together," she said. "Thirty thousand down, the balance on land contract at eleven percent."

"I see," I said. "Is your buyer a guy named Carney?"

"Yes, it is. Have you two already discussed this?"

"Not exactly. He mumbled something about it. On his way out. Look, I don't mean to put you on the spot, but I don't know doodley about local real estate values. Is this a good offer?"

"It's . . . a legitimate offer," she said.

"That wasn't the question," I said.

"No," she said, meeting my eyes. "Frankly, it's a lousy offer. The Crow's Nest alone is worth that. Still, it's on the table and I thought you ought to know."

"I appreciate your candor," I said. "But the truth is, I couldn't sell now if I wanted to. The properties will be tied up in probate for at least sixty days, maybe longer. Some of my father's papers seem to be missing."

"I see." She nodded. "Well, I apologize again for intruding. If you decide to sell, please give me a call. Thanks for your time." She turned to go, a bit reluctantly, I thought.

"Miss Stepaniak? Forgive me if I'm out of line, but a lady

seems to have left some clothing here. I wonder if you could do me a favor and take it with you. To give to Goodwill or whatever?"

"It's Mrs. Stepaniak, actually," she said carefully. "I, um, suppose I could. Strictly as a courtesy, of course." She took a deep breath and walked directly into the bedroom. Without asking where the clothing was.

I wandered into the living room and straightened up, tossed my sleeping bag behind the couch, carried the dishes to the sink. I glanced into the bedroom as I passed. Karen Stepaniak was sitting on the edge of the bed with her eyes closed, holding one of my father's crumpled shirts pressed over her mouth, breathing a memory. I rummaged through the chipped china mugs in the cupboard, found a fit-for-company Rookwood cup and saucer my father'd probably scavenged from a wreck, and poured her a cup of coffee.

She looked shaken when she came out, her eyes misty, her mouth a taut line. "Please, stay a moment," I said. "I think we could both use someone to talk to."

She slumped down at the kitchen table, looking a decade older than when she arrived. She sipped her coffee gratefully and visibly knit herself together. She was an attractive woman, sharp features, taut skin, tightly coiffed blond hair the shade that never ages. "So," she said quietly, "I gather you know about your father and me?"

"Mrs. Stepaniak—"

"Call me Karen, please."

"All right, Karen. The fact is, I didn't know, about you or anything else that's been happening with my dad lately. Shan and I exchanged Christmas cards and occasional phone calls. I sent him Corey's school pictures, and I mailed him an article the Houston papers ran when Corey saved a friend from drowning at school, but that was about it. I haven't seen him or spoken to him for more than a few minutes in ten years."

She eyed me oddly for a moment. "Men," she said at last.

"What is it?"

"Nothing. Just that Shan gave me the impression things were improving between you two. He was very proud of you, and Corey, too. Especially after you sent him that article. He even had the local newspaper run it. He . . . felt very badly about the trouble between you. We were going to try to set it right."

"We?"

"Yes, we. Your father had asked me to marry him."

"No kidding? And you took him seriously?"

Surprisingly, she smiled. She had a good smile. "Touché. My God, you even sound like him. He meant it all right. Oh, I know he had a long string of ladies in his life, but we were a match, your dad and I. We were going to start fresh together, and his first priority was to rebuild the bridges you two had burned. He said he handled things pretty poorly when you . . . left home."

"Yeah, well, maybe I didn't handle it all that well myself. What did he tell you about it?"

"The basics. That you'd . . . gotten pregnant and that he tried to bully you into having an abortion. And that you ran away."

"That pretty much covers it. I needed his help badly at the time, but I learned to survive without it—which was probably for the best, anyway."

"And Alec? Didn't he help?"

I blinked, surprised by the question.

"It's all right. Shan told me Alec Deveraux was the father, but I would have known anyway when I saw your son's picture. There's quite a resemblance."

"If there is, I try not to see it. He isn't part of our lives. He never has been."

"He must have been at one time—"

"Not even then," I said, cutting her off. "There was no . . . relationship. We weren't lovers. I thought we were friends, but . . ."

"I don't understand," she said softly. "What happened?"

"Nothing complicated," I said, taking a deep breath. "My, um, my boyfriend dumped me for Alec's sister. So I tried to even things up by getting friendly with Alec. We were at a party, had a few drinks too many, and . . . he took advantage of the situation."

"Date rape," she said.

"That's what they call it now. At the time, the words for it were a lot uglier. And they only applied to the girl."

"Did you tell Shan what happened?"

"Not all of it, no. I was afraid to. God only knows what he would have done."

"Killed Alec, I imagine," she said, shaking her head. "And not a bad idea, either. Alec lives in New York now, if you're curious. Still spends summers here, though. With his wife and kids."

"No problem," I said, trying to keep the acid out of my tone. "By summer, I'll be long gone."

"To where?"

"I . . . You know, I'm not sure. I'd planned to keep working on the Gulf. But I also hoped Dad and I would straighten things out eventually. I thought we had lots of time. Now . . . Hell, I don't know. Everything seems to be falling apart."

"I thought you were were engaged."

"Past tense," I said simply. "I was seeing a terrific guy, a marine biology prof I met at school a few years ago. We even picked out a 'happily ever after' house."

"But it didn't work out?" she prompted.

"He expected me to quit my job, move to Dallas, and live a . . . normal life. But when it came down to it, I couldn't give up deep water. Not even to give Corey a real home. So I'm back on the Gulf and my son's in boarding school, being raised by strangers. And now Shan . . . It's all too much. I'm not even sure how I'm supposed to feel about it."

"A little lost, I imagine. That's certainly how I feel. But if there's a silver lining in all this, maybe it's that we've inherited each other."

"How do you mean?"

"I think we're two ladies who've been run over by the same

bus. So if you need a friend, I'd like to volunteer for the job. If I can help you in any way at all, Mitch, I'll do my best, okay? For Shan. And for me, too."

"Thank you," I said. "That's very kind."

"Not at all. Just talking to you makes me feel like . . . I don't know. That maybe I haven't lost him completely. So," she said, gulping down the dregs of her coffee, "first things first. Somebody said you've started remodeling the Nest. By pitching a chair through the front window?"

"It seemed reasonable at the time," I said. "And to be honest, it felt terrific. I just hope it's not habit-forming."

"It sounds like something Shan might have done, and the Nest needed an airing, anyway. Are you planning to stay on a while, then?"

"Long enough to clear up the probate paperwork at least. After that, I'm not sure. This thing has shaken me up more than I expected. I need to think. If I decide not to sell and blow your commission, will you still want to be my pal?"

"If you want me to be," she said, smiling. "You really are a lot like Shan, you know, like it or not. But you're quite different, too. You're civilizing the place already, for one thing," she said, indicating her cup. "You probably even sleep in the bed."

"I beg your pardon?"

"It's nothing, really. I . . . stayed over now and again, but I always woke up alone. I'd usually find him asleep in his chair in the living room. He'd sit out there all night, watching the lake, or the ice. And dream. He said sometimes he could hear her singing."

"Hear whom?"

"The Lady of the Lake. He must have told you about her."

"Yes," I said slowly, "I guess he did. A long time ago."

"God, what a line of blarney he had," she said, misting up. "I'm going to miss him more than I can say. Thanks for the tea and sympathy, but I've got to get back to work." She rose briskly and folded her nightclothes into her briefcase. "If you're going to run the Nest, let me offer some friendly advice. Show some black ink on the books. Shan always ran it in the red to avoid taxes, which makes it a tough sell. If you show even a small profit for a few months, I can probably get you half again as much as he was asking."

"Wait a minute. Are you saying that Shan was trying to sell the Crow's Nest? And the cottage?"

"Of course. I thought you understood that."

"No, I assumed Mr. Cohen listed it to settle the estate."

"Shan listed both properties a couple of months ago. We planned to leave for Baja before spring. He said he'd had enough snow for a lifetime, that he was getting too old for cold water. . . ." She swallowed hard and looked away.

"I'm still not sure I understand. Was Carney trying to buy the Nest before the accident?"

"He'd made an offer, but Shan turned it down."

"So he was planning to leave whether the Nest sold or not? With what?"

"I'm sorry, you've lost me."

"What did he plan to live on? According to Mr. Cohen, he had only a few thousand in the bank."

"I'm afraid I don't know. We never really discussed his finances. But I gathered that money wouldn't be a problem, especially since he could have gotten considerably more for the Nest if he'd waited to sell during the tourist season."

"I see. Forgive me for being blunt, but I don't suppose you were planning to support him down there?"

"Me? Support Shan?" she said, straightening to her full five three. "If we're going to be friends, maybe we'd better clear up a point. I'm not some bimbo your dad picked up in the Nest. I was slogging along in a bad marriage when I met him. Maybe he was my midlife crisis, or maybe it was just chemistry, but we clicked, Shan and I. We were good for each other. He asked me to go to Mexico with him, and I agreed. I'm no gold digger, but I'm not independently wealthy, either. I'm just a working girl. The car I'm driving belongs to the agency, and I'm as much a gofer there as an agent. And since I'm presently in the middle of divorce proceedings, I hope I can count on your discretion."

"Of course," I said, "and I apologize for . . . well, for everything. Just one last thing. Did my father seem at all worried the past month or so?"

"Worried? How do you mean?"

"I found two of his guns stashed in strategic spots when I arrived last night, his pistol behind the door, a rifle in the living room. Both loaded."

"I don't recall seeing them," she said, "and I was here quite often. But worried? You really didn't know him well, did you?"

"No," I said, "maybe I didn't."

"That was your loss. He was a complex man, not easy to understand, but . . . always interesting. I seem to have a weakness for dangerous men. The way you must like dangerous work. In any case, your father was probably the least-fearful man I've ever known. I don't think he was afraid of anything on God's green earth."

"Considering how things turned out," I said, "maybe he should have been."

CHAPTER 4

LESSON ONE for a new businesswoman: If you're late, everybody else will be on time. And everyone but you gets paid by the hour. Red, Mr. Misiak, and his blank-faced teenybopper assistant were waiting none too patiently for me in the parking lot when I rolled in at ten-thirty. Misiak and company hung a sheet of heavy gray canvas over the wall to keep the weather out, then promptly disappeared beneath it and began sawing an opening for the new window.

Red was dressed for the job today, blue jeans and a sleeveless U of M T-shirt that showed off her graceful toreador's build. She began scrubbing the walls where we'd quit the night before. I decided to check out the tackle shop to see if I could turn up the papers my father's attorney said were missing.

The shop is adjacent to the Nest but has its own entrance, an ancient oaken door with a brass porthole and a massive old lock, all faux of course, but very realistic. They look as though they've slept for a century on the lake bed. Plunder from a wreck? Hell no, my father would say, all outraged innocence. Looting's not only a crime against history; it can cost you two years in the joint per piece and forfeiture of your boat. What do you take me for, a damned grave robber?

And of course they did. And he meant them to. He could lie with total sincerity or make the absolute truth sound completely unbelievable. A useful talent. One I didn't inherit. A pity. He used to say that white lies are the threads that keep the social fabric from ripping apart. Of course, I couldn't be sure he meant it.

The dive shop hadn't changed much, racks of fishing tackle along the east wall, iridescent Blue Fox and Rapala lures, Shakespeare reels, transparent nylon lines, and snells in a dozen gauges. The rest of the shop was all diving supplies: an air compressor at the rear for refilling tanks, Scubapro masks and snorkels in translucent colors, flippers and weight belts. Nothing too expensive, and only American equipment. I prefer to use one of the high-tech European imports myself, but this was tough utilitarian gear for divers who take the sport seriously, the only way to take it.

The rafters overhead were rough wooden beams festooned with antique diving gear, coils of tarred rope, a beautifully discolored brass diving helmet with canvas-shielded air hoses, a cast-iron sturgeon spear, its barbed blade worn to the width of a knitting needle. The most striking piece was a single oaken keel timber, sculpted by a century of sand and current to a naked elemental arc. Shan almost died digging that timber out of Lake Erie muck, working for days in silt-clouded black water, stretching his safety margin to the max with every dive. A crazy thing to do. But I understood it, and so did every diver who walked into the shop. It was just a piece of wood, but divers would gaze at it as if it was a spar from the True Cross. A gift from the Lady of the Lake.

The shop was chilly, dusty, and deserted, closed for the winter. I expected the stock to be low this time of year, and it was. I'd have to replenish it in the spring, assuming I was still here. And had the money. At least the place seemed reasonably neat. My father always kept . . .

But it wasn't. As I glanced around the room, I realized that everything was at least slightly out of place. Gear'd been dumped in the wrong bins; the sliding doors beneath the display counters were open; the stock boxes had been rifled. The shop had been ransacked, and none too carefully. I popped open the porthole in the wall between the shop and the Nest.

"Red?"

"Yeah?" She was on a ladder, wiping down the ceiling beams over the bar.

"The shop's a mess. Has anybody been in here?"

"Not that I know of. Shan closed it down after Christmas." She clambered down the ladder and strode over. I moved aside to let her look through the porthole. "Sweet Mamma Mary." She whistled. "It wasn't like this when we closed it up, or even a few weeks ago. I got a couple of hooks for an ice fisherman and it was fine then."

"Did Dad's lawyer do an inventory?"

"No, no one did that I know of. Is anything missing?"

"You'd be a better judge of that than I would. But if somebody broke in, they left an awful lot of expensive equipment lying around loose. Did Dad keep money or anything back here?"

"No, that's all in the office. What do you think, should we call Sheriff Bauer?"

"Not yet. I'd better take a quick inventory, see if anything's missing first."

I closed the porthole to save heat, then started for the office. But I didn't make it.

A wolf came to the door, literally. Someone began pounding on the shop door, I opened it, and a wolf was sitting there, eyeing me like a potential lunch. Not a Malamute or an Alsatian, but an honest-to-God Canadian gray wolf. It must've weighed close to a hundred and forty pounds, coarse charcoal pelt, intelligent amber eyes.

"Hey, Mitch, how you been doin'? You remember me?"

I managed to tear my gaze away from the wolf long enough to glance at her owner—a big guy in a grubby red plaid hunting coat, a corduroy cap with one torn earflap, an ugly wine-stain birthmark leaking down from his cap over one cheek. His face was moon-shaped, like a pimiento loaf, with unknown bits of stuff sticking in it.

Ratshit.

I almost said it. It was the only name I could come up with,

28

one that kids hung on him in school and taunted him with until his teens, when he suddenly bulked up to near polar bear size . . . and temper. Radowicz. That was it. Judgment Christ Radowicz.

"Jud," I said cautiously, "how are you?"

"Good, I'm good. I heard you was back in town. I stopped by your dad's place this morning, but you was already gone."

"You still live out there on the point?"

"Yeah. In my mom's ol' shack. But I'm alone out there now. Ma died, you know."

"No, I hadn't heard. I'm sorry."

"Shit happens." He shrugged, looking away. "Look, I was wonderin' if maybe you got any work for me? My truck's broke down and I need some cash money. Any kinda manual labor, you know."

"I, um . . . You know, maybe I do. Do you know anything about diving gear, Jud?"

"Sure. I gofered for your dad plenty a times. I can't work more'n thirty feet down, though. I got the bad ears."

"I don't want you to dive. I need somebody to clean up the dive shop, straighten up the equipment, and make a rough count of the stock. It's a lot of bull work. Six bucks an hour sound fair?"

"Damn straight." He nodded eagerly. "That'd be great. You want me to start right away?"

"Anytime you like, but I'm afraid you'll have to do something about the wolf first."

"You mean Dog?"

"That's a dog?"

"Nah, Dog's her name. She's a cross-wolf. But you go around yellin' wolf, people think you're nuts. She won't be no trouble. She don't bother nobody long as they stay clear."

"I'm sure she doesn't, but we've got a food license, Jud. We can't have animals on the premises."

"Oh yeah, I see whatcha mean." He frowned. "Well, I guess I could drop her off to home. Probably take me a couple hours."

"Why should . . . You mean you walked all the way to town? From the point?"

"Sure," he said, puzzled. "I told you, my truck's broke down."

"So you did. All right, tell you what, you can keep Dog with you out here in the dive shop for today, but leave her home tomorrow. Okay?"

"Whatever you say, Mitch," he said, pumping my hand in his grimy fist. "You won't be sorry." The cross-wolf's eyes never wavered from my belly. She didn't offer to shake hands. Neither did I.

CHAPTER 5

I WAS HOLDING THE LADDER for Red while she wiped down the ship's wheel chandelier over the pool table when the canvas tarp the glaziers had draped over the window billowed aside and an honest-to-God ghost stepped from beneath it, a trim, compactly built man in a navy peacoat and jeans, wind-tousled dark hair, and pirate's eyes. He stared at me a moment, then nodded slowly. "You know, I got thrown out a saloon window once," he said, glancing around. "Don't believe I've ever come in through one before. It's a lot less painful. How've you been, Mitch?"

"Terry Fortier," I said, unable to keep from grinning, feeling my spirits lift. "I thought you'd be dead or in jail by now."

"Not so far, but it's still early in the day. Sorry to hear about your dad. Never figured he'd die of old age, but . . . Anyway, I'm sorry."

"Thank you. Me, too."

"Right. But before you start blubbering about how glad you are to see me, I'd better warn you. I'm supposed to slap the livin' bejesus outta you and maybe break one of your arms."

"Why? Just because I didn't write?"

"Nope. Because your ex-bartender Joe Carney slipped me fifty bucks to knock you around."

"Only fifty? I'm insulted. Think you're up to it?"

"Seemed like easy money at the time, but now I'm not so sure. You look pretty sturdy to me, lady. And you never did fight fair."

"Shan always said people who fight fair lack imagination."

31

"Can't argue with that. Besides, it does seem kinda short-sighted to whup up on a lady who just inherited a saloon. Tell you what, buy me a drink and we'll call it even."

"Buy your own drink. You're the one with the extra fifty."

"Cold, Mitch, very cold. But at least you were always a cheap date. Fair enough. I'll buy; you pour. The office, say? It's a bit noisy out here."

"What about Carney?"

"Hell, he'd have to hire a small army to stomp both of us," he said, following me through to the office. "It'll teach him to be more careful about who he hires. Speaking of hiring, was that Ratshit I saw working out in the dive shop?"

"Do people still call him that?"

"Not me"—Terry grinned—"at least not to his face. Baggers Gant made a wisecrack about that mud-pie birthmark of his last summer and Rats beat him half to death and pitched him in the harbor. He's Mr. Radowicz, sir, far as I'm concerned, but I wouldn't want him working for me. He's always been two bricks shy of a load, Mitch, and since his mom died, he's probably certifiable. Lives in that old shack past your father's place with a damn wolf—"

"Dog," I corrected, pouring a fair-sized jolt of Courvoisier into a brandy snifter. "Her name is Dog." I opened a bottle of Perrier for myself.

"If that thing's a dog, Cujo was a hamster. You're not drinking?"

"It's a bit early for me."

"Me, too." He nodded. "But I'll make this one exception for your sake. You want to hire Rats, it's your lookout, but keep an eye on him, okay? He's definitely crazier than he used to be. The only talent Jud's got is for makin' people uneasy."

"He said he'd been working for my father."

"Yeah, he rousted for Shan on his boat, did scut work around the cottage. Shan could always handle him. He'd josh with him when he got down or slap him upside the head if he got too hostile. No offense, Mitch, but you aren't your father."

"No, I'm not," I said, raising my glass, "but I think I can probably manage Jud. Happy days."

"And happier nights," Terry said. He knocked back half the brandy, baring even white teeth at the bite of the liquor. Damn. In his scruffy way, he looked even better than I remembered. Ralph Lauren peddles that rugged outdoor look for five hundred bucks a pop. Terry owned it as a birthright. He'd weathered a bit, acquired the beginnings of crow's-feet from squinting into the wind, and there was a scar above his lip that looked fresh. There's no justice. Some of us age, but Terry just seemed to season, like oak, or bronze. The years had only made him more interesting. At least to me.

"This is your boy, isn't it?" he said softly, picking up the framed photo of Corey from the desk. "He looks like you. Looks even more like his father. Definitely got Deveraux eyes. Do, um, do you and Alec keep in pretty close touch?"

"Not at all. Not word one."

"Really? He pays child support, though, right?"

"No. I never asked for any."

"You never . . . What the hell, Mitch, it's not like he can't afford it."

"That's not the point. I didn't want Alec in my life, or Corey's, financially or any other way. We're doing fine on our own. And let's change the subject."

"Okay by me," Terry said. "Maybe we'd better talk about Shan's boat."

"What about it?"

"I bought it from him a few weeks back. Wasn't the bill of sale in the estate papers or whatever?"

"No. Actually, quite a few papers seem to be missing—the title to the house, a few other things."

"Well, I've got a copy of the bill if you want to see it. But you won't like it. He had a four-year-old, twenty-seven-foot Bayliner. He sold it to me for a grand."

"A grand?" I echoed, sipping my Perrier, reading Terry's face. It was a good face, almost matinee-idol handsome. I'd known

33

him since I was thirteen. We were best friends and kissy-face lovers in high school. A long time ago. Maybe too long.

"So," I said, "why don't you tell me about it?"

"About what?"

"What my father was into."

"I'm not sure what you mean."

"C'mon, Terry, something was going on. Shan was dumping his house and the business. He practically gave you his boat. It looks to me like he was getting ready to leave town in a hurry. Why? Was he afraid of somebody?"

"Shan? Not likely. Most people with any sense were afraid of him. He had a helluva temper, your old man. He mellowed some lately, though. Maybe because of his latest lady friend. He was always a cun—a fox in the henhouse with women, but his new lady was special. He wanted to marry her, I hear."

"Karen Stepaniak?"

"My, my, what big ears we have."

"She stopped by the house this morning—on business."

"Well, I hope you got it all finished up. The lady's got a surly son of a bitch husband the size of New Jersey. Hacksaw, they call him. He and your father tangled a couple months back."

"What do you mean, they tangled?"

"The usual thing. Hack came to the Nest, made a scene, cursed your old man out, said he was gonna stomp him into hamburger for taking Karen away. He charged around the bar after him. Shan came up with that forty-five he kept by the register, shoved it under Hack's chin, eared back the hammer, said one more step, they'd have to scrape his brains off the ceiling with a trowel. I saw Shan's eyes, Mitch. I swear, I really thought he was gonna do it. Hack did, too. He backed off, but not by much. Told your old man he'd break his back if he didn't stay away from Karen."

"And now he's dead," I said.

"But not from a broken back." Terry shrugged. "From what I understand, he ran off the road, lost his way in the dark, and . . . died out there."

34

"The forty-five was hanging behind the door at the cottage," I said, "and my grandfather's Winchester was in the living room. They were both loaded."

"Then I'd guess he took Hack seriously. He damn sure should have."

"Maybe. But I think there had to be more to it than a jealous husband. He'd had problems with husbands before, but he never ran to Mexico to dodge one. And he wouldn't have sold you his boat for chump change, either. So why don't you tell me about the rest of it?"

"The rest of what?"

"Money, Terry. It all comes down to the money. I can see why he might take a low-ball price for the Nest and the cottage if he was in a hurry to get out. But not his boat. He could've sold it for double what you paid him any day of the week. Something was going on, right? Like what?"

"I heard you got married," he said.

"I came close," I said. "It didn't work out."

"Doesn't surprise me. Maybe the guy might've hung around if you'd lightened up a little."

"Actually, I was the one who walked. Tell me about the boat."

Terry glanced away, chewing his lower lip—a gesture I remembered. "I gave Shan a name," he said.

"What kind of a name?"

"A salvage buyer's name. There's a heavy market up here for contraband from deepwater wrecks. The penalties are pretty stiff, but sometimes the money's just too damn good to pass up."

"And you're involved in the trade?"

"Let's just say I know people who are."

"And my father, was he involved?"

"Not really. Oh, I'm not saying he wouldn't buy a brass lamp or a ship's wheel off a diver who needed money, but he usually kept the stuff for his own collection or donated it to the Deveraux Institute museum here in town. He never actually dealt in artifacts, as far as I know."

35

"Until last month."

"Could be. I just gave him the name."

"Which means he must have had something to sell."

"I honestly don't know. A deal like that, I didn't ask questions—especially not of Shan. I've seen him in action."

"Me, too," I said. "What was the dealer's name?"

"Why do you want to know?"

"I'm not sure, but if Shan was getting ready to pull out, he needed cash. Maybe the gentleman owes me something. Money, or a lot more."

"What, you think the buyer ripped your father off? Maybe did him in somehow?"

"He's your pal. You tell me."

"I suppose it's possible," he said, nodding slowly. He wandered around behind my desk to the small window that looks out over the harbor. "This dealer's definitely a hard case. He's got an antique store and a couple of pawnshops down in Saginaw. Supposed to be mobbed up. But I don't think he and your father tangled. The buyer called me last week to ask if Shan had made a deal with somebody else. He didn't know he was dead."

"And you just took his word for that?"

"I had no reason to doubt it," Terry said evenly, turning to face me. "I still don't. The guy's always been straight with me."

"I'm afraid that's not quite good enough. Not anymore. I want to meet him. Can you set it up?"

"I could try, but I don't think it'd do any good. I doubt he'll talk to you. He's more'n a little paranoid about who he deals with."

"He can either talk to me or we can all talk to Sheriff Bauer. Your choice."

Terry eyed me for a moment, then shrugged. "So much for auld lang syne," he said. "All right, tell you what, I'll make a couple calls, see what I can find out. Of course you realize that if something heavy went down with your dad, the buyer'll be edgy as a pit bull on amphetamines. I could end up in the same shape as your old man."

"Then just give me the name. I'll take it from there."

"No, I hooked Shan up with him. If it went bad, I'm at least partly responsible. I'll handle it. Unless you think maybe I'm involved in whatever happened?"

"No, of course not. How much time will you need?"

"I don't know. A day or two."

"Take three," I said. "And be careful, okay?"

"You know," he said, "for a minute there, I was actually glad to see you. I forgot what a major pain you can be."

"I know," I said. "I've missed you, too."

⟅⟆ Mr. Misiak and his helper finished installing the new bay window late that afternoon. And a very odd thing happened. When he swept the canvas away to reveal a Rockwellesque view of the snowbound harbor, it was as though a new door opened in my life. For the first time, I could sense a pattern, a possible future that didn't include working on an endless parade of drilling platforms in Texas or Alaska or God knows where. Where I could bring up Corey in some semblance of a real home. No more boarding schools and living with strangers for him. And for me, just having him with me would be enough. I could survive here; I was almost certain of it. I knew the business. Hell, I grew up in it. Maybe, just maybe . . .

"You've gone awfully quiet, lady," Red said. "What's wrong? Don't tell me you want it half an inch to the left?"

"No, it's just fine where it is," I said. "In fact, I like it so much, I want another one. Maybe just a little smaller. In my office."

"I doubt I've got a unit that size in stock." Misiak frowned. "Might take me a few days to order one in."

"No rush," I said. "I'll be here."

CHAPTER 6

TERRY WAS BETTER than his word. His black Jeep Cherokee rumbled into the Nest parking lot at three the next afternoon and he stalked in, wearing a scruffy leather jacket and a surly outlook.

"I talked to our friend," he said brusquely. "He's not a happy camper about any of this, but if you want to talk to him, we've got one shot. Right now. His place, tonight."

"Where's his place?"

"Downtown Saginaw. Which is a two-hour run south, in case you've forgotten. He'll wait in his shop a few minutes after closing. If we're not there, the meet's off."

"What's the rush?"

"The guy's ultraparanoid. Whatever he had going with Shan probably was less than legit, so with Shan dead, Johnno's afraid we might be setting him up for a bust. This way, we've got no time to arrange anything. Look, I'll tell you straight up, the guy's bad news, Mitch; it could be risky. You sure you want to do this?"

"You're damned right," I said, grabbing my parka, tossing Red my keys. "Red, lock up for me, will you? I've got a heavy date."

"Hang on a minute," Terry said. "Is Shan's forty-five still behind the bar?"

"No. It's out at the house. We could stop—"

"Nope, no way," he said, checking his watch, "we barely have time to make it as it is. We'll just have to chance it."

"Do you really think we'll need a gun?"

"Lady, I'd feel a lot happier if I was drivin' a tank down there instead of my Jeep. Let's go."

"Hey, wait up," Jud called through the porthole of the dive shop. "Can you guys drop me at the point? It'll save me a walk."

Terry blinked once, then smiled slowly. "Mr. Radowicz, sir," he said. "I think I can do better than that. How would you like to take a little ride south with us?"

⚓ It's funny. Over the years, I'd daydreamed away more than a few off-duty hours, lying in my bunk, wondering what had happened to Terry. Had he ever married Andrea, the girl he'd dumped me for?

Apparently not. He wasn't wearing a ring and he hadn't mentioned her—which left a much bigger question. Had we blown a chance for the Real Thing all those years ago? Or was I just looking back at puppy love in a rose-colored rearview mirror?

And now we were driving into the dusk, a perfect opportunity for catching up and asking the questions that mattered. But the timing was all wrong. Terry was edgy as a panther, totally focused on threading his Jeep through rush-hour traffic on U.S. 23, the two-lane highway that snakes along Lake Huron's sunrise shore.

And of course we weren't alone. Too tall to sit erect in Terry's hard-topped Jeep, Jud Radowicz hunched in the backseat in a Quasimodo crouch. His presence permeated the cab, a feral scent of wood smoke and damp earth. Not unpleasant. Elemental. Like burying your face in a dog's mane. Or a wolf's, I suppose. He must have been uncomfortable back there, but he never complained. He just stared out the window into the dusk, absently massaging the three-day stubble on his cheek, eyeing the scenery with knit-browed concentration as though he'd never seen it before. Perhaps he hadn't.

I glanced casually at Terry now and again, and answered at least one of the questions. He wasn't just a teenybop dreamboat memory. Oh, perhaps nostalgia helped a little. But there was more to him than that. I could remember how he looked in high school quite clearly. He was a good-looking boy then, but just a boy. And now? My feelings were a lot more complicated than auld lang syne. I still found him magnetic. A bit more brutal than I remembered, but a decade had passed, and it's a rough world out there. God knows, I'd picked up a few scars of my own.

"Okay," Terry said quietly as he swung off Interstate 75 on the 675 Saginaw exit. "This is how things are gonna go. The guy we're going to see is Johnno Habash. He's Syrian, I think, or maybe Lebanese. He owns a place called Antiques Incroyable, a three-story building stuffed with more goodies than the *Andrea Doria*. He also owns four pawnshops in the north ward district. Nobody ever rips him off—which says all you need to know about him. Be straight about two things. One, I don't scare easy, but Johnno makes me edgy. Two, he doesn't *have* to meet with us, Mitch. He's doing it as a favor to me. So be polite. Jud, you just be your usual charming self. Keep your eyes open, but don't say doodley. Okay?"

Jud nodded, unconcerned. Or so he seemed. I couldn't imagine what he was thinking, how his mind worked. Behind his birthmark mask, his face was as unreadable as Dog's.

I remembered Saginaw as a city teetering on the edge of the urban-blight abyss, its downtown district struggling gamely against the creeping commercial cancer that had devoured the heart of Flint and parts of Detroit.

It looked like the north end of the city had already lost the battle, gutted cars dumped in weedy lots, abandoned houses, vacant storefront businesses. But the downtown district was still hanging on, anchored by an upscale Jacobsen's department store and the restored Art Deco Temple Theater, plus half a dozen blocks of smaller businesses, from Wade's Military Surplus to Michigan National Bank. Antiques Incroyable was just east of the central business district, a garishly painted three-story concrete fortress that occupied most of a city block. Its steel-grated display windows were cluttered with antique furniture, a rack of flintlock rifles, upright Starck Victrolas, Civil War sabers, Victorian silverware.

"Showtime," Terry said, wheeling the Jeep smoothly up to the shop's side door. "Jud, they may wanna search us, for weapons or wires or whatever. Just go along with them. Don't get upset, okay? If you've got a blade, leave it behind. And remember, be cool, right?"

"They aren't gonna strip-search us like they do in jail, are they?" Jud asked anxiously.

"I hope the hell not." Terry sighed. "On the other hand, if they decide to strip-search Mitch, don't argue. It might almost make the trip worthwhile."

As we climbed out of the Jeep, the shop door slid open electronically. A mountain of a man stood just inside, black, in a black suit, white shirt, red skullcap, and maroon bow tie. A Remington automatic shotgun was cradled casually in the crook of his arm.

"Yo, Terry," he said softly, smiling. "How you been doin'?"

"I've been better, Mr. Bass," Terry said. "Like I said on the phone, we've had a death in the family. Sorry to barge in like this on short notice. This is the lady I told Johnno about, Miss Mitchell, and my friend Mr. Radowicz."

Bass barely glanced at me, but he looked Jud over warily.

"Boy don't look like he gets to town much. Do you, cracker?"

"Never been here before," Jud said, glancing around calmly. "It looks nice. You sell mostly old stuff here?"

"That's right," Bass said dryly. "Old stuff. All right, this the trip, folks. Mr. Habash says you got five minutes to talk. You say anything Johnno don't wanna hear, the meeting's over. I ain't gonna pat ya'll down for iron outta respect for the lady's b'reavement, but I ain't the only one workin' the store tonight. Understand what I'm sayin'? And Terry, any shit comes down, you'll be the one pickin' up the tab, dig?"

"Absolutely, Mr. Bass. Johnno in his office?"

"Like Muhammad on the mountain. You know the way. Go

41

ahead on. I'll just tag along behind. And farm boy, you watch them brogans o' yours. Wouldn't want you breakin' none of our . . . old stuff."

"You don't know the half of it," Terry said cheerfully. "This way folks." Jud and I followed him in. Antiques Incroyable was a huge open warehouse, with metal roof supports clearly visible nearly three stories overhead. Its walls and aisles were stacked with metal shelving, every inch of them jammed with an incredible array of antiques, everything from Wedgwood china sets to crosscut saws.

The center of the store was dominated by a two-and-a-half-story office tower encircled by a winding wrought-iron staircase. Terry started up the steps without a word and I followed. At the second landing, I glanced back at Jud. He was moving very warily, staying close to the wall, keeping a hand on the railing for comfort. He looked uneasy, which made me uneasy. Was he afraid of heights? I hoped not. We were already above the second-story light fixtures and it was a long way down.

The top of the mesa was an elegant open-air square, guarded by a waist-high oaken railing on all four sides, offering a spectacular overview of the aisles of antiques two stories below. The only furnishings were an exquisitely carved mahogany desk and an IBM 386 computer off to the side. There were no chairs, not even a footstool. And I instantly understood the need for the giant with the shotgun. Johnno Habash was a bloated dwarf of a man with a silhouette like a suet block. He was wearing an expensively cut black suit that made him look like a toad in a tuxedo. Even his face seemed amphibian, fleshy, with an unhealthy frog-belly pallor, petulant lips, bulbous brown eyes.

He looked us over with ill-concealed distaste, like soiled goods he wasn't interested in buying.

"Johnno, you're lookin' good," Terry said. "I appreciate your seeing us on such short notice."

"I'm not seein' much," Johnno said. "And I won't be seein' it long. Time's money, Terry. So what's this all about?

"Mr. Habash," I said, "I understand my father, Shannon

Mitchell, contacted you about some kind of a business deal. I was hoping you could fill me in on the details."

Habash looked right through me as though I were invisible. "What is this bullshit, Terry? You said the bitch might have somethin' for me."

"Lighten up, Johnno," Terry said, smiling brightly, a danger sign I remembered from years before. "She's been working down in Texas, hasn't talked to her dad for a while. Maybe we can do each other some good here. Sometimes you gotta give to live."

"I don't have to give squat," Habash said bluntly. "You're on my ground now, playin' by my rules. Rule one is, I don't talk business with people I don't know."

"You know me," Terry said equably.

"Maybe, but I don't know this chick, or your Davy Crockett buddy there, and I guess I don't know you as good as I thought, Terry. Figured you for better sense. Look, this guy Mitchell's dead. That's too bad. Sorry to hear it, but it ain't no skin off my butt, you know? People die in this town every day. Sometimes even hicks from the sticks. You're wastin' my time, Terry. Maybe I better have Bass here haul your young ass down to the alley and straighten you out."

"Bad idea," Terry said calmly. "Nobody makes money that way. Besides, Bass here's a good man. You'd have a helluva time tryin' to replace him. Come on, Johnno, we know Shan Mitchell had something goin' with you. Help the lady out. Maybe we can all salvage something out of this."

Habash bridged his fingertips, eyeing me across manicured nails. "These're sorry-ass times we're livin' in," Habash said at last. "People fightin' over scraps. Cops and the IRS bustin' hump tryna nail honest citizens like myself. So I tell you what I'll do. Since they got little tape machines nowadays that can fit in your damn navel, I won't do any talkin'. But I'll listen. This here is Mr. Yes," he said, holding up his right hand, "and this is Mr. No." His left. "You got two minutes. Talk to me."

"Did my father contact you?" I asked. Habash cooly opened his right palm: yes.

"About doing some kind of a deal?" Again yes.

"What kind of a deal? What was involved?"

Habash's face told me nothing, nor did his hands.

"How much action was he into, Johnno?" Terry put in. "What was it worth? Twenty grand? Fifty?"

Still no response.

"More?"

"You really don't know shit about it, do you?" Habash frowned, shaking his head slowly. "Too bad. Thought maybe we could do some business. Forget it. Meet's over. Take your pals and take a hike, Terry. And I don't ever wanna see your ass again, about this or anything else. I don't do business with amateurs. Ever."

"Time's up, folks," Bass said, moving away from the railing. "The door's two floors down. You can use the stairs, or you can try flyin'. Your choice."

"You're making a mistake," Terry began, but Bass raised the shotgun a half inch. Terry sighed, took my arm firmly, and started toward the stairs.

But Jud didn't follow. "Wait a minute. This ain't right," he said slowly. "We came a long ways to see you, mister. You think you're some kinda big deal just because you own a fuckin' store? Mitch here owns a store, too. And she sells new stuff, not old junk like you got."

"Yo, shitkicker," Bass said, prodding Jud in the side with the shotgun muzzle, "maybe you don't get the picture—"

"You poke me with that thing again, I'm gonna feed it to you," Jud snapped, slapping the gun barrel away so quickly, I barely saw him move. Bass pivoted, whipping the gun butt up in a blur, slamming it savagely into Jud's cheek.

"Oh Jesus!" Terry said. "That tears it. Get outta here, Mitch! Head for the door!"

Jud wobbled but shook off the blow. For a frozen moment, Bass stared at him in disbelief. Then he tried to swing the gun muzzle up again, too late. Jud ripped the shotgun out of his grasp and spun it, cartwheeling, out over the railing.

Bass hit him, three solid body shots. Jud barely wavered.

"Sons a bitches!" Jud roared, his eyes blazing, his cheek streaming blood. Bass tried to knee him, but Jud avoided it and hammered Bass across the temple with a grimy fist, spinning him into the corner. Terry grabbed my wrist, jerking me back from the railing as the shotgun hit the floor two stories below and went off, punching a jagged hole through the ceiling.

Johnno was frantically scrabbling in his desk for a weapon when Jud reached across and hauled the small man out of his chair like a sack of potatoes.

"Now you're gonna talk to her, you little pimp," he snarled into Habash's face, "or I'll throw your punk ass out through your fuckin' front window!"

"Put him down, cracker," Bass said quietly, clawing an ugly little automatic from beneath his coat. "Do it now!"

Terry stepped between them, hands up, palms open. "C'mon, Bass, chill out. You shoot Rats with that popgun, you're just gonna piss him off and he'll bounce Johnno halfway to Motown."

"Damn it, Terry, your ass is dead meat!" Habash raved. "I'm gonna—" His ranting strangled to a squeak as Jud swung him out over the railing, suspending him in space, holding him one-handed. "Jeeeeeezuz! Wait a minute!"

"Mr. Habash," I said as calmly as I could, "I think you'd better tell us about the deal you and my father worked out."

"Christ, it was nothin'! I bought some merch from him!"

"What kind of merchandise?" Terry asked. "Ship's jewelry?"

"No, cargo! China. He had a couple cases of saucers. Prime stuff. Rookwood, '91. Untraceable. No historic value. A clean load."

"How much was involved?" Terry asked.

"Hell, I don't know. He wasn't sure himself, said he didn't have it all. He said twenty-grand worth, maybe a little more."

"Twenty grand?" Terry echoed.

45

"That's what he said, Terry, honest to Jesus! He sold me the stuff; I paid him seventy-five hundred cash. That was it. He said he'd have more later, but he never showed!"

"And you didn't wonder why?" I said. "And maybe pay him a visit to find out?"

"For some lousy china he maybe didn't have? Gimme a break, lady!" Habash babbled. "People offer me deals every damn day! This wasn't nothin' special for me. I figure he gets more, he'll bring it! If he don't, who cares? Now Jesus, please, tell your gorilla to let me down!"

"No problem," I said. "But first you'd better ask Mr. Bass to loan me his gun. Just so we all feel comfortable. Then we'll all walk down to the front door together. Can you carry him that far, Jud?"

"I can throw him that far," Jud snarled.

"Johnno?" Bass asked anxiously. "What you want I should—"

"Give her the goddamn piece, dumbshit! Before this crazy fuck drops me! Give it to her for Chrissake!"

Bass hesitated a moment, eyeing me carefully, as if memorizing my face. Then he passed me his weapon.

"Thank you," I said, and jacked a round into the chamber to show him I knew how to use it. "After you, Mr. Bass?"

CHAPTER 7

"TERRIFIC." TERRY SIGHED. "You're back in town exactly three freakin' days and you've already cost me the best contact I ever had." We were in his Jeep, cruising north on I-75 in sparse traffic, a light snow falling.

"Contact, my foot. He's a fence, Terry," I said. "What kind of business does he handle for you, anyway?"

Terry flared. "Whatever it takes. It's fine for you—you've been hangin' out down on the Gulf, drawing a fat-city Exxon paycheck, diving warm water with a ten-man backup team up top. Some of us have to scuffle."

"Don't talk to me about scuffling! I've done plenty of it!"

"Hey, Terry," Jud growled from the backseat. "You got a rag I can bum? I'm bleedin' on your seat covers."

I swiveled in the seat. The shotgun butt had opened a gash in Jud's cheek, a nasty purplish bruise that was trickling blood into his wine-stain birthmark. I groped a tissue out of my coat pocket and passed it back. "Turn your head. Let me—"

"No!" he said, snatching the tissue out of my hand and turning away. "I'll do it. It ain't about nothin'." He moistened the tissue with his tongue, then pressed it firmly against the wound. The bleeding slowed to a trickle but didn't stop entirely.

"I think we'd better have that looked at," I said. "You may need stitches."

"No." Jud scowled. "I'm okay. I been hit harder plenty of times. Just lemme alone."

"Terry?"

"You heard the man, Mitch. He says he's okay," Terry said. "Hell, his head probably did more damage to the shotgun than it did to him."

"Nice friends you have," I said.

"They weren't friends. . . . Well, maybe Bass was. But not anymore. I'll be lucky if Johnno doesn't have me whacked out for this. Jesus, Rats, did you have to——"

"Don't call me that, Terry," Jud said coldly. "I ain't tellin' you again."

"Yes, sir, Mr. Radowicz." Terry sighed. "Sorry, I forgot. But do me a favor. Next summer when you're bummin' around the harbor lookin' for work, ask me last, okay? Better yet, don't ask me at all."

"You still want me to work for you, Mitch?" Jud asked. "Or are you pissed off at me, too?"

"No, I'm not angry. I'm grateful. Habash wasn't going to tell us anything until you . . . did what you did."

"I lost it is what I did," Jud said gloomily. "It happens sometimes. My mom used to say be nice to people and they'll be nice to you. Bullshit. Most people ain't nice. They don't like me, and I got no use for them, neither. And now my mom's gone, I don't hafta fake bein' nice no more."

"Terrific upbeat attitude you have there, *Mr.* Radowicz," Terry said. "It'll take you a long way. The sooner the better."

"Lay off him," I snapped.

"Yes, ma'am," Terry said cooly. "Why doesn't everybody just lay off everybody?"

We drove the rest of the way to Huron Harbor in silence. Nearly two hours without a word.

"You want me to drop you at your dad's place or the Nest?" Terry said at last, as we approached the Ponemah Point turnoff.

"The Nest. My car's still there."

"Let me out when you pass the point," Jud said.

"I can give you a lift home if you like," I offered.

"Nah, I better walk. My head hurts. The cold will help.

'Sides, Dog won't know your car. She'd be waitin' all night by the road. Lemme out here, Terry."

Terry eased the Jeep to the shoulder. Jud climbed out and trudged off into the dark without a backward glance. If Dog was lurking in the area, I couldn't see her.

"I warned you about Rats," Terry said, gunning the Jeep back onto the highway. "He was on your side tonight, but I've seen him flip out like that over nothing at all. Cut him loose, Mitch. Next time, it could be you he tosses off a balcony."

"He may have a shaky grip on reality," I conceded. "Still, you've got to admit, he came in handy tonight."

"Handy? Is that how you see it? Lady, from where I'm sittin', we blew a piece of my action and bought me a boatload of trouble for nothing."

"What do you mean?"

"Look, as I understand it, you think your father may have been involved in something heavy and got himself killed, right? That maybe somebody arranged his accident?"

"I don't know," I said carefully. "Maybe."

"Okay, for the sake of argument, let's say you're right. God knows, Shan drew trouble like a honey bear draws bees. Hell, I could probably make you a list right now of a dozen people who might've taken him out, but Johnno's name would be a lot nearer the bottom than the top."

"Why?"

"Because he may be a first-class jerk, but he's also a businessman, and according to him, the only business he had with Shan was a few grand's worth of china."

"Or so he said."

"Granted"—Terry nodded—"but since he was hangin' three stories in the air at the time, I think there's a fair chance he was tellin' us the flat-ass truth. You have any reason to think he wasn't?"

"No." I sighed. "In fact, I think he probably was, too."

"You know anything about the china he was talking about?"

"I may have one cup. It's Rookwood all right, but there's only one."

"Maybe there wasn't any more. But either way, I'd say if Habash was telling the truth about the china, that about wraps it up."

"Why should it?"

"C'mon, you saw Habash's place. He wouldn't get all hot and bothered over a twenty-grand deal. He probably bets more'n that on the Pistons."

"Suppose there was a lot more. He said Shan didn't know how much there was."

"Even so, he'd have waited until after he had it, unless . . ."

"What?"

"Unless Shan tried to cheat him somehow," Terry said, frowning. "Johnno's got a rep as a bad man to cross. That might change the picture a lot. I can't see him going after Shan for twenty grand's worth of pie in the sky. But to get even? Maybe."

"Want to move him higher up on your list?"

"No, I don't think so. For openers, Shan never cheated anybody I ever heard of. Besides, he died in the swamp, a few miles from his house. Do you think Habash or Bass, or a half dozen more like them, could've handled your father on his own ground?"

"No," I conceded, "probably not."

"I guarantee they couldn't. Messin' with your old man was like slam-dancin' with a train. And I'm speaking from experience."

"What experience? When did you ever have trouble with my father?"

"Once, a long time ago. It doesn't matter now," he said, wheeling the Jeep into the Crow's Nest parking lot. "I was just a kid. And I lost."

"I see. Do you want to tell me about it?"

"Maybe sometime. Not tonight. Look, I'm gonna be out of town for a few weeks, maybe longer. Baggers picked us up a job working high steel down in South Bend, and after the way things went with Johnno, I'd better be hard to find for a while. I did you a favor tonight, Mitch. Now I want one back. Get rid of Rats. Please. He's crazier'n that wolf of his. Okay?"

"I'll think about it," I said, climbing out of the Jeep. "Thanks for your help, Terry. I'm sorry if it worked out badly for you."

"I'll get by. Or maybe I won't, depending on how long Habash stays ticked off. Think you'll still be here when I get back?"

"I don't know," I said honestly. "Maybe."

"Well if you're not, leave a forwarding address. I, um, I don't want to lose track of you again."

"No? Why not?"

"Damned if I know." He sighed. "I must be a glutton for punishment. You're a dangerous woman, Mitch. Swear to God, you're riskier to be around than Shan ever was. You watch yourself, hear? Promise me."

"I will, I promise." Our eyes met and held for a moment, and then he nodded and drove off without looking back. Terry Fortier. Last of the romantics.

But he was right about one thing: My father had been a dangerous man to be around. And in a way, he still was.

CHAPTER 8

THE COTTAGE LOOKED DIFFERENT to me when I drove up that night. I'd always thought of it as lonely and isolated. But after the kind of day I'd had, it just seemed . . . secluded. Private.

I made myself a cup of coffee and gazed out the beachfront window, marveling at the moonlit shadows on the ice and the shore, turned away to see what I could find for dinner, and—stopped. I had that nagging feeling that something was odd. Out of place.

I turned back to the window, scanning the yard, the beach, and the ice beyond. No, whatever it was wasn't out on the ice. It was open and empty as far as the eye could see. Something in the yard? It took a moment to register. The boathouse on the beach—something was there that shouldn't have been. In the wan glow of the yard lights, I could see a padlock on the boathouse door: a large one. But if my father sold Terry his boat, why bother to put a lock on an empty shed, especially out here?

Unless it was being used to store something else.

I pulled on a pair of heavy snow boots, grabbed my parka and a flashlight, and trotted across the yard. The boathouse was a garage-sized white clapboard outbuilding built over a narrow artificial channel that led out into Thunder Bay like a frozen driveway. The padlock on the side door was definitely brand-new, a combination-type Master lock, massive and damn near indestructible. The only way to get past it would be to pry the hasp out of the doorjamb with a crowbar. Unfortunately, my father kept his tools in the boatshed. Stalemate? No way.

I fetched the tire iron from the trunk of my rental car and grunted and cursed and barked my knuckles for twenty minutes prying the damned lock off. For nothing. As soon as I swung the door open and flicked the flashlight into the gloom, I could see the shed was empty. No boat, no plunder, just the gray ice of the frozen channel for a floor and my father's cluttered workbench along the far wall.

Something crawled across my legs. Spider? I played the flashlight down at my feet—and froze. A clear monofilament fishing line stretched across the open doorway, tugging against my shins, almost invisible in the shadows: a trip wire. I traced it with the light beam, following it along the wall, then across the room to the workbench. To my father's shotgun, locked in the bench vise, its barrel aimed directly at the door. And at my kneecaps. Sweet Jesus.

I was instantly drenched in cold sweat, chill as an ice-water shower. The line felt taut against my leg. How much slack was left? I couldn't tell. Keeping the light beam on the line, I slid my left hand down my pant leg to keep the trip wire from snapping back when I stepped away. I took a shallow, ragged breath, then very slowly started shifting my feet backward, a millimeter at a time, until my legs were clear of the filament. Then I eased my finger back until the line returned to its original position across the open doorway.

I sidestepped out of the line of fire, sagged against the wall, and the damn gun went off, hammering a round of buckshot through the doorway beside me.

That bastard! The shot had erased the line, and I stormed into the empty shed, unlocked the vise, jerked the shotgun free, and smashed it over the bench, shattering the stock. Christ, he could have killed me! What kind of a psycho would booby-trap an empty shed? He . . .

He wouldn't have. As my panicky heart rate slowly subsided, that realization gradually sank in. He had a murderous temper, my father, one I'd inherited. But he wasn't crazy, at least not altogether. He wouldn't have set a death trap to stand guard over nothing. So what was in here that was worth killing some-one?

I tossed the broken shotgun aside on the bench and played the flashlight around the room. The boat entrance door was barred from the inside, so whatever it was should still be in here. But there was nothing! An empty room, nothing on the walls, only a few odd tools on the bench, the floor a frozen sheet of . . .

Ice. But it wasn't smooth. There were tracks embedded in it, gouge marks from a tread and metal skis. A snowmobile had been driven in here through the channel door. And something heavy had apparently been unloaded onto the ice, something heavy enough to mark it with deep grooves in a six-foot square.

Frowning, I eyed the square. It was too large. You couldn't possibly carry anything on a snowmobile that would take up this much space or weigh enough to make impressions like these. I knelt and ran my fingers over the grooves. They were jagged, of uneven depth. But they hadn't been pressed into the ice by something that had rested on it. They'd been cut into it. And I only knew one way to cut through ice this thick.

I jogged back to the house and found the chain saw I'd fallen over in the entryway that first night—a 2-horsepower Stihl with a sixteen-inch blade. It had seen some hard use. The chain teeth were worn, much too dull to use for cutting wood—but sharp enough for ice.

Back in the shed, it took four or five pulls on the starter cord to get the unfamiliar saw running, but eventually it fired up, blatting away like a machine gun. I revved the engine, getting it warm, then lowered the blade to the ice. It bit in fiercely, spray-ing the room with chips and splinters, howling like an air-raid siren in the enclosed metal shed. I should have been wearing safety goggles and earmuffs and heavier gloves, but I didn't care. I was too close now, and much too pumped up.

The blade chewed through to the water beneath, and I traced the line of the square around until the slab broke free, rocking beneath my weight. I shut off the saw and set it on the bench, my head clanging like a fire alarm in the sudden silence.

I stepped on one edge of the slab. It sagged in the water, tilting the opposite side up. When the far edge was high enough, I simply thrust it up and over the rim like a sliding door.

The water was roiled from the movement of the slab, so it took a few moments before I could see anything clearly. But they were down there: wooden crates, six of them, streaked with lake-bottom mud, with wisps of sodden excelsior sticking through the slats. I knelt beside the hole, trying to read the faded print on the cases. I couldn't make it out. It was too faint. The top of the uppermost box had been pried off, so I shucked my parka, rolled up my sleeve, and reached down into the roiled water, feeling the icy bite of it clamp onto my arm like a bear trap. I fumbled gingerly inside the box, feeling for metal, or another trip wire. If my father'd booby-trapped the shed, maybe he'd . . . My fingers brushed something smooth, and curved. I closed around it and carefully lifted it out.

A cup. A single china cup. With a familiar pattern: Rockwood. A mate to the one in the house. I set it carefully aside, dried my arm as best I could, and slipped into my jacket. Six cases of antique china in mint condition. I wasn't sure how old the stuff was. Habash had said '91, and it certainly looked old enough to be turn of the century or earlier from the condition of the boxes. I'm no expert on china, but I know enough about salvage to know the crates were probably worth a couple of thousand each, maybe more. But not nearly enough.

The figure Johnno had mentioned was twenty thousand or so. Even at $2,500 per case, this cache wasn't worth that. It wouldn't come close to making up the loss my father was willing to take for a quick sale of the Crow's Nest. Besides, he'd stored the boxes underwater to keep the excelsior from freezing and pulverizing the china, but if these six cases were the lot, he wouldn't have bothered to keep it here. He would have carried it into the cottage.

So there had to be more of it. Perhaps a whole shipload more. And maybe I even knew where it was. Or where it had been, anyway.

I'm not sure I would have called Sheriff Bauer even if there'd been a phone. In any case, there wasn't. I went back to the house and took a bearing on the crossed-finger ice spire where I'd seen movement the first night. It appeared to be about two miles out on the bay, a serious hike over the ice. But not impossible, especially since I was fairly certain there'd be a trail of some kind out there. Leaving the yard lights on to give myself a homing beacon, I loaded a full clip into the butt of my father's .45 automatic, slid it into my parka pocket, and set off.

CHAPTER 9

FOLLOWING THE NICKS and chips the snowmobile cleats had gouged in the boat-channel ice was easy enough, but once I was clear of the lakeshore, the wind and the swirling snow devils made walking difficult and making out the faint traces of the narrow track even harder.

At least visibility wasn't a problem. High above the bay, mountainous clouds drifted like ice floes in an indigo sky. The moon was partially occluded but still bright as a beacon. It was nearly full, and the ice served as a giant reflector for it, throwing everything on the surface of the lake into glistening crystal relief.

The pack stretched out ahead and around me like a moonscape of thrusting slabs, jagged craters, and occasional ebon pools of lustrous black glass, scoured and polished by the wind. From shore, the ice appears white, but out here on the cap it's dappled, the skin of an ancient lady, beige patches of windblown beach sand, grayish soot smudges, and inky shadows that stretch like fingers from every ridge and turret.

I moved cautiously out from the shore, following the scrapes and gouges of the snowmobile tracks. The only sounds were the crunch of my own footsteps on the snow and the whisper of the wind. And, of course, the night sounds of the Lady of the Lake.

Beneath her alabaster shroud, I could feel her moving in her dreams. Her tides follow the moon, harrying the waters of a thousand rivers ever eastward to the St. Lawrence and the sea. The floating pack responds like a lover, with gentle shifts and moans and murmurs. And occasionally, a sharp crack instantly reminds you of the depth and darkness of the waters below. And of the spirits who sleep there. You can't grow up in the north country without knowing someone who has died on the ice. Fishing, or snowmobiling. Or just walking across it.

The firmness of the pack is an illusion. It's riddled with holes, air pockets hidden by crusted snow, gaps in the plate seams camouflaged by a thin ice skin. I knew this, of course, but I also knew that as long as I kept to the snowmobile track, I should be safe enough. Even a small machine weighs roughly fifteen hundred pounds, and one hauling cargo, probably a ton or more. Anywhere the snowmobile had been, I could follow.

The only flaw in this comforting theory was that I kept losing the trail beneath drifted snow or where a plate had shifted and erased the track. When it happened, I had to slow my pace and choose my steps cautiously. But each time, I managed to find the track again simply by picking out the smoothest direct route. Ordinarily, a snowmobile could sprint through this kind of broken icescape like a mustang, but the one I was following would have needed a level road to keep from smashing up its fragile cargo.

I was nearly a mile from shore when the moon broke through, bringing the surface of the ice to life with the ghostly dancing of cloud shadows. The poignant, untouchable beauty of the night was hypnotic, and not for the first time I felt the lure of the Lady below, calling to me in the half-remembered voice of the mother I never knew. Come down, come down to me. . . . Leave your world. Sleep with me. Stay with me. . . .

And I almost did.

I found the crossed-finger ice marker two miles out, but the track continued beyond it, northward. How far, I couldn't be sure. And at that point, I was so entranced by the silvery spell of the night that I would have followed the path another five hundred miles. To Canada, or oblivion. So I trudged on, nudged by the night wind, hearing only the crunch of snow beneath my boots and the murmur of the pack like low voices from another room. . . .

And then I stopped—so suddenly, I surprised myself. There was a faint pattern in the ice ahead: a crude square. It could have been natural, but somehow I knew it wasn't. The snowmobile track veered sharply to the right and ended a few feet away.

I cautiously stepped to the edge of the square and stamped my foot over the line. And punched through the crust so easily, I nearly stumbled in. This was the place, then.

I switched on my flashlight and played it around, not looking for anything in particular, more to be seen than to see. I found a few marks, mud splotches and frozen puddles on the ice where the crates had been lifted free. I knelt beside them, looking for footprints, but the surface was too rough. . . . And I gradually felt a psychic touch, the uneasy sense that I was being watched. But I knew it couldn't be true. The ice pack was swimming in moonlight. I literally could see for miles in every direction, and there was nothing *to* see but ice and snow and shadows. . . .

And yet I had that feeling, as sharp and cold as an ice pick between my shoulder blades.

I played the flashlight around in ever-widening circles. And suddenly caught twin reflections, eyes staring at me unblinking from fifty yards beyond the square out on the pack. A shape rose up out of the snow and began moving slowly toward me, head down, circling. And I felt a soul-deep shiver of dread older than my life, older than words. A gray shadow, drifting across the snow silent as smoke. A wolf. No, not a wolf.

Dog.

CHAPTER 10

———————

THE CROSS-WOLF MOVED toward me in total silence, no growling, not so much as a whisper of her pads gliding over the ice. At times, she seemed to disappear, melting into the moon shadows so perfectly, I couldn't define her form until she moved again. And each time she was closer. Much closer.

I closed my fist around the butt of the .45 in my coat pocket, but it didn't offer much comfort. In the moonlight, I'd have no chance of hitting her until she was close enough to charge, and that might be too late.

I heard a faint whine from behind me and risked a quick glance away from Dog, toward the shore. Another shape was moving out there, coming in our direction, but not silently. A snowmobile, low and black, was running without lights, towing a sledge behind it, snaking through the broken surface of the pack like a slalom racer. Dog heard it, too, and slowed her advance, crouching in the shadow of a snow hummock, a formless threat, invisible except for the metallic glint of her eyes.

The snowmobile whined to a halt a few yards away. Judgement Christ Radowicz unfolded himself from the machine, a hulking scarecrow figure, the night wind snapping his tattered coat. And part of me was glad it was Jud. I'd been half-expecting Terry. He unstrapped a tool from the sled, a double-bitted brush ax. He didn't threaten me with it. He just held it. "Turn out the light," he said. "Somebody might see it."

"Maybe they have already," I said.

"Nah, it don't look that bright from shore. I wouldna seen it if I wasn't watchin'. I was gonna talk to you about this," he said, gesturing toward the ice patch behind me. "I was hopin' I could wait awhile, see what you was like, but it don't matter now. How did you find out? Shan leave a note or somethin'?"

"No. I saw you out here the night I arrived. I didn't know what it meant at the time."

"I been comin' out every night to bust up the ice," he said, hefting the ax. "Otherwise, it'll freeze over; I'd have to use the saw again. Noise carries a long ways out here. You know what's down there?"

"A wreck." I said. "With a cargo of china."

"Ain't much to it." He nodded. "Superstructure's all tore away. Only thing left is the keel. Shan tried to figure out who she was, looked her up in some books he had. She might be the *Victorine* outta Chicago, 1891, but there ain't enough left of her to be sure. I found her fishin' last fall. Sunlight was just right, and I made out her shape on the bottom. She's fifty feet down, too deep for me—I got the bad ears. But Shan didn't have no trouble and you won't have, neither. We can go partners."

"Can we? Things didn't turn out very well for your last partner, Jud."

"No," he said, shaking his massive head slowly, "they didn't. But it didn't have nothin' to do with me."

"Didn't it? Maybe you'd better tell me about it. What happened to my father, Jud?"

"We had it all worked out. Shan said he had a guy who'd take the stuff. I din't know who he was until today. We figured we could make three, maybe four runs a night durin' the dark of the moon, stash the cases in his boathouse. He said there was at least twenty boxes down there."

"I only found six in the boathouse," I said.

"We could only make a couple runs a night. Two cases are all the sledge'll carry, and we had to get 'em ashore fast before they froze up and crushed the china. We got three cases that first night, the ones Shan sold to that little pimp in Saginaw.

"The second night, by the time we brung in the third load,

lights was startin' to go on along the bay shore, you know, people gettin' up, gettin' ready for work? Couldn't risk gettin' spotted, so Shan figured we better pack it in, try again the next night. Only there wasn't no next night."

"Why not?"

"I . . . I went outta town for a couple days. Took longer'n I figured. They killed him while I was gone."

"Who killed him?"

"I don't know." He frowned, looking away. "Everything was all messed up by the time I got back. Cops'd been all over the place, screwed up the tracks, but I could read enough to tell Shan was haulin' ass way too fast for that road. He wouldna done that. He knew how dangerous it was. It was like he was runnin' from somethin'. Or maybe to somethin'. But I don't think it was no accident. Hell, he drove that road a million times drunk and sober without crackin' up. And even if he ran off, he coulda made it back to the bank easy, steada . . ."

"Instead of what?"

"Insteada crawlin' away to die in the dark like he done. Like he was afraid, scared to death of somethin'. Swear to God, that ol' man wasn't afraid of nothin'."

"Maybe he was afraid of you."

"Me? Nah, Shan had no call to be scared of me. He could whip my ass anytime. Done it more'n once."

"Did he? And how did you feel about that?"

"About what? Gettin' slapped around? It didn't mean nothin', Mitch. I had it comin' both times. And it ain't like it was the first time I been beat on. You look like I do, ass whuppin' kinda comes with the territory. I mostly give better'n I get, but even when you win, you still get hammered. I'm used to it. I been gettin' it all my life." He swallowed and looked away. His face was in shadow. I couldn't read it at all.

"Why didn't you go back for the stuff in the boathouse?" I asked, risking a quick glance over at Dog.

"I could have, easy. Shan gave me the combination to the

lock, warned me about the booby trap. I just left it be, waitin' for you to come back. They tried, though."

"Who did?"

"I don't know. Maybe the ones who done him. They come out to the house twice snoopin' around, but I set Dog on 'em, fired a couple shots in the dark, and run 'em off. I never got a good look at their car, and they never come back."

"But if you two were partners, why didn't he tell you about Habash, Jud? Didn't he trust you?"

"He didn't have to. I trusted him. Anyway, deep down I don't think Shan really trusted nobody. It's just how he was."

"But I can trust you, right?"

"Sure you can. Look, I waited for you, didn't I? I mean, if I wanted to cut you out, I coulda got somebody else."

"Maybe. Or maybe you just didn't know anybody you could trust. Or more likely, you couldn't find anyone who'd trust you."

"I coulda got Terry. He'da gone for it, and you know it. But I didn't. I waited for you, Mitch. You always treated me decent, never called me names, and you had more reason than any of 'em. Look," he said, starting forward, "we can work things out between us back onshore, but right now we gotta bust up the hole again and get outta here before somebody spots us."

"Don't come any closer," I said, pulling the .45 out of my parka.

"Damn it, Mitch, don't be stupid," he said, halting. "We can't stay out here."

"We'll go," I said, "but first, toss that ax away."

"I'd never hurt you, Mitch. You must know that."

"All I know is, my father's dead and you were involved in it somehow. Maybe it happened the way you said. But it's also possible you and Dog just kept him from climbing out of the water long enough for him to lose consciousness. Then you let the cold finish him off and faked the accident."

"That's crazy. Why should I do that?"

"Maybe because you heard he was taking off with his girl-friend and thought he was going to cheat you."

"He woudna done that. Hell, he already gave me half the money he got from Habash. I blew most of it, but I got some left."

"That's just one more reason I should doubt you, Jud. Maybe you just got greedy and wanted it all. Figuring motives is Charlie Bauer's job, not mine. But one thing I am sure of. I've got a chance for a new life up here, and I'm not going to start it by plundering a wreck, with you or anybody else."

"No," he said, "that ain't fair. I've never had nothin'. This is the only chance I'll ever get. Shan promised to do right by me before he left. You can't just throw it away. You got no right."

He shuffled toward me, a ragged Neanderthal, ax in hand. "Jud, back off," I said, raising the .45. "I don't want to shoot anybody, but I'm up to it if I have to."

"Look, at least let me bust up the hole, and we can—"

From the corner of my eye, I caught a flash of movement, Dog snaking rapidly toward us, belly to the ground, fangs bared, snarling a deep rumble that seemed to emanate from the ice itself. "Call her off, Jud!" She rose suddenly and I fired a warning shot toward her, the gun blasting like a lightning strike in the darkness.

"*Noo!* Don't!" Jud howled, hurling himself at me. I slashed him across the temple with the gun barrel as he slammed into me chest-high, but the force of his rush hurled us backward onto the broken ice field. We came down hard together, hammering at each other, and then the ice crust collapsed and we plunged into the freezing dark.

CHAPTER 11

THE SHOCK WAS INCREDIBLE, the chill so fierce I almost cried out. Jud's weight was carrying me down, deeper into the icy blackness. I twisted free of him, forgot about the damned gun, forgot everything but clawing my way back up to the gray jumble of ice above me, breaking through, gasping for air, then flinching backward as Dog lunged at me from the edge of the hole, her fangs clashing only inches from my face.

Jud thrashed to the surface a few feet behind me, flailing blindly about, blood streaming from the gash on his temple over the stain on his cheek, dazed, desperate. I tried to grope my way to the edge, but the ice chunks broke away in my hands, freezing to my arms like iron leeches. Dog was berserk, charging frantically back and forth, snarling, whining. Then suddenly, she launched herself into the water with us, crashing into my shoulder, smashing me aside as she tried to get to Jud. God, it was horrible. She couldn't swim in the broken ice, and we were all plunging about, churning in the freezing cauldron like souls in hell.

I thrust myself away from them, struggling through the broken ice toward the far side. I managed to find a fingerhold on the pack, then slowly, agonizingly dragged myself up out of the water a millimeter at a time, my fingernails breaking away, hands slipping, too numb to grip. I inched my shoulders onto the ice, then gave a scissors kick and rolled my legs out.

For a moment, I just lay there, barely conscious. Then I forced myself up to my hands and knees, head down, chest heaving like a spent animal, water streaming from my hair, my clothes.

A howl from behind me brought me out of the haze. Dog was half out of the water, scrabbling desperately at the rim, Jud clinging to her pelt, but neither of them could hold on, and they slid back into the black water. Jud lost his grip on her fur and went under, and Dog quit trying to save herself and tried to paddle to him. Then something snapped in me.

An atavistic *no* came roaring up out of my subconscious. Get up! Move! Move! You can't let them die like this! You just can't!

I crawled on my hands and knees around the edge of the pool, toward them. I groped in the water for Jud, managed to tangle my fist in his hair, and hauled his shoulders clear of the water. I didn't have strength enough to pull him out, but he weakly squirmed free of the ice and onto the pack, then collapsed beside me, moaning like a child, blood trickling down his cheek, staining the snow crimson.

Dog tried to struggle toward us, but she could make no headway in the broken ice, and her endurance was nearly gone. She sank once, then managed to fight her way to the surface, but I knew she couldn't do it again. Damn it!

I took a deep breath, then gingerly reached out, fumbling for the scruff of her neck, but the moment I touched her, she whirled and clamped onto my arm, her fangs tearing through my coat, my arm instantly afire with agony.

I yelled and tried to pull free, and saved her miserable life as she came boiling up onto the ice. I hammered her face with my left hand, jabbing at her eyes, and she let go and spun away, snarling, crouching to spring again.

But she didn't. She stood her ground, glaring at me, eyes alight with fury, and if I'd had the damned gun, I would have shot her on the spot. Jud tried to stand, but his legs folded and he fell, more dead than alive. And so was I. The wind was picking up, whining out of the dark, dusting us with frost, slowing us, chilling us to death. We had to get away from this place, to find shelter and warmth, or we'd die.

I managed to coax Jud to the sledge. He had to crawl on his own, because whenever I reached for him, Dog lunged at me, warning me off, and there was no doubt in my mind she'd tear me apart if I touched him. He finally dragged himself aboard the sledge, then collapsed, unconscious or nearly so. The snow-mobile fired up with the first touch of the switch, thank God, because my strength was nearly spent and my will to go on seemed to be fading with it. I flicked on the headlight and gunned the machine forward, with Jud unconscious on the sledge behind and Dog trotting alongside.

Following the track out on foot, where I could pause and look around, had been difficult, but picking it out in the glare of the headlight was almost impossible. And I had to stay on the trail. To stray off course in the dark would be death. If we broke through the ice again, or even got stuck, we'd never make the shore. It was too far to walk, and much too cold.

Dog had the better of it. At least she was moving. The night wind howled down from the moon, sweeping across the ice, freezing my clothing to me, numbing my face, my senses, freezing my hands to the grips. The snow began to shimmer and dance. . . .

And apparently I blacked out.

Somewhere on the trip back, I must have lost consciousness completely. I don't remember smashing up the machine near shore, or crawling to my car, or driving it until I ran into a road sign on U.S. 23. They tell me I did. I honestly don't remember. I was unconscious until noon the next day, nearly fourteen hours later.

And only then did anyone go to look for Jud.

CHAPTER 12

"NOTHING," Charlie Bauer said. "We found the snowmobile wrecked about a hundred yards out on the ice. I don't know how you made it ashore. There was no sign of him near the machine. Maybe he . . . dropped off farther out. With the wind blowing the way it was, it would have erased his tracks in minutes. We checked at his shack and your house. He wasn't there and it didn't look like he had been, either. Nothing was disturbed. I sent a Coast Guard chopper out in the afternoon. Visibility on the lake was good from the air. They didn't see anything but ice."

"You think he's dead, don't you?" I asked. We were in the hospital dayroom at Huron St. Joseph's. The wan winter sun was slowly fading to dusk. Twilight time.

"I don't know," Charlie said. "But there are patches of open water out there. If he stumbled into one . . . On the other hand, he grew up on that point. Lived on it all his life. It's possible he found shelter somewhere. God knows, he's strong as an ox."

"Or a wolf," I said.

"Look, I hope you won't take offense at this question, Mitch, but are you absolutely sure he was there at all? You were in pretty bad shape when they brought you in."

"He was there all right. He came out on the snowmobile. But beyond that, I'm not altogether clear on what happened. He, um, he told me they killed my father."

"Who killed him?"

"He didn't know. It didn't make much sense. He said it must

68

have been someone Shan was afraid of. But he wasn't afraid of anyone."

"You're right," Charlie said. "That doesn't make much sense. What do you think it meant?"

"I'm not sure it meant anything. I think more likely, Rats was involved in his death somehow. They were plundering the wreck together. Maybe they fell out over the money, I don't know. Maybe Rats ran him off the road or something. Could it have happened that way?"

"No, no chance."

"You seem very sure."

"I may be a small-town sheriff, Mitch, but I know my job. I didn't like the way your father died. It didn't seem right to me, still doesn't. But no matter how I worked the evidence, I couldn't make it add up to foul play. One, there were no signs of a collision on your dad's truck, and no tracks at the scene other than his. He just . . . Walked away from the wreck. Into the dark."

"Could he have been chased? Maybe by Jud's wolf?"

"I don't see how. Even a wolf leaves sign, and anyway, he could have just stayed in his vehicle until help came."

"But if Jud was—"

"Radowicz wasn't there, Mitch. Couldn't have been. He had a perfect alibi, absolutely ironclad. He was in jail down at Oscoda the night Shan was killed. He was out drinking the night before, got in a bar fight with a couple of lumberjacks, busted them up pretty good. State police tanked him four days, drunk and disorderly, then cut him loose when the 'jacks wouldn't press charges."

"I see," I said slowly.

"No," he said, "you don't. I've got a problem here, Mitch. And I'm honestly not sure how to handle it."

"What kind of a problem?"

"The worst kind, a matter of ethics. I've lived in the north country all my life, been on the department since I got out of

69

the army. I know the people around here—too well sometimes. I remember when you came to live with your dad, back when you were in high school. I thought you were just about the prettiest little tomboy I'd ever seen. I still do."

"That's . . . nice," I said evenly. "But that's not what you want to tell me, is it?"

"No," he said, turning away from the window, facing me. "And maybe I'm making a mistake telling you at all. But it's likely to come out now, so maybe it's best you hear it from me."

"Hear what?"

"Look, there's no easy way to say this, so here it is, straight up. One of my duties as sheriff is to oversee the Friend of the Court's office, you know, collecting child support? Your dad sent us a check every month. He was never late."

"What are you talking about? He never paid me a dime—"

"Not for you," Charlie interrupted. "To Stella Radowicz, Jud's mother. He paid her child support until Jud turned eighteen."

"What are you saying?" I asked. But it was only reflex. Some small part of me knew instantly, bone-deep, that it was true.

"I'm sorry," he said. "I know this is a bad time for you, but I thought you should know. You told me once I had a lousy bedside manner. You were right."

"Yeah, I guess I was," I said. "Still, I, um . . . Thanks for telling me, Charlie. It was the right thing to do. I just don't know what to . . . make of it right now."

"I understand. And I'm sorry, Mitch, sorry as hell about everything. We'll keep looking, you know."

"I know."

"Well, I'd better get back to it. You do know the DNR will seize the cargo, right? It's technically state property."

"They're welcome to it. I want no part of it."

"Right. I'll tell 'em," he said, turning to go. "I'll see you tomorrow."

"I won't be here," I said.

"You're not leaving town?" he said, his face showing so much concern that I smiled in spite of myself. It was a good face, strong and honest. Funny, I hadn't really noticed before. I hadn't ever looked past the uniform.

"Not the town, Charlie, just the hospital. I don't like them. I've never had much fun in one."

"I know the feeling. But don't try to rush things, okay? You've had a rough go of it. Try to take it easy for a few days, anyway. I'll see you later."

He left, but I really didn't see him go. I was already drifting away, back out on the ice in the moon shadows. They killed him, Jud said. Somebody he was afraid of killed him. . . . And then he started walking toward me, carrying the ax. . . .

—⟐ I left the hospital the next day and spent a night at Red's apartment, then went home to the point. I worked only half days at the Nest for the next week. I didn't seem to have much stamina. I left early every afternoon to drive out to Jud's shack to check on it. There was no trace of him, no tracks, no sign at all he'd been there. After the first few days, I knew there wouldn't be any.

But I kept going back, anyway.

I wanted him to be alive. I needed him to be. He might have been involved in my father's death somehow. I needed to ask him about that and look into his eyes when he answered. But most of all, I wanted to ask him about the checks, canceled checks I found in the dive shop in a box with the rest of my father's missing papers. Paid monthly to Stella Radowicz, Jud's mother. By my father.

Eighteen years' worth, just as Charlie said.

I know what they were for. What they must have been for. We were all of a size, my father and me. And Jud. But I'll never truly be sure until I look into his face and, for the first time, try to see past that damned birthmark.

But I never will.

He's gone. I think the Lady must have taken him, down and down, to sleep in the deep green halls of her icewater mansions.

In my heart, I knew it was true. Because ten days after Jud disappeared, Dog came back. I saw her on the beach at dusk, gaunt as her own ghost, her gray pelt rimed with ice, her pads bloody and swollen. I called her, but she wouldn't come to me. She roams the point now, guarding Jud's house, and mine. I put food out for her, and sometimes she eats it, but mostly she kills her own. She was a one-man Dog. She's all wolf now.

And sometimes I wake in the moonlight, and I see her sitting on the lakeshore, staring out over the ice, waiting for someone she's lost.

And so do I. And so do I.

CHAPTER 13

Spring

THE EARTHQUAKE shook me out of a dream. I sat up in bed, dazed, still half-asleep, disoriented by the deep bass rumbling that seemed to be coming through the floor. I threw off the covers, groping for my robe, trying to remember where to take shelter. . . .

Crazy. I shook my head, trying to wake up. It couldn't be an earthquake. Not this far north. But it was. In the dull pewter glow of a March dawn, the bedroom was shuddering like an overloaded freight elevator. I wasn't dreaming. I could feel the vibration, hear the roaring off in the distance, like a train or heavy earth-moving equipment. Then a tree snapped, loud as a gunshot. And suddenly, I realized what it meant. I checked the outdoor thermometer through the porch window. The temperature read forty-two degrees Fahrenheit. And it was raining, a steady gray drizzle.

I scrambled into jeans, a sweatshirt, and boots, grabbed my parka, and sprinted out to my spanking new pickup, a loaded metallic blue Chevy S-10 I'd bought with my father's wreck and a bite out of my savings.

I drove warily down to the Silver Creek Bridge. A second tree snapped off as I approached. I parked well away from the bridge for safety's sake, then walked slowly toward it through the downpour. Fat droplets spattered my face, soaking my hair, trickling down my neck. I should have brought an umbrella. But it didn't matter.

The river ice was moving, not in bits and chunks but in great jagged slabs the size of boxcars. Two days of steady rain combined with snowmelt had raised the level of the stream, lifting the anchor ice away from its riverbank moorings, and now the unrelenting pressure of the current had broken it free, sending massive plates hurtling pell-mell downstream toward the great lake.

The floes did not go gently into that good night. They raged, thundering, gouging black loam from the banks and rocks from the riverbed, lunging ashore to snap off small trees or to rip them bodily from the earth, root systems and all, carrying them along like trophies, offerings to the mother of waters.

I watched for nearly an hour, soaked to the skin, transfixed by the sheer inexorable power of this upstart little stream, swollen beyond the shackles of its channel, literally moving mountains of ice and earth lakeward. It held a message for me. Not one that I understood completely, but I felt it nonetheless, to my soul.

A dual message, actually. The second part of it was that it was still March and I was soaked to the skin and freezing to death. Time to go. I turned away but then hesitated, held by the feeling that I was missing something. . . .

And I realized that the snowbank beside the road was gone, erased by the rain. There was no longer any mark to show where my father's truck had plunged off the shoulder and into the swamp. The ice he'd broken through was gone, too, swept away by the flood. Only black water remained now, lapping gently at the muddy banks and the hardy tag alder saplings that grew there. Perhaps I could have found some traces on the roadside where the wrecker had winched the pickup out of the mire, but I didn't see them. And I didn't want to. Not anymore.

My father and Jud had been raiding a wreck. And somehow it all went wrong, and now they were both gone. And I couldn't change it. Hell, I couldn't even make sense of it. I had no way of knowing how much of what Jud had told me was true, and

74

probably never would. Maybe it was time to let it go—with the ice. To wherever the ice goes.

The morning was as gray and cool as sheet steel, but there was freshness in the air, too, and I was ready for an end to winter. Ready for a new season.

I went home, took a long, hot shower, slipped into a robe and slippers, then made myself a cup of cinnamon coffee and carried it out onto the small deck at the rear of the cottage. The rain had passed and the sun was peering through, melting away the pearl-and-silver overcast. The breeze off the lake was damp, soft as a caress. A spring breeze, surely. A wind of change.

I took my time finishing my coffee, leaning on the deck rail, listening to the murmur of the waves, looking out over the lake but not really seeing it. Then I changed clothes and drove in to work.

—⚓ "I thought I heard you pull in a couple of minutes ago," Red said. "What are you doing out here? Checking out the harbor?" She was wearing her usual workaday sleeveless U of M sweatshirt and jeans, trim and muscular as a surfer.

"Exactly right," I said, leaning against the back wall of the Crow's Nest, eyeing the masts of the few hardy cold-water sloops scattered among the four long bays of the harbor marina. "The ice is going, and in a few weeks the summer people will start taking their boats out of local storage or sailing them up from Detroit or wherever. The harbor will fill up. And it'll be party time for the rest of the season. Is that still pretty much how things work up here?"

"More or less."

"I thought so. You know, I can almost see them already, sloops and cabin cruisers and dive boats."

"No kidding? What'd you have for breakfast, peyote granola?"

"Nope, just coffee. And anyway, the boats aren't the most interesting part. It's where I'm seeing them from."

"Let me guess," she said, eyeing me oddly. "It looks to me like you're standing beside the garbage cans by the kitchen door."

"True at the moment, but I'm also looking out over the harbor from our new afterdeck, four feet above the beach, fifteen feet deep along the full width of the building. It'll have balustered railings, canopied tables, sunny in the morning, cool in the afternoon, and a terrific view all day long. The boating crowd can sit out here and sip Perrier or Chablis and schmooze while their kids run amok on the beach. What do you think?"

"Since it's too overcast for sunstroke, I'm guessing you either copped some bad drugs or you're serious."

"Oh, I'm serious all right."

"In that case, there are a couple of minor flaws in your little fantasy, Mitch. For openers, how are we supposed to serve people out here? We can't very well trundle everything through the kitchen."

"You're right—we can't. So we're going to walk right through the middle of the back wall."

"Through the wall?"

"Well, actually, through a set of oaken French doors with etched glass inserts. And with luck, we'll not only attract the harbor trade; maybe some of the downtown office crowd will munch lunch out here and mix business with pleasure. All kidding aside, what do you really think?"

"Okay, kidding aside, I think you may be onto a helluvan idea." Red nodded thoughtfully. "Times are changing; people don't drink as much anymore. It might just work. Building a deck that size won't be cheap, though."

"I know. I called around and got some ballpark figures. I have enough left of my Exxon severance to cover it."

"Are you sure you want to do that? I thought you were going to run the Nest only long enough to show some black ink on the books, then sell out."

"Maybe I am. But summer's coming and I haven't done any

freshwater diving in years. Why not have some fun while I make up my mind, right?"

"Why not? Speaking of fun, your pal Terry was here earlier looking for you. Said he had to talk to you."

"Terry? What did he want?"

"Actually, I was kind of wondering how you were fixed for money," Terry said, striding around the corner of the building.

It was the first time I'd seen him since the trouble at the antiques shop. He looked a little worn and needed a shave but otherwise looked unfashionably fit and hard-edged as ever. He was wearing a battered bombardier's jacket over a T-shirt and faded jeans. No belt, no need for one with his narrow waist. He could have modeled for a Remington painting just as he was. There oughta be a law against looking that good without having to work at it.

"Money?" I echoed. "Gee, it's nice to see you, too, Fortier, but it's been so long, you've apparently confused me with somebody who works at a bank."

"I don't need their money; I need yours. Got back last night, heard talk you might be staying on."

"So?"

"So if you're gonna dive, you'll need a boat, right? And I came across a beauty a couple days ago. Absolutely the right boat for you. Problem is, she was scheduled for auction this morning, so I wired 'em fifty bucks against the base price to hold her."

"You did what? You had no right to do that."

"I'll risk it. But I'll have to wire 'em the balance before noon or she goes on the block. I need another seven hundred."

"Damn it, Terry, I'm perfectly capable of finding a boat—"

"I know, but you're not gonna find another craft like this one for that kind of money. Tell you what, you don't like her, I'll sail her out in the bay, pull her plugs, and go down with the ship. So how about it? You trust me seven hundred bucks' worth or not?"

He expected me to say no. I could see it in his eyes. And so did Red. And maybe I should have. It would have been the smart, businesslike thing to do. But there was more on the line here than buying a boat, sight unseen, and we all knew it.

What the hell. It was spring.

"Will a cashier's check be all right?" I said.

CHAPTER 14

"C'MON, ADMIT IT," Terry said. "You wondered whether you'd ever see me *or* the seven bills again, right?"

"Wrong. I never doubted you'd come through. Because you knew if you didn't, I'd hunt you down like a dog. Where is this little gem of yours, anyway?" We were in his Jeep, towing an empty boat trailer with a power winch attached, heading northwest along the Lake Huron shore on U.S. 23. Typical Terry: He'd called just after two, said he'd bought the boat and would be by to pick me up in ten minutes. And I went.

"She's in a little inlet, just south of Point Nipigon, out in the middle of no place."

"And that's all you're going to tell me about it?"

"Absolutely. Why spoil a surprise?"

"And if I don't like it?"

"You'll like her; I guarantee it."

"You keep saying that. Why are you so sure?"

"For one thing, you've got no choice. She's all yours now."

"Gee, that's a comfort. And what are you getting out of the deal?"

"A clear conscience. That warm glow you get from doing the right thing, or knocking back a shot of Jim Beam neat."

"I'm serious."

"You're always serious. No wonder you're still single. But okay, the bottom line is, Shan sold me his boat dirt cheap, and then things . . . worked out badly afterward. I heard about the trouble you had with Rats. I'm sorry. I tried to warn you about him, remember?"

79

"I remember," I said quietly. "What happened wasn't his fault, or at least not altogether. And I'd rather not talk about it. Tell me more about your conscience. It shouldn't take long."

"True enough. Anyway, I figured after what happened, if I didn't come up with a replacement boat for you, Shan might haunt me. Or you would."

"Then why not just sell me back his boat? At a modest profit, of course."

"Not a prayer, lady. I sold my old beater last fall and I had to bust hump on Shan's to get it ready for summer. She's been refitted, and even renamed. She's mine now. Sorry."

"What did you name it?"

"The *William Kidd*. Two *d*'s."

"After the pirate? Appropriate. Has my new boat got a name?"

"She's had a couple of them. The *Sheba*'s the most recent."

"Which I'll probably change to *For Sale Cheap*. It's an hour's drive to Nipigon. Catch me up. What have you been doing all winter? And the past ten years?"

"Winters, I mostly work high steel down south to make enough money so I can dive and charter on the big lake all summer. Used to think it was a romantic way to make a living, but it's gettin' tougher all the time. Been at it ten years, and all I got to show is a secondhand boat, some beat-up gear, and a houseful of ship's artifacts too hot to sell."

"If they're hot, why keep them around?"

"Because they're . . . beautiful, I guess. Shan had some nice pieces out at the cottage, right? I know because I sold him a few. You turn 'em over to the DNR?"

"No," I admitted, "not yet."

"Right. I rest my case. Shan said you got a degree. True?"

"In marine biology, University of Texas. I only had to be on campus a couple of semesters. No big deal."

"Sure it is. Had to be killer juggling a job and school and a kid. Hell, I still find it hard to believe Alec didn't pay child support. I thought he was a better man than that."

"Maybe you don't know him as well as you thought. I certainly didn't. End of subject."

"Okay, okay. On the other hand, maybe some of your friends would have come through if you'd let us know."

"We managed, Corey and me. On our own. And I think it's better that we did."

"I'm not disputing that; I just wish you'd asked, is all. I, um, I tried to find you after you left. Even waltzed a round with Shan about it one night in the Crow's Nest parking lot."

"You fought with my father?"

"I don't know if *fight's* the right word. He did most of the punching; I did most of the falling down. Eventually, I noticed he quit hitting me when I was on the ground, so I took a short nap."

"I'm flattered. Thanks for . . . trying, anyway."

"If I'd known you needed help, I'd have tried harder. Still, you did fine on your own. A damn sight better than I have."

"Not true. I did what I had to, to survive. As near as I can tell, you've always lived pretty much the way you wanted to. Most people never have that chance."

"Sure they do." He smiled. "They're just too smart to try it. Too busy gettin' rich."

"When did you ever care about being rich?"

"Lately. Maybe Shan buyin' it put it on my mind. My life's goin' no place, Mitch. I'll never make any real money diving or working construction. I'll either have to try robbing banks or marry rich. Maybe find a lady who owns a saloon."

"Bank robbery would be safer."

"I think it might be, at that. How about you? You gonna stay on awhile? Or just for the summer?"

"I don't know yet. But while I'm up here, I'd like to spend some time, see some of the country. It's as close to a home as I've ever had. And I'd really like to do some diving in fresh water again."

"You could do that on a weekend."

"Or in a summer," I said. "Maybe that's all it'll be."

"I hope not," he said. "Having you around isn't always easy, Mitch, but at least it's never dull. Maybe your new boat will convince you to stay on."

"Why should it?"

"You'll see," he said, smug as a goose the day after Christmas. God, he could be insufferable sometimes.

We turned off U.S. 23 onto a narrow unmarked gravel road that soon petered out to a barely discernible sandy track. Terry shifted the Jeep into four-wheel drive, following the crude trail a half mile through copses of scrawny tag alders and aspen showing their first leaves of the season. The track ended on the rocky shore of an empty inlet. Lake Huron stretched away iron gray to the horizon, dotted with the distant whale shapes of dying ice floes.

I glanced at Terry. He was frowning, scanning the beach.

"Don't tell me," I said dryly. "Gee whiz, looks like somebody stole the boat."

"Not your boat," he said, climbing out. "At least I hope not. But there was a skiff here last week. Figured I could use it to hook up to the *Sheba*."

"Hook up? Where?" I said. "There isn't even a dock here."

"Won't need a dock. Your boat's underwater, maybe sixty, seventy yards out, thirty feet down."

"Underwater?" I repeated.

"What'd you expect for seven bills? Top of the line at Boat City?"

"I thought she might at least be afloat."

"She will be. It'll be a little tougher without the skiff, but we can still get her up. She's only been down there ten days. She's damn near cherry, and definitely worth the extra trouble, trust me."

"Trust you? Are you kidding? I gave you money to buy a boat—"

"And I did. So do you want to see it or not? Or maybe you'd rather wait until August when the water's warmer?"

"It's not the water. I can swim in anything you can, Fortier, but . . . Ah hell, how do we work it?"

"I'll back the trailer into the lake. It slopes away pretty steeply here, so the trailer should submerge all the way, no problem. Then I'll just swim out with the winch cable, dive down, hook her up, and you can winch her out."

"Suppose she snags on something? She could pull the Jeep in."

"The bottom's mostly shale and sand. She should come clear okay. If you feel the Jeep start to move, stop the winch. I'll go back down and rock the boat free."

"Go down how? You didn't bring any scuba gear."

"Jesus, Mitch, she's at thirty feet, not two hundred. I can free dive that far. So, do you want to try this or not?"

"It'll be worth it just to see you turn blue out there, Fortier. Let's rock'n'roll."

"Good, hang on." He gunned the Jeep around in a half circle on the beach, then slowly backed the trailer out into the water, inching it along until it disappeared under the shallow chop. The Jeep's rear axle was submerged as well, waves lapping against the tailgate. "Show time." Terry grinned. "Pardon me, ma'am, but I didn't bring a suit, so I'll just have to improvise. Try to hold yourself in check, Mitch—until afterward, anyway."

"I think I can manage."

Terry kicked off his deck shoes, shucked his jacket and his jeans, stripping down to blue bikini briefs. I hadn't seen him in swim trunks in a decade. But I remembered perfectly the way he looked. He looked even better now, chiseled by the years down to elementary muscle and bone.

"Lord, I hate gettin' wet this time of year." He stepped out of the Jeep into knee-deep water. "Ahooooah! Jesus Jenny on a bicycle, Mitch, hurry up and release the damn winch!"

I scrambled up on the boat trailer, switched on the winch, and began playing out the cable as Terry waded out into the surf. Waist-deep in ten meters, chest-deep in twenty-five, and then he began swimming, a powerful sidestroke, smooth as a seal, trailing the cable behind him. He was fine for the first forty meters or so, but then the drag of the cable began to slow his progress. He was holding his own against the waves but just barely inching ahead.

Damn it, damn it, damn it. "Hold on a minute!" I yelled. "I'm coming out." No time for modesty. I stripped to my bra and panties, grabbed an empty Styrofoam ice chest out of the backseat, and stepped into the water.

My God, it was cold. Wading out from the shore was too painful, like dying by inches. I plunged into the surf, swimming hard, pushing the cooler ahead of me out to where Terry was treading water, waiting.

"Hang the cable over it," I shouted, my teeth rattling like castanets. "I'll help you tow it out." He didn't argue. With two of us swimming, we made fair time the rest of the way.

"You sure you know where it is?" I gasped, shivering. A small ice floe was bobbing gently on the chop only a few feet beyond us.

"She was out here last week," he said, treading water, looking around for his bearings. "How's the water, Mitch? Warm enough?"

"It's just ducky, you bastard. Now get down there and find the damned boat."

"Yes, ma'am, since you ask so nicely." He power-breathed a moment, saturating his lungs with oxygen. Then he disappeared, sank without a word, for what seemed like a century. A full two minutes at least. And then he broke the surface a few yards away, grinning like a Viking on a raid.

"Got her, Mitch, and she looks even finer'n I thought. Tell you what, if you want to trade, I'll give you the *Kidd,* even up, right now. What do you say?"

"Ask me again after we reel her in," I said, wheeling, swimming strongly for shore. Terry stayed put, using the cooler for support while I climbed back aboard the Jeep and switched on the winch. The reel whined to life, snaking the cable out of the water, taking up slack. Then it slowed as the line drew taut, vibrating with tension. The Jeep began rocking, bucking against the strain of the cable.

"Shut it down!" Terry yelled, but the cable was still inching aboard, so I hung on instead, riding the trailer. Out there, beneath the dark water, the boat was stirring, answering to the tug of a steel umbilical, coming to life. I could sense it. The Jeep shuddered, then settled again as the *Sheba* began to rise. The tension on the winch eased and it began slowly reeling in the cable. Terry whooped and began swimming in, ducking under every few moments to check the boat's progress.

Twenty meters out, she surged to the surface like a porpoise, then settled again, obediently following the cable ashore, water streaming off her sides. She'd surfaced too far to port, and I plunged back into the shallow chop, too excited now to worry about how cold I was. I tugged at her bow cable, guiding her toward the trailer. Terry joined me, thrusting his shoulders against her stern, and we managed to get her lined up.

She made it halfway up the trailer before the combined weight of the boat and water aboard her overloaded the winch. Its circuit breaker kicked open, shutting it down.

No problem. Terry scrambled aboard over her stern and opened her seacocks, letting the lake water drain out. I waded slowly around her, hugging myself against the chill, lips numb, shivering, but unable to take my eyes off her.

Terry was right: She really was a beauty. A Chris-Craft Sea Skiff, wooden-hulled, probably thirty years old, but none the worse for it. And she was achingly familiar. I'd seen her before, or one very much like her. My father'd owned one the year I moved in with him. My first boat. I cried when he sold her. On Terry's shoulder, as it happened.

I glanced up. Terry was watching me intently from her stern. Our eyes met and held a moment—an honest exchange of empathy and affection. And more. And I realized that the water had turned my bra and panties transparent. I was nearly nude.

"Well?" Terry said quietly. "What do you think?"

"I think she's beautiful, and I think you're cute when you're blue," I said, swallowing hard. "I also think I'm freezing and I'd better get dressed."

"What's the rush? If you're worried about hypothermia, maybe we should shuck our soggy duds and huddle together. Strictly for warmth. One nice thing about Jeep seats—they recline."

"Somehow that doesn't surprise me," I said. "Thanks for the offer, but I think I'd better keep my pants on. For now."

He shook his head, smiling ruefully. "Some things never change. Isn't this how we got jammed up the last time?"

"That's not quite how I remember it," I said.

⟶ "Tell me something, straight up, okay?" I said. We were cruising back to Huron Harbor in the late afternoon, the *Sheba* proudly in tow. "You remembered that my father owned a skiff like the *Sheba* way back when, didn't you?"

"Absolutely. I've been known to lose my car after too many brews, but I never forget a boat. You were nuts about that old Chris-Craft—for reasons not obvious to a serious seaman."

"How did you find this one?"

"I didn't. She found me. I dove on her last week for the state cops. I dive bodies for 'em sometimes."

I blinked. "There was a body aboard her?"

"So what if there was? You're a pro; you must've seen bodies before."

"Just once," I said. "I dove for a little girl in a river. We found her. It was . . . grim business. I'll never do it again."

"I know the feeling." Terry nodded. "But the staties pay sixty bucks an hour. Anyway, it turned out the guy wasn't actually aboard her. He swamped her and then swam for the beach, without a vest. Less than a hundred yards from shore, and he couldn't make it. Drowned like a duck in the rain. Stupid bastard had no business ownin' a boat, to say nothing of runnin' one on the big lake in a storm, God bless him. As soon as I saw her down there, I thought, Terry, you probably know the only bozo on the face of the planet who'll pay cash money for that hulk."

"Is that what you thought?"

"No"—he smiled—"not exactly. But I did think of you. You cross my mind from time to time, Mitch. Once a decade or so."

"I'm flattered."

"You should be. I'm a busy guy and—no." He shook his head slowly. "No. All kidding aside, Mitch. I've thought of you a lot. Wondering if we blew it. If I blew it. You were the best girlfriend I ever had. Probably my best friend ever. And I know that your running away was at least partly my fault. If I'd handled things better—"

"Don't flatter yourself," I interrupted. "Maybe you could have let me down a little easier when we broke off. But the rest of it? You weren't to blame for that."

"You're right," he said, brightening. "I guess maybe it was all your fault. Gosh, I feel better."

"One thing I would like to know, though," I said. "Whatever happened with you and Andrea? You've never said."

"Nothing heavy," he said curtly. "It was a summer thing with her. Fun and games. She got married a few years ago. Some society type, I guess. Just as well. We never had much in common, Andy and I."

"Other than the usual."

"Which is more than you and I ever had." He grinned. "You, um, do like men, don't you? I mean, you and Red are big pals, right? And I know she's gay. Hell, she's proud of it."

"Yes she is. And as much as I'd love to jerk your chain, Fortier, it wouldn't be fair to Red. We're friends. We work well together; we get along. Sometimes when I work late, I crash on her couch for a night. But she doesn't sleepwalk. We're not lovers. Semi-serious question for you. How would you like to run the dive shop for me this summer?"

"Aren't you going to run it yourself?"

"I'll help out, but I've got plans for the Nest that'll keep me busy. I need somebody good, somebody I can trust."

"No," he said slowly, "bad idea. What would I call you? Ma'am? Boss? It wouldn't work. I'm a stray dog, Mitch. I don't do well on a leash. I'm glad you're back; I've missed you more than I can say. But I won't work for you."

"Fair enough."

"I know a guy, though, a college kid who'll need a summer job. I'll send him around. No strings."

"Thanks. And thanks for finding me the boat, and for, well, for everything."

"No charge. I took you down to see Habash and I helped get you a boat. The way I see it, we're even now, Mitch. We can start over fresh, see how it goes. Friends again, right?"

"Something like that," I said.

CHAPTER 15

LIKE HER NEW OWNER, *Sheba* looked a little rough first thing in the morning. Terry recruited a couple of Crow's Nest regulars when we'd returned the night before. And for the price of a few free beers, we got enough volunteer muscle to wrestle the *Sheba* off the trailer onto sawhorse-style cradles, high and dry on the beach behind the bar. And she looked so good to me that if she hadn't been waterlogged, I might have slept in her.

As it was, I was back at first light to look her over. I knew that much of the warmth I felt for her was that my father had owned one like her and that Terry had remembered after all this time, but that passed. And after a more thorough examination, I began to appreciate her for what she was, sound and sturdy, and more or less shipshape.

But more important, she had soul. Or so it seemed to me. I must have circled her twenty times, examining every inch. Red found me there when she came in at nine to open the Nest.

"So this is the lady all the fuss was about, huh? So, do you think it's worth the seven bills or not?"

I nodded. "She's worth ten times that to me."

"I don't know," Red said doubtfully. "Looks like it might take more'n a little mascara and some lipstick to make this lady presentable."

"She won't need makeup," I said. "She's a natural. Sonia Braga, or Kate Hepburn."

"Say what?"

"She's got a few years on her, but she's still strong, and pretty in a way they just don't make anymore. With a little fixin', she'll still knock your eye out in the right light. Like Sonia Braga."

"Or maybe Michelle Mitchell. You going to call her the *Sonia?*"

"No. *Sheba*'s her name. She's been manhandled and sunk all the way to the bottom, but she's up again, and with a little help from her friends, she'll be ready to kick ass and take names, as they say."

"Who are you talking about?" Red said dryly. "Your boat? Or yourself, sister?"

"Maybe a little of both." I grinned.

"I'd better open up," Red said. "Mr. Misiak's bringing the contractor today to scope out the new deck, remember?"

"I remember. When he gets here, send him around. I'll be out here for a while."

As the first glow of ownership wore off, I could see *Sheba* definitely needed some semiserious work. But it was nothing I couldn't do myself, and I had a beautiful day to make a start on it. The sun was glowing through the gray haze over the lake, gulls were wheeling and circling high overhead, occasionally plummeting into the harbor after fish or scraps. And it occurred to me that for the first time in my working life I had no time clock to punch, no one to tell me what to do. If I wanted to work on *Sheba*, no one could order me not to.

I liked the idea. A lot. Maybe being a small businesswoman wasn't all overdue bills and inventories and hassles.

A previous owner had fiberglassed *Sheba*'s hull below the waterline, probably when she got a little too sprung to take caulk. The glass was weather-checked, scraped to the fur in a few spots, but with some sanding and a couple of coats of marine epoxy paint, it could be brought up to par.

Mr. Misiak showed at ten, with his construction contractor in tow, a tall, red-faced Swede who looked much too young for the job. Still, he had a can-do attitude and he seemed to know which end of a hammer to swing. He took thorough measurements, did some figuring with a calculator and a small notebook, then gave me an estimate well below what I expected. And I gave him the job. He set off to get the proper building permits and I went back to work on the *Sheba*.

I was well into sanding down *Sheba*'s fiberglass, feathering the seam smoothly into the wood beneath, breathing the tang of sawdust mingled with the lake breeze, when a shadow fell over her.

"Nice boat. Yours?"

"She will be," I said, squinting up at the silhouette. A striking figure, tall, with shoulder-length sandy hair pulled back in a neat ponytail, an open, boyish face, blue eyes behind frameless glasses, dressed in a trimly tailored three-piece pinstriped suit. A sorority party dream boat, the kind your sister wants you to bring home.

"Ken Robinette," he said, offering his hand. "We're going to be neighbors, sort of. I'm down here getting my boat in shape, the *Mai Tai*, fourth berth down."

"The thirty-two-foot sloop? She's nice. I take it you sail."

"No more than I have to. I'm strictly a landlubber, had a hired crew sail her up from Detroit two years ago. I live aboard her during the summer months. I moved up here to get out of the rat race. Haven't quite managed to do it yet. Speaking of which, this isn't entirely a social call."

"Don't tell me—you're selling insurance."

"Even worse," he said, smiling easily. A good smile. "I'm an attorney. In fact, at one point, I was your father's attorney."

"His attorney?" I said. "You mean you work for Mr. Cohen?"

"No, I'm in private practice. Cohen and Jansen handled his estate. I acted as an intermediary on another matter—the negotiations with the Deveraux Institute."

"You've lost me. What negotiations?"

"Your father didn't tell you about them?"

"No, I hadn't spoken with him for some time. Why?"

91

"I see," he said slowly. "Well, I'm afraid I have a bit of a problem, then. You see, we were only in the preliminary stages at the . . . time of his death."

"What were you negotiating about?"

"I'm afraid that's the crux of my problem. Since I was more or less a go-between, I'm really not free to discuss the matter without permission from the other party."

"Who was . . ."

"The Institute. Mr. Jason Deveraux was handling it personally, in fact."

"Jason? I'm surprised the old bear's still wheeling and dealing. And dealing what, exactly? My father didn't have anything to sell the Institute but some contraband china, and that's not the kind of thing they display."

"Gee, I hate to sound like a lawyer, but I'm truly not at liberty to say. I can tell you a considerable amount of money was involved, though."

"How much is considerable?"

He hesitated a beat, then shrugged. "How large a figure would you consider a lot of money, Miss Mitchell?"

"Depends on the situation. A hundred bucks some days."

"I know that feeling." He smiled. "Suppose we say that by our mutual standards, the negotiations involved a *very* substantial amount. And I'm afraid that's really all I can say."

I eyed him a moment, then shook my head. "No way. This has to be a joke, right? Red sent you out here to bug me. You don't even look like a lawyer."

"You have my word it's not a joke, Miss Mitchell," he said, unoffended. "If it'll help, I'll trot over to my boat and dig out my degree."

"I don't understand. My father didn't have anything worth a substantial amount of money. He was nearly broke."

"I wouldn't know about that. But since you said you hadn't been in contact with your father for some time, perhaps you should meet with Mr. Deveraux to discuss the matter. I take it you know the family?"

"Of course," I said evenly, "so does everybody else in this town. But as you can see, I'm busy. If Jason thinks we have something to discuss, I'm here seven days a week."

"I'm afraid his coming here is out of the question. Mr. Deveraux had a coronary last fall, and a quadruple bypass. He seldom leaves his home these days. Would you be able to meet him out at the estate? Say sometime this afternoon?"

"You're kidding. What's the rush?"

"If I were you, Miss Mitchell, I'd treat it almost as a matter of life and death. I know we've just met, but I hope you'll take me at my word. It's definitely in your best interests to look into this."

"I'm touched by your concern. Tell me, Mr . . ."

"Robinette. My friends call me Rob."

"Rob. An appropriate nickname for a lawyer, *Mr.* Robinette. You said you were the go-between, right? So whose side are you you on now?"

"My own, of course." He smiled. "Just like everybody else. But I'm also concerned about Mr. Deveraux's interests. And yours, as well. Now let me ask you one, Miss Mitchell. Aren't you the least bit curious?"

"I suppose I'll have to be. Okay, counselor, set it up. Will three this afternoon be all right?"

"I'll see that it is. You won't be sorry."

"I'd better not be," I said. "Or some dark night, your little home down the pier might sink."

CHAPTER 16

So. It had finally come. A decade ago, when my world flipped upside down, I'd half-expected to be summoned out to the Deveraux estate. To be browbeaten or bought off. But it never happened. And now it truly didn't matter anymore. I'd made a life for myself and my son on my own, and Alec's family was irrelevant to me now. Or so I kept telling myself as I drove out that afternoon. In my heart, I think I still needed to prove something—to myself, if not to them.

I hadn't been there for years, but I had no trouble finding it. I could probably find my way to it in my sleep. And I often have, in dreams. I'd worked at the estate back in high school, taking care of the pool, and later trying to teach Alec and Andrea to scuba dive in it—unsuccessfully, as it happened. Alec was game enough, even though he carped about taking lessons from a slip of a girl, but he had a lame knee from an old riding injury, and it couldn't take long immersions in cold water. Andy simply didn't like getting her hair wet. Or maybe I was just a lousy teacher.

A few things had changed since my last visit. The old decorative split-rail fence had been replaced by a spear-tipped wrought-iron palisade ten feet tall that snaked around the grounds and uncoiled off into the hills. I had to identify myself to a tinny speaker phone in the stone gatepost, like ordering takeout from a McDonald's drive-through. When I was a kid, we never locked gates. Now we talk to them. America, America.

The house is essentially a Yankee clone of an Antoinette-era French château in brick and granite, twenty rooms or so, a six-car garage, stables, a greenhouse, Olympic-size swimming pool, tennis court. It's a small palace really, dreaming like Brigadoon on the crest of a seven-hundred-acre bluff overlooking Huron Harbor. The view will stop your heart, if the house hasn't done so already.

I parked my pickup between a British Land Rover and a silver Mercedes 450SL, stalked up to the outsized oaken doors, and took a deep breath. I hadn't bothered to change clothes for the occasion. I was still wearing a flannel work shirt, faded jeans, and boots, and I was glad of it. The hell with them. I tapped the buzzer. Chimes sounded from within like a whisper of raindrops on Waterford crystal. But no one answered.

I tried again. Still nothing. I checked my watch. I was ten minutes early. I started to turn away, then hesitated. I could hear splashing from the rear of the house. I followed the porch around, and found Jason Deveraux.

He was in the heated pool, churning the china blue water to a froth, steam boiling into the cool spring air like a cannibal stew. Jason's arms were sweeping fiercely, legs scissoring in a crude, energetic breaststroke, but he wasn't making much headway. A nylon line attached to a canvas belt around his rubbery waist was tied to the pool ladder, tethering him in place a few meters out from the edge. He was a huge man, Jason, broad as a bear, probably 250 plus, but not noticeably overweight. Except for the tether belt and an incongruous yellow swim cap, he was completely nude, with thighs like tree trunks, his broad back and slablike buttocks covered with a thick silvery pelt, matted by the water.

A second man was seated with his back to me at a cabana table by the pool, frowning over paperwork in a manila folder. For a moment, I thought he might be Alec, but his thinning hair wasn't dark enough, and he was too short.

"Hi," I said. "Sorry to barge in. I rang, but nobody answered."

The smaller man glanced up, sharp as a ferret. There was an unhealthy chalky cast to his features, as though he wasn't quite well. He was wearing a khaki safari jacket and shirt, a dark rep tie, not a military uniform exactly, but almost. I half-expected him to salute.

"Miss Mitchell, I presume? I'm Gerald Hoffman, Mr. Deveraux's assistant. You're early." He had a trace of an accent, an affected southern drawl. He picked up a large terry beach towel and stalked around the edge of the pool until his shadow fell across Jason's churning form. It didn't register for a moment; Jason just kept thrashing away, mindless as a Galápagos turtle. Then he sensed the shadow over him and abruptly stood upright, chest-deep. He peeled off the swim cap, knuckled the water out of his eyes, and squinted up at me in the afternoon glare. Neither of us spoke for a moment, each frankly evaluating the other. Jason had changed, aged a bit more than I'd expected. He had a beard now, gunmetal gray. It suited him. Reminded me of pictures of Hemingway late in his life. His eyes hadn't aged at all, though, still alert, lit from within, and fierce as a feral cat.

"Well, well, little Michelle, my favorite tomboy, all grown up," he said at last, his voice a well-modulated rumble I could feel in my heart. "Kind of you to come see an old man." He lumbered to the side of the pool, hoisted himself out, and sat on the edge, his large feet dangling in the water.

He accepted the towel from Hoffman with a nod, mopped his face with it, then draped it casually over his lap. His chest was scarred with a narrow seam that ran from his throat to his navel. "You look fine, girl. Favor your father, I believe, same dark eyes."

"You look the same," I said.

"Don't bother bein' polite, Mitch. People still call you that, do they?"

"My friends do," I said.

"Then I hope you'll allow me to as well. I want to be your friend, Mitch. Maybe the best friend you ever had. We're family, after all."

"Are we?" I said, smiling in spite of myself. God, he was as glib as ever, a charming, urbane, vindictive son of a bitch. For a time, he'd been my fantasy father figure, a civilized contrast with my own unpredictable dad. I'd always liked him. Everybody did. Even people he'd eaten alive liked him.

"Friends?" I said. "Family? I got the impression you wanted to see me because you were doing some kind of a deal with my father. About what, by the way? Your Mr. Robinette wasn't exactly forthcoming."

"Robby can be the soul of discretion, a rare talent in a lawyer. And he's not *my* Mr. Robinette; he's a hired gun, belongs to anybody with a fee." He mopped his face off with an end of the towel, exposing his genitals with every swipe. He either didn't notice or didn't care.

"You didn't answer my question," I said. "What were you and Shan negotiating?"

He hesitated, then gave a barely perceptible shrug. "A salvage arrangement. A substantial one, by his standards."

"How substantial?"

"His end was a quarter of a million."

I blinked. "You're joking," I managed.

"I joke all the time, dear heart. Never about money."

"But a quarter of—for what? What did my dad have to sell that was worth that kind of money?"

"Salvage rights," Jason said.

"Salvage rights? To what?"

"Do you expect us to believe that you really don't know?" Hoffman put in. "We have your letters, Miss Mitchell."

"What letters? What are you talking about?"

"The letters your father showed—"

"Shut up, Jerry," Jason said calmly. "My God, you can be dense. She doesn't know."

"I think she does. I—"

"Leave us, Jerry. Now." Jason hadn't raised his voice, but it was no less a command. Hoffman nodded, pointedly collected his manila folder, and stalked off without a word.

"A good man," Jason said absently. "Ex-CIA. Can dig up dirt

on people their own mamas don't know about. Depressin' to be around, though. His mind's as squirmy as matin' snakes. Always thinks the worst of people. Usually rightly, I might add. But he's wrong about you, isn't he? Shan didn't tell you a damn thing about this."

"Except for an occasional card at Christmas, I haven't heard from him in years."

"I see." He nodded, smiling ruefully. "I believe I truly do. It's all . . . symmetrical. I almost died last fall. Did you know?"

"Robinette told me you were ill."

"Ill? Now there's an understatement. Look at this railroad track down my chest. I'm a flatliner, girl. I was dead on the table for nearly four minutes. They did a quadruple bypass, gutted me out like a ten-point buck and sewed me back together again. I'm healthy enough now, or I will be if I keep swimming and walking. Still, a thing like that makes you think. Made me think about you, for instance, and how unfairly I'd treated you all those years ago."

He paused, waiting for a response. I had nothing to say.

"So I contacted your dad to see if I couldn't make up for it in some way," he continued. "And apparently, I got myself taken. Hoffman tried to warn me. I guess I should have listened."

"I don't understand. Are you saying my father cheated you somehow?"

"Cheated you far more than me, Mitch. I knew your father a lot of years, and I won't speak ill of the dead, but by God, he was a lot harder than I thought. Especially where you were concerned. But, since Shan's not here to tell his side of it, perhaps we'd best start fresh, you and I. Put our heads together, work something out."

"Work what out?"

"Well, the money for openers. I want you to understand that the money isn't a problem. If you're not satisfied with Shan's arrangements—"

"Mr. Deveraux, I hate to disappoint you, but if my father offered to sell the Institute something, say a cargo of contraband china? I don't have it anymore. I turned it over to the state police."

"I know, I heard about your . . . trouble. I'm sorry. But this isn't about crockery, it's . . . about family. My family. Has Alec been in touch with you at all over the years?"

"Alec? No. Not a word. Why?"

"Just wondered. He's never said one way or the other, but he might not have. We aren't as close as we once were. He's his own man. Done very well for himself, too. Lives in New York now. He and Andrea still come home for the summers, though. Alec's married. Did you know?"

"Someone mentioned it."

"Good. It's the reason we're talking. He married a fine girl, good Boston family. They have two girls, cute as buttons, the both of 'em. Lovely girls."

"I'm happy for them, but I don't—" But suddenly, I did understand. Enough. "My God," I said. "Alec wants custody of Corey now, is that it?"

"Not custody necessarily," Jason said, watching me carefully. "But he does have certain rights."

"Rights?" I echoed, unbelieving. "And my father offered to—" I swallowed, gagging on the words. "To sell Corey to you, or something like that?"

"You're making it sound far too sinister, Mitch. Corey is legally my grandson, perhaps the only one I'll have. I just want to be sure he has every opportunity. The money I paid Shan was only a down payment, a goodwill gesture. I'm prepared to settle a much larger sum on you and your—"

"Don't," I said, cutting him off. "Don't say anything else to me. Not about Corey. Ever. If, um—" I swallowed. My eyes were stinging, and I was so enraged, I could hardly breathe. But I wasn't going to cry. Not now, not in front of him. "I don't know anything about this, Mr. Deveraux, and I don't want to. We've managed just fine, Corey and I. On our own. Let's leave it at that. I don't know anything about any arrangement you may have had with my father. If you think he owes you something, file a claim against his estate. Beyond that—" I broke off. I wanted to say more but couldn't. I turned and tottered away, a hundred years older than when I'd arrived.

I paused at the corner, then turned back, wanting to shout my anger out at him. He was already lowering himself gingerly back into the steaming pool. He pushed off from the side and began to swim, slowly at first, until he felt the gentle tug of the tether. Then he gradually increased his pace, churning the water to foam, as though he was surrounded by a school of frenzied sharks. And still I had the impression he was holding himself in check. That if he strained just a bit harder, that old man could have snapped the cable like a thread, or perhaps ripped the pool right out of the ground. And his whole damned mountaintop along with it.

Hoffman was leaning against my truck door when I rounded the house. He straightened.

"I trust you worked things out satisfactorily?" he said.

"Get out of my way."

"Of course." He smiled sourly. "I warned Mr. Deveraux about your father. He chose to go ahead anyway, and he paid the price for it. But don't think for a minute I'm buying your innocent act. It was a nice ploy, having someone else write the letters. Gives you leverage to renegotiate. My compliments. But if you think you can just take Mr. Deveraux's money and run—"

His voice was drowned out as I fired up the engine, and then he was scrambling out of the way to keep from being run down as I gunned the truck past him. He shouted something after me, but his words were swept away by the windblast.

CHAPTER 17

I DROVE THROUGH THE HILLS above Huron Harbor for over an hour, windows down, chill spring air blasting through the cab. I was trying to cool down, to collect myself. It wasn't working. The anger kept building, feeding on itself like a fire, one I couldn't check. I'd seen my father out of control like this, in a killing rage, but I'd never truly understood it—until now. I'd loved him, and hated him. But I'd never thought him capable of this kind of betrayal. How could he do such a thing to me? How could anyone? I needed answers. And I knew where to get them.

It was after five when I roared into the Crow's Nest parking lot. I didn't go in. Instead, I marched around the building and down the harbor boardwalk. The *Mai Tai* was easy to find, sleek and slick as her owner. There were lights in the cabin. Permission to come aboard, my foot. I stomped across the deck and pounded on the cabin roof.

"Robinette! Open up! We have to talk!"

He opened the door, shirtless, clad only in fashionably faded jeans and scuffed Bass deck shoes. He was sunlamp-tanned and smoothly muscled, like a marathon swimmer. "Hi. Thought you'd be back. Excuse the clothes, or lack of same. I just got back from working out at the gym. I take it you're upset?"

"*Upset* doesn't come close to covering it."

"I see. Well, come on in, or aboard, or whatever sailors say. Sun's over the yardarm; can I offer you a drink?"

"Not unless you want to wear it," I snapped. "All I want from you is an explanation. For openers, exactly what kind of a deal did you arrange between Jason and my father? And don't give me any crap about being unable to talk."

"Look, I understand why you're angry, and I sympathize," he said, tugging a faded U of D sweatshirt on over his head. "But if you'll just calm down—"

"Don't tell me to be calm, not about this. Just tell me about it. All of it."

"All right," he said, taking a deep breath. "The truth is, I never liked being a party to it. I was retained by Mr. Hoffman to act as an intermediary, to draw up the papers and make sure everything was legal. Frankly, I was glad to get the work. As the new kid on the block up here . . ." He shrugged. "Anyway, I took the job. I met with them twice, both times at the estate. They put the best face on it they could, talking about Corey's education, a trust fund for him, et cetera, but the bottom line was basically a straight exchange: custody of your son to his father, Alec, in return for an even million. In cash."

"A million," I echoed stupidly. "But Jason said it was a quarter—"

"Quarter of a mil down, the balance on delivery, so to speak. Since the arrangement couldn't be shown as a sale, on paper it was a salvage contract, with Jason hiring Shan to recover goods unspecified. The rest of it was an oral agreement between them, with myself and Jerry Hoffman as witnesses."

"An agreement between them? What about me? What about Corey?"

"Your father assured us that you'd been fully apprised and had consented to the arrangement. He showed us your letters to that effect."

"What letters? I didn't write any letters to my father about this."

"No? Well, be that as it may, your father showed us two letters, purportedly written by you, agreeing to the transfer of custody."

"And you just . . . went along with all this?"

"I did what I was hired to do," he said coolly. "I don't know about you, but I'm not a rich man, and since I don't have a child to sell, I'm—"

I slapped him, hard. A reflex. His head snapped halfway around and he grabbed my shoulders, pinning my arms. For a moment, I thought he was going to hit me back. He didn't. But it was a close thing. I could see it in his eyes.

"I'm . . . really sorry I said that," he said, releasing me, stepping back, massaging his cheek. "Especially since I think you may have broken my jaw. You ready for that drink yet? I think we could both use one."

"I'm sorry, too," I said. "I don't normally go around slapping people, even when they deserve it. I'm just . . . so angry about this. I'm sorry. I know it's not your fault."

"You're wrong," he said, filling two glasses from a crystal decanter on a mahogany bar at the end of the cabin. "Part of it is certainly my fault. It bothered me at the time, and it still does. But basically, I did the lawyerly thing and kept my mouth shut, partly as a matter of professional ethics, but also economics. Heck, you're probably morally entitled to sock me a few more times. I hope you won't," he added hastily. "Maybe I should have warned you, but . . . Do you have any idea what the Deveraux family is actually worth? The Institute, Deveraux Shipping, the paper mill?"

"No, I don't," I said, accepting a tulip glass of white wine. "A lot, I suppose. But they don't have enough to buy my son. The U.S. mint doesn't have enough."

"That isn't my point. I'd guess the family's worth close to a billion, give or take a few mil. And since I'm a guy with simple needs," he said, gesturing at the *Mai Tai*'s cabin, "even ten percent of their legal work would do me quite nicely. Which is a roundabout way of saying that I held my nose and did as I was told when they put this deal together. I shouldn't have touched it with the proverbial ten-foot pole. And I'm sorry I did."

"Like you said, you were just doing your job."

"True, but there must be easier ways to make a buck. For instance, have you ever considered a boxing career? With me as your manager and with a punch like yours, we'll make millions. You'll need a new name, though. Mitch the b—nope. Wrong. How about Rockyette? What do you think?"

"I'm wondering if that's your first glass of wine or your second gallon," I said.

"My first, Scout's honor. I take it that's a no?"

"Look, I appreciate your trying to jolly me out my snit, but I'd rather stick to business. This deal Jason and my father cut, is it enforceable?"

"No, ma'am. The written agreement was for salvage, and you're under no obligation to fulfill it—unless they can prove you were a party to it. You're, um, sure you didn't write those letters?"

"Absolutely. I didn't know a thing about this until today."

"I see. Did your father leave you any cash or substantial assets that Deveraux could suggest were purchased with his funds?"

"No, he was nearly broke when he died. Are you saying money actually changed hands?"

He hesitated. "Is . . . that what Mr. Deveraux told you?"

"Yes, but at the time, I was too angry to care. And why do I get the feeling you're backing away from something?"

"Because you've got good instincts," he admitted. "Look, I want to do the right thing, but I'd rather not get burned for it. If either Jason or Hoffman find out I told you . . ."

"I don't owe them any favors. What about the money?"

"They lied to you," he said, facing me squarely. "They didn't pay your father a cent. Hoffman wanted to verify your signature on the letters. Shan wouldn't agree to it, so the negotiations stalled. After your father's death, Mr. Deveraux suggested we wait for a decent interval, then try again."

"Decent interval?" I echoed bitterly. "He doesn't know the meaning . . . Forget it. Is there any way they can pressure me now?"

"Not for the money, no. And I doubt that Mr. Deveraux would sue to get it back even if you had it."

"Why not?"

"Because if the details of the agreement came out, it could damage his legal position. He doesn't care about the money. He wants custody of the boy, for Alec."

"But surely he can't win it legally, not after all this time."

"That depends. Is there any question that Alec Deveraux is the boy's father?"

"On my son's birth certificate, I listed the father as unknown."

"That wasn't the question."

"But that's my answer. I don't owe Alec a thing, nor do I want anything from him, or his family. Except to be left alone."

"Fair enough. Where's your son now?"

"In boarding school in Texas. As a single mother working out on the Gulf, I don't have many options."

"A good school?"

"The best. His class is going to tour Europe this summer. He's an honor student and a competitive swimmer. He's doing fine."

"So I understand. In fact, it was a news item in the local paper about him that aroused Mr. Deveraux's interest. It was his impression . . . well, that you'd had an abortion at the time."

"Why would he think that?"

"Because your father told him so. That when you left, it was to get an abortion."

"But . . . He knew that wasn't true. Why would he lie about it?"

"I'm not certain, but it was my impression that they'd had an . . . arrangement at the time."

"You mean my father was . . ." I swallowed. "Paid off? To push me into getting an abortion?"

"Something like that, yes. Sorry. I assumed you knew."

"No, I didn't. Apparently, there's a lot I didn't know. Both then and now."

"So it seems. Well, with regard to custody, did you accept any money at the time from the Deveraux family?"

"Not a dime, then or since. We've had no contact at all."

"Then the only legal avenue left would be to prove you an unfit mother somehow, child abuse, moral turpitude, something like that."

"How could they do that?"

"They probably can't. Forgive my bluntness, but is your private life . . . orderly?"

"More or less. There aren't any pictures of me swinging naked from the chandeliers at a Hell's Angels kegger, if that's what you're wondering."

"Glad to hear it." He smiled. "In which case, it's my considered legal opinion that it would be very difficult for Alec to win custody of your son at this late date."

"Difficult? Not impossible?"

"Be realistic, Mitch. This is America. Nothing's impossible, especially for a billionaire. I think that you'd almost certainly retain custody in the end. But you might well bankrupt yourself fighting the suit. Fortunately, you have an attorney who'll work very, *very* cheaply."

"No kidding? And why would he do that?"

"To quiet his guilty conscience, of course. I have to shave this chin every morning."

"That shouldn't be so tough," I said. "It's a nice chin. Too bad it's glass. Thanks for the information, Mr. Robinette. I know you put yourself at risk by telling me the truth. It'll stay between us. And I'm sorry about the slap."

"My friends call me Rob. And I hope we'll be friends, you and I. Tell you what, why don't you let me cook you dinner some night? Right here. I'm not much of a sailor, but I know my way around a galley. What do you say?"

"Sorry, I'm not really in the mood to—"

"Consider it an open invitation. Anytime. Preferably after you've cooled off."

"That may take a while."

"I can wait," he said.

CHAPTER 18

I COULDN'T JUST TAKE Robinette's word that my father hadn't been paid. I spent half the night searching the Crow's Nest and the cottage, top to bottom. I knew both buildings inside out, but I found exactly nothing. Except a few signs that indicated that they might already have been searched by someone. Jud? Maybe. But I could think of a more likely candidate.

I pulled my pickup into the Century Realty parking lot a little before noon the following day. The office fronted a new subdivision built in the Black River foothills, split-level ranch-style homes, all prefab construction, varied only by the color of their vinyl siding. Most of them stood empty.

The realty office itself was rustic-modern, trimmed with slanted rough cedar planks, huge round bubble windows. A vacation cottage for Martians.

The interior was all business: blue plush carpet, metal desks with leatherette tops. The only people in the room were Karen Stepaniak and an overweight salesman in a maroon blazer, oozing oil into his phone. Karen looked terrific, trim and pert, in a tailored blue suit and impeccable makeup—the Lana Turner look. I've always envied women who can achieve that perfectly finished effect. I look anemic without makeup, but if I add more than the bare essentials, instant hookerdom. It must be a great comfort to know you can look a lot better than that first grim glimpse in the morning mirror.

Karen glanced up with a reflexive receptionist's grin, which faded when she recognized me. A more cautious smile took its place. "Mitch, nice to see you," she said, offering her hand.

"You may not think so in a minute. I want to talk to you, about some letters I think you wrote for my father."

"Right." She nodded, paling a bit. "I thought you would eventually. Please don't make a scene, Mitch. I need this job."

"You should have thought of that before you wrote the letters."

"We can't talk here. Bernie? I'm going to lunch early, okay?"

Maroon Blazer scowled and tapped some papers on his desk with a pudgy forefinger without missing a syllable of his pitch. "Damn it, I have to finish typing up these contracts before I can go. It'll just take a couple of minutes. Can you wait? Please?"

"It's waited this long. I'll be outside."

She came out twenty minutes later, looking like a lost puppy. "Hi," she said ruefully. "You're really angry with me, aren't you?"

"Shouldn't I be?"

"You have every right to be. Look, I don't eat lunch, so I usually walk my boss's dogs on my break. Join me?"

"You walk his dogs?"

"Sad but true," she said grimly. "God, the things a girl has to do to hang on to a job these days." She unlocked the tailgate of a gray Taurus station wagon and a matched pair of blond cocker spaniels scrambled out, scampering in frantic circles around us. But when Karen said, "Heel," they settled down immediately and took up station a pace behind as we followed a path around the back of the office.

"I take a walk out here every day, weather permitting. Otis and Ernestine get to stretch their legs, and I can see some countryside without worrying about how much it's worth. There's a terrific view of the hills a half mile or so back."

"I didn't come for the view," I said.

"I know. What do you want to know?"

"Everything. I already know my father was working out an arrangement to peddle custody of my son to Alec's family."

"It wasn't quite like that. For what it's worth, I was against the idea, but your father could be very persuasive, and I had to admit there was some poetic justice to it."

"What's poetic about selling children?"

"That's not fair. We never intended to go through with it. It was a sting. A payback. I wouldn't have written the letters for him otherwise."

"What are you talking about? A payback for what?"

"Back when you . . . became pregnant, the Deveraux family put heavy financial pressure on your dad to make you get an abortion. Did you know?"

"No. But it . . . might explain a lot I didn't understand at the time," I said slowly. "My God."

"The hell of it was, Shan really thought an abortion would be best. So, um, after you ran off, he told them you'd gone away to have one. But he never forgave Jason for interfering. So when Rob brought the offer to him, Shan flipped. A gift from the god of revenge. We wanted to go away together, and Shan loved the idea of letting Jason pay for the trip. He intended to share the money with you, of course. He thought it might help patch things up between you."

"He didn't need money to do that."

"Maybe not, but he thought he did. You know how men are, always trying to earn things that we're perfectly willing to give."

We walked in silence for a few minutes while I mulled over what she'd told me. It was a beautiful day for it, golden sun, air moist and sweet—fresh, the way it can be only in a forest in spring. The path was bordered by stands of maple and yellow birch. Otis and Ernestine gave up tagging along behind us and went scooting off into the underbrush. I thought better of them for it.

"Why didn't you tell me about all this that first day?" I said at last.

"I should have, I know, but I'm . . . not like you, Mitch. You know, independent? I've always needed men in my life to tell me what to do. But I should have told you. I'm sorry I didn't."

"Do you know if Shan actually collected any money? Jason told me he paid him."

"I can see why he'd want you to think so, but the truth is, Shan never got a red cent," she said wryly. "Too bad. It'd be nice to be lying on the beach in Acapulco instead of walking my boss's damned dogs just to keep my nickel-dime job."

"Why didn't it work out? What happened?"

"Shan said Hoffman blocked the deal, something about checking the signatures. Shan could hardly agree to that, so that ended it. Didn't he call you?"

"No, why?"

"He meant to tell you about it, in case they ever contacted you directly. I thought he might have called. I didn't see much of him during those last weeks."

"Why not?"

"He and Rats had something going, raiding that wreck, I guess. And after Shan and my ex tangled at the Nest, Shan thought it would be safer for me if we didn't see each other until we left. Hack can be a handful, and I've got the scars to prove it."

"Where's your ex now?"

"Seattle. I filed for divorce in December and he pulled out shortly afterward."

"Are you sure?"

"That he's in Seattle? Yes. I've called him there a couple of times about odds and ends from the divorce. He's not such a bad guy, just a little wild. Although when it came to wild, your dad could have given Hack lessons. It was part of his appeal, that craziness."

"I know the feeling," I said.

"What are you going to do about the . . . situation?"

"Nothing," I said flatly. "I didn't know anything about it and it isn't my problem. I just want to get on with my life."

"I understand. I can only say I'm terribly sorry about my part in it. Please believe me, we never meant to hurt you, ever. It was just a scheme that . . . got out of hand. At least I can prove I wasn't fibbing about the view. Isn't this something?"

We'd come out onto a narrow shelf on the crest of a hill. The leafy roof of a birch forest sheltered the valley below, stretching off in the distance to the Black River hills. White and silver birches stood out in stark relief above the forest floor, their upper limbs gleaming like burnished copper, bathing in sunlight.

"God, it's lovely," I said. "Sometimes I wonder how I ever left this country, trouble or not."

"You did what you had to. It took more guts than I would have had in your place. I'm sure your father never meant— Oh! Damn, damn! Otis, no! Sit! Sit!"

She pushed past me and grabbed the female cocker by the collar. The male had barreled out of the brush, holding a small rabbit in his jaws, dripping blood and drool on the ground, wall-eyed with excitement. The female was trying to grab his catch, and Karen dragged her bodily away by her collar. The rabbit was struggling feebly, eyes glazed, then it started to cry, wailing like a human child. Otis shook it fiercely.

"Oh Jesus," Karen said, tears streaming down her face. "Otis! Put it down! Put it down!"

"Start back with the other dog," I said. "He won't drop it while she's near. Go on. I'll catch up."

She nodded, tight-lipped, hauled the female along for twenty yards or so, then let her go and trotted back down the trail, calling her name. The female hesitated, then followed Karen back into the woods.

"Good boy, Otis," I said, kneeling beside him, running my hands over his flanks. He was shivering, taut as a coiled spring. "Good boy. Put it down. Come on now, give it to me." I ran my fingers around his face to get him used to my scent, then hooked my thumb and index finger in the hinge of his jaw and began squeezing gently. If he growled now, we were in big trouble, but he didn't. He slowly released his squirming catch

111

into my hand. I placed it on the ground as far away as I could reach, while keeping a tight grip on the dog's collar.

The rabbit's forelegs were broken and its rib cage was crushed. Still, it tried to push itself along with its hindquarters, scraping through the leaves, leaving a crimson trail. The movement excited the dog and it was all I could do to hold him back.

"Sit!" I roared, then stood up, clutching his collar, forcing him down. Otis sat, but he was drooling, eyes locked on his wounded prey, quivering like a drawn bow. Then suddenly, he relaxed a fraction, and I realized the rabbit had stopped moving. Dead. Damn!

I let Otis sniff the carcass, feeling the tension drain out of him as he realized the game was over. Touchdown. Nothing else to it, as far as he was concerned. A fireside dream for his old age. It wasn't his fault. He was descended from ten thousand generations of hunters. Just a guy doing his job. Still, it was all I could do to keep from slapping him silly.

I gingerly picked up the rabbit and tossed the body as far as I could over the ledge. Otis watched it tumble down through the canopy of birches to the forest floor below, then looked up at me in utter disbelief. He shook his head hard, as if to clear it. I obviously didn't know the rules of The Game.

I let go of his collar. He trotted over to the edge of the shelf, nose in the air, sniffing, but made no move to go after his fallen prey. Instead, he circled the clearing once, looking for another score, then loped back down the road, nose to the ground, trailing Karen and the female.

I lingered a moment, looking out over the beauty of the treetops, trying to collect myself and absorb what Karen had told me. All these years, I'd been seeing what had happened to me one way: that my father hadn't understood, that he'd driven me away. I hadn't known half of what was going on. And I wondered how many more of my memories were lies.

Even the view of the valley below looked different—magnificent, but dangerous, as well. Still, I recognized it for what it was: home.

The big lake, these hills, they were truly my home. I belonged here, and I wanted to stay. I'd run away once. But not again. Not again.

I closed my eyes a moment, offering a silent prayer for my dad, and my son. And for Jud. And a small one for the rabbit. God help us all.

And then I took a deep breath and trotted back down the trail after Otis.

CHAPTER 19

———◆———

Sheba saved me. Over the following weeks, I worked through what could have been a very bad time for me. The Nest was literally a shambles, disrupted by the din of carpenters hammering and saws whining as they built on the back deck and ripped out a wall for French doors. My life wasn't in much better shape. Things I'd believed about my past and my father weren't true. I tried to tell myself it didn't matter, that it was over and done. But, of course, it wasn't. The past may be gone, but it's never truly . . . finished.

I heard nothing further from Jason Deveraux. But I knew I would. I guessed he was waiting for Alec to come home for the summer. I was Alec's problem, after all. Or rather, Corey was.

Did Alec want custody enough to start a court fight? Rob assured me Alec had no chance of winning. And yet at four in the morning, when you wake and wonder . . .

I called Corey each Sunday, but for the first time in our lives, we had trouble talking. I wondered if he was angry with me for leaving him behind in his private school while I went off adventuring on my own. Or perhaps he was just coming to the age where boys have less to say to their moms, especially over the phone. The distance between us involved more than miles and we couldn't seem to bridge it. Too many things had happened that I couldn't control or even understand. But by God, I understood *Sheba*.

I made it a point every morning to go into the Nest an hour or two early to work on my boat. It was slow, painstaking scut work, but it was what I needed, and *Sheba* never complained. I began by refinishing the fiberglass on her hull below the water-line. I could have patched it; no one would have known but the fish. But I would have known, and so would she. So I took my time and sanded her down completely, then gave her two thick coats of marine epoxy paint. Then I recaulked her, stem to stern, replaced a cracked section of taffrail, and polished her brightwork. And suddenly, she didn't look like a hulk any-more. She looked . . . seasoned, but still handsome, still strong. Katharine Hepburn.

Terry helped me go through her engine. And strange as it sounds, we had fun. It might not have looked like it, both of us hunched over a grubby marine inboard, cursing rusty bolts and lubbers who don't change engine oil from season to season. But in the end, we got her mill running, a bit rough when first started, but it evened out as it warmed, smooth as the prover-bial baby's bottom. A glorious, sensual rumble.

And Terry kissed me. And it meant something. We both knew it. But we didn't talk about it. We didn't have to. And anyway, trying to talk to Terry when he's working is like shout-ing down a hundred-foot well. Replies are long delayed and cryptic, if he answers at all. Some people don't change.

And some do. I began to see Charlie Bauer and his deputy, Jackowski, two or three mornings a week, jogging on the beach past the harbor. They were a mismatched pair, Jackowski hard and trim, wide shoulders, narrow-waisted, a muscle builder who obviously spent a lot of time working out. Sometimes they stopped. Charlie would compliment me on the way *Sheba* was coming along. Jackowski was usually too winded to talk much. His gym-crafted build seemed to be more for show than go, and I remembered Red's crack about steroid-laced beef. Maybe she wasn't kidding.

From his few sour comments, I gathered Jack didn't think much of women working on boats, or diving. Or not swooning at a glimpse of his bulging pectorals. He quit running with Charlie after the first week or so, and I didn't miss him a bit.

Charlie kept gamely at it, though. He stopped almost every

day to chat, to catch me up on local gossip or cop stories. He was surprisingly funny, with a sense of humor so dry, I couldn't always tell when he was kidding. He had wonderful eyes, too, deep and thoughtful. And I found myself thinking of him, and things he'd said, at odd times.

As the weeks passed, Charlie's tenacity gradually began to pay off. He was shedding pounds, and years as well, paring himself down to muscle and bone. He was still big, the size of the middle linebacker he'd been at Michigan State, but the flab was gone. Had to admit it, he was looking good—rangy and bony and hard. But he was always courteous, always correct. An interesting man, definitely, and interested, too, I thought.

I let it pass. I know my own limits, and I was very close to them. But at least I wasn't entirely alone anymore. I was forging new connections, to Red and Terry and Charlie, and even to Dog.

I began seeing her more often as the weather warmed. She still wouldn't come to me, but at least she'd stopped eyeing me like an hors d'oeuvre. Part of her seemed to need human companionship, or perhaps proximity.

And then one morning in mid-May, she carried a dead squirrel into the yard and laid it on the bottom step of the porch. It was a brutal offering, especially so soon after the incident with Karen's dogs, but I accepted it in the spirit in which it was offered: peace. We were, after all, family. We'd shared the same brother, which made us sisters, I suppose. Or pack mates. Either way, the connection was real: blood.

Karen did her best to maintain our ties, too. We met several times for coffee and talk. She advised me on local politics and bookkeeping and the dependability of local merchants. She was a big help and we became friendly without truly being friends. Sometimes you can't *make* friends, even when both of you try.

Business at the Nest gradually increased as the permanent slips at the harbor began filling. I had to hire a cook, and I let Red choose two more waitresses. The college kid Terry recommended stopped by to talk about running the dive shop for me, but he struck me as patronizing and I didn't hire him. I've endured the presumption of male superiority all my working life. Damned if I'll subsidize it. Instead, I hired a green local girl with some diving experience and a hunger to learn. A girl like I'd been once. Her name was Jeanette and she was a godsend. She worked hard, was good with the customers, and by the second weekend she'd memorized our entire stock.

That left me free to concentrate on overseeing both businesses, with time left over for my first love: diving.

I began going out on the *Sheba* almost daily to dive, or sometimes just to snorkel. Mostly, I dove alone, relearning coldwater techniques, reacquainting myself with the solitary, ghostly grandeur of the big lake, and, in a sense, revisiting my childhood.

When I wasn't actually in the water, I spent every spare moment poring over my father's books on lake shipping, memorizing the names of the wrecks, their routes, cargo, and final resting places. And how they died.

As Memorial Day approached, the harbor slips were ninety percent filled and business at the Nest nearly doubled. Things were looking much brighter. And I had all but decided that when Corey's European summer was over, I would bring him . . . home. It was time we had one together, and I was working like a dog to make it happen—and perhaps I was trying too hard. Because in studying the lore of the deepwater ladies, I'd overlooked the most obvious lesson of all: that life on the big lakes can be a very, very chancy thing.

CHAPTER 20

THE NIGHT OF MAY THIRTIETH, the Crow's Nest was jammed, wall to wall, a mixed bag of tourists and locals. A few hardy souls were out on the new deck, enjoying the harbor view and a fresh breeze off the lake. I was in my office, catching up on paperwork, feeling insufferably smug about the profit-and-loss statement, when I glanced up. And the earth shuddered beneath me like a seismic tremor.

Alec Deveraux had wandered in with his sister, Andrea, and another man, a tall blond. I tried not to stare but couldn't help it. Alec was changed. And not for the better. He'd always been fashionably gaunt. He looked haggard now, like his own undertaker, in a dark tweed jacket, black turtleneck. He was using a cane, and his dark hair was flecked with premature gray.

The years had sculpted him into a skeletal version of his father, but he looked more like Jason's sibling than his son.

Time had been much kinder to Andrea. She'd always been a strikingly attractive girl. She was even more so now: petite, broad-shouldered, with ebon hair that gleamed like a raven's wing. Her features are too angular to be conventionally pretty, but she always had a feline magnetism about her that more than compensated. And eau de money is a marvelous scent. Meow.

Her escort was male-model handsome, trim and tan, with a shaggy sun-bleached mane, collar-length. His white linen blazer probably cost as much as airfare to Australia. Andrea stopped off to chat with friends; her escort said something to her, but she waved him off. He shrugged and sauntered through the crowd back to my office, rapping politely before he stepped in.

"Miss Mitchell?" he said, offering his hand. "I'm Harvey Addison. I've been told you're the lady to see about scuba diving in the area." He had a distinctive British accent, polished and elegant. Probably too good to be true.

"I've been known to get wet," I said. "What can I do for you, Mr. Addison?"

"I'm hoping we can do some business," he said smoothly. "Visited your shop earlier. Quite a selection, but I didn't see any of the newer Genesis air tanks. Do you carry them?"

"Not yet," I admitted. "I only took over the business a few months ago, and my father only stocked American gear. A matter of honor. I use European tanks myself, though, and I've got several backup sets if you're interested in trying them."

"Bought a pair in the south of France last year and promptly sold the rest of my gear," he said, flashing a five-thousand-watt smile. Up close, I revised my male-model impression. Addison was gorgeous, a stone hunk, grade-A beef. Firm jaw, ice blue eyes. And yet I found myself glancing past him, watching for Alec.

"I'd like to discuss chartering you and your boat for a few weeks," he said, easing into one of the captain's chairs in front of my desk. "I understand there are some interesting wrecks in the area."

"Quite a few," I said. "There are roughly a hundred and fifty hulks within fifteen miles of the harbor, over six thousand major wrecks in the Great Lakes that we have records of. God knows how many smaller ships there are. The big lakes are hard on boats. On people, too, sometimes."

"Actually, there's a specific wreck I want to dive on, the *Queen of Lorraine*. Do you know anything about her?"

"The *Queen*? She was built in 1926, flagship of the Deveraux Mills Fleet," I recited, showing off. "She was bound for Chicago out of Erie, Pennsylvania, with a cargo of rolled steel in November 1972, when she was rammed in a fog by a Swedish freighter, the ah . . . the *Halmstad*. Her captain apparently didn't realize how badly she was damaged and tried to run her for the beach on North Point: He didn't make it. She rolled and sank. Most of her crew got off, but several of her officers didn't, including her captain."

"Very erudite, ma'am, I'm impressed," Addison said. "You've dived on her, then?"

"No, but I may know someone who has." Terry was shooting pool in the lounge, and I motioned him in. I introduced them, and they shook hands, looking each other over. Quite a con-trast: Addison, the impeccably dressed WASP, and Terry in a faded T-shirt and jeans, trim, tousled, and tanned dark as a Spaniard. Terry got my vote. I told him Addison was interested in the *Queen*.

"I looked her over last year," Terry said, parking a hip on the corner of my desk, resting the hilt of his pool cue on the floor. "She's a mess. She's roughly six miles out, two hundred feet down, smack in the middle of the Huron Bottomlands Pre-serve. The reef tipped her over when she settled, so she's upside down, with her masts and stacks buried in the mud."

"What's this about a preserve?" Addison frowned.

"The state outlawed the looting of wrecks back in '80," I ex-plained. "You'll need a permit to dive in the preserve. The law's tough to enforce, though. There's quite a black market for ship's 'jewelry,' running lights, portholes, things like that. In fact, I heard a rumor that some gear from the *Queen* was on the market recently."

"Yeah," Terry said blandly, "I heard that, too. Why the par-ticular interest in the *Queen*, Harvey? There are plenty of wrecks a helluva lot safer to dive on."

"She was built by my wife's family, the Deverauxes? Perhaps you know them?"

"Sure, Andrea and Mitch and I did high school together. I heard she got married. Congratulations, you're a lucky guy."

"In some quarters, the lady was considered equally lucky," Addison said evenly. "In any case, my father-in-law's rather keen on recovering the *Queen*'s dedication plaque for the Deveraux Institute's museum. Here, I have a photograph."

He slipped an old photo of the *Queen of Lorraine* from an inside pocket of his sport coat and passed it to Terry. "The plaque is bronze and quite large. It was mounted on a bulkhead in the passengers' lounge when she was launched, all the way forward in the bow. From the blueprints, it appears the only way in there is the corridor from the main entrance amidships. Could we get to it, do you think?"

"I'm not sure," Terry said, examining the photo carefully. "I haven't been inside that end of the ship, but her bow area's clear of the bottom. Maybe."

"You said 'we,' Mr. Addison," I said. "Are you planning to dive on the *Queen* yourself?"

"Certainly, that's the whole point. I want to retrieve the plaque as a sort of . . . get-well present for my father-in-law. I've never been down two hundred feet, but I'm quite athletic and I've done a bit of diving."

"In the Great Lakes?" I asked.

"Mostly in the Caribbean, the Bahamas, Jamaica, that sort of thing. I don't imagine there's much difference."

"Actually, there's quite a bit," I said. "The lakes are dark and murky and cold as a witch's kiss. Visibility's lousy because of the silt, and the currents are unpredictable. On the upside, since the wrecks deteriorate very slowly in fresh water, they're often in remarkable shape. Which can make them seem deceptively safe sometimes. They're not."

"And of course, there may be a body or two," Terry put in, "which may be why Mitch here hasn't been down to the *Queen* herself. How do you feel about bodies, Harvey?"

"There was a skeleton on one of the wrecks off Jamaica," he said wryly. "I managed not to wet myself. Though I suppose that might have been difficult to prove at the time."

"I'm not talking about skeletons," Terry smiled. "I'm talking about bodies."

"But the *Queen*'s been down over twenty years, surely—"

"At two hundred feet, the lake temperature only varies from thirty-four to thirty-eight degrees, at considerable pressure," Terry said. "If you wanted to preserve something permanently, you couldn't pick a better spot. Lake fish don't scavenge that deep and bodies decompose slowly. The *Griffin* disappeared in 1689, but if she's deep enough, whoever went down with her might still be aboard, and maybe even in one piece. More or less."

"You're joking, of course," Addison said.

"I'm afraid he's not," I said. "Three men went down with the *Queen*. It's possible they're still aboard her. It's something you might want to consider."

Addison eyed us with obvious suspicion. "I'm sure it's local custom to bugger about with the new boy in school, but I'm quite serious about going down to the *Queen*. I'm not a puddle diver. I've worked at nearly a hundred feet and I can doubtless manage two hundred with a bit of coaching. So, are you interested or not, Miss Mitchell?"

"Don't let the locals get your goat, Harvey," Andrea said, leaning over the back of his chair, her lips brushing the air beside his cheek. "Especially not these two. They're past masters of the art. And don't get up on my account, Fortier, if the thought had even occurred to you." She eased gracefully into the chair beside Harvey's, withdrew a cigarette from her bag, and paused just long enough for Harvey to light it.

"Mitch"—she nodded, blowing a plume in Terry's direction—"how are you? It's been awhile."

"You wouldn't know it to look at you," I said honestly. "You look terrific." And she did—almost. She was wearing an unbleached muslin sunsuit that showed her trim figure to good advantage, but the tequila sunrise in her hand looked suspiciously like a triple to my practiced eye. She'd kept her sunglasses on, though the Crow's Nest is dim as a dungeon. Charlie'd told me her mother was summering at Betty Ford's clinic. I wondered if Andrea was going to make it a family tradition.

"My father said you were back, Mitch," Andrea said, "running the Nest. Frankly, I was surprised."

"Why surprised?" I said. "Some of my best friends are saloons."

"As I recall, you were annoyingly ambitious, always screwing up the class curve for the rest of us. I assumed you'd go on to bigger things."

"I have, in a way," I said, indicating the window.

"You mean the harbor?" She frowned, puzzled.

"No. The lake."

"I don't follow you, but then I seldom did," she said. "Is your ah . . . son with you?"

"No," I said.

She arched an eyebrow, waiting for an explanation. I didn't offer one. "What a shame," she said. "I've heard there's quite a resemblance."

"There is," I said evenly. "He looks a lot like me."

"Then he must be a very good-looking . . . boy," she said.

Harvey hastily interjected, asking Terry about the difficulties of obtaining a salvage permit from the DNR, but I didn't pay much much attention. Jason could finagle a permit to cede Ontario to the Bulgarians if the mood struck him. Andrea appeared to be listening politely, but I had the feeling she'd tuned the conversation out. And so had I.

Instead of listening, I switched on an imaginary slide projector in my mind and tried to align my memories of Andrea from that last chaotic summer with the woman sitting beside Harvey now.

The images didn't quite match. The changes were slight but significant: the cigarette, the tequila triple, lines of petulance etched around her mouth. But then I noticed the way Terry was looking at her, his head cocked, staring without seeming to. And my little projector went out of control and memories came rushing over me in a torrent: Terry in skimpy bikini briefs, dozing in sunlight on the foredeck of his little sloop, or on a beach blanket at dusk, his breath warm on my neck as he fumbled with the snaps of my bathing suit, peeling it away. . . . He always stopped when I asked. I wouldn't have asked much longer.

And then Andrea took him away from me, as casually as borrowing pocket change. The party at the estate, Andrea and Terry dancing on the tennis court in the shadows away from the rest of us. And I was so enraged that I deliberately got drunk and threw myself at Alec. . . .

They were staring at me expectantly, all of them.

"I'm sorry," I said, "I was . . . woolgathering. What did you say?"

"Harvey asked if he could charter you and the *Sheba* for a month or so to have a go at the *Queen*," Terry said.

"No. Sorry, but I have other commitments."

"What sort of commitments?"

"I'm going to teach dive classes for beginners, mostly girls."

"I might be able to make it worth your while to adjust your schedule," Addison said.

"The answer's still no. Thanks anyway."

"Fortier might be the better choice in any case, since he's already been down to the *Queen*." Harvey frowned, annoyed. "Unless you're busy also?"

"I've got a few things going," Terry said, "but having a go at the *Queen* sounds like more fun. Sure, let's do it."

I was having trouble breathing. My chest was constricted by a long-forgotten ache.

"Good," Harvey said, rising. "It's settled then. Come out to the estate tomorrow, Fortier, and we'll work out the details. Nice meeting you, Miss Mitchell."

Andrea glanced at Terry a moment, and back at me, then smiled and stalked out without a word. Addison hurried after her.

I watched them make their way through the crush, Andy moving a bit unsteadily, I thought. Terry crossed to my liquor cabinet and poured two snifters of Courvoisier.

"Here," he said, handing me one, "you look like you need it."

"Was I that obvious?"

"Probably only to me. What's the problem? Seeing Alec again?"

"No. It's . . . I don't know. All of it. It feels like it's all coming back. Like bad karma or something."

"That's a natural reaction. You had a rough time. But hell, you were just a kid. Things are different now. Or at least some of 'em are," he said, absently warming the brandy with his palm. "She hasn't changed much, has she?"

"Everybody changes."

"Not Andy. She's like one of the deepwater ladies. I don't think she'll ever change."

It occurred to me that Terry might have memories of his own to savor, so I let it pass. I sipped my brandy, trying to let its smoky warmth ease the chill on my soul. It didn't work. I could feel myself regressing, feel the pain of the bad years rolling toward me like a dark wave. And the shame. And the rage. Especially the rage.

CHAPTER 21

TERRY WANDERED BACK to the lounge, and I returned to my books, losing myself so fiercely in the figures that I missed Alec's entrance. I'd waited ten years for it, and I missed it. I glanced up and he was there in the doorway, looking jaded, gray as a shadow.

"Hello, Mitch," he said. "How are you? Can, um, can we talk?"

I didn't answer for a moment. Couldn't. Finally, I managed a nod. He walked stiffly to the chair Harvey Addison had used and lowered himself into it carefully, bracing himself with a silver-headed cane. Except for his eyes, there was almost nothing of the boy I'd known in him.

"You look terrible, Alec. What happened?"

"A horse," he said easily. "The one that racked my leg up when I was kid. Its ghost gives me another kick now and again. I wanted to make a mark in the world. Instead, it's making them on me."

"So sorry," I said evenly.

"No reason you should be. You, on the other hand, look wonderful, Mitch. Dad said you did. He also said you were . . . formidable now. Like your father. So before you rip into me, let me at least get this out. I'm sorry. I'm sorry I . . . handled things so badly. I, um . . ." He took a deep breath, looked away.

"That's it?" I said. "That's the speech?"

"It was a long time ago. We were kids, Mitch. Kids make mistakes."

"That's how you see it? Rape as a prank?"

"No, of course not. We both had a little too much to drink. And things . . . happened. They do sometimes."

"I won't dignify that with a response. But I trusted you, Alec. Like a brother. My God, I was a virgin. Or were you too drunk to notice? Do you have any concept of what it was like to wake in a strange bed? Without knowing what . . ." I swallowed hard, collecting myself. "Funny. For years after I left, I must have run through this scene a thousand times. What you'd say. What I'd say. A chance to tell you what a bastard you . . . The hell with it. It isn't important now. And neither are you. What do you want, Alec?"

"A chance to correct a mistake. To set things right."

"It's a bit late for that. Why now?"

"I didn't know until recently that you had the child," he said simply. "At the time I thought you'd . . . had it taken care of."

"Which was what you wanted at the time."

"I didn't know what I wanted. I was sorry about . . . your situation, Mitch. I would have helped if you'd asked. But to be fair, I had no real reason to believe it was mine. You'd been much closer to Fortier than to me."

"Maybe you were right."

"No," he said, shaking his head slowly. "I've seen his picture, Mitch. The ah . . . the resemblance is striking. Look, you have every right to be angry, I realize that. And since nothing I can say could mean much at this late date, I'll be direct. If there's any way that I can make amends for what happened, say it. I'll do it. Anything at all."

"Just like that?"

"Mitch, you're a professional person now. And I'm a businessman. Which makes us both practical people by necessity. So, as one professional to another, what more can I do? I can't change the past."

"No, I suppose not. All right, there is one thing you can do. Write a statement, right now, summing up what happened. If the term *date rape* offends you, use *droit du seigneur*. Put any spin on it you like. But at the end, give up any claims you think you have on my son. I'll get somebody to witness our signatures and we'll call it even. What do you say?"

"*Droit du seigneur?*"

"My accent may be lousy, but I can read Cousteau in French. Can you?"

"Probably not. And I'm afraid I can't do as you ask, either."

"Why not?"

"For one thing, our recollection of the . . . events differ. Sorry, but I just don't remember it that way. Maybe it's selective memory, I don't know. And my father said you already agreed to—"

"Alec, I give you my word, I didn't have anything to do with the deal Jason and my father cooked up. I didn't know a damned thing about it and don't want to. All I'm asking is that you let us alone. I'll sign away any claim to child support or anything else you like."

"But suppose I want to contribute? I don't see why we can't work out some sort of agreement."

"You can't be serious."

"Just hear me out. Would granting some kind of minimal visitation rights be so terrible? Especially when you could do so much for yourself and the boy with the money. You wouldn't have to work so hard—"

"Christ, you're incredible! If you'd raped me in an alley instead of your bedroom, would you still expect me to agree to visitation rights? I don't want a damned dime from you! I just want to get on with my life. Stay away from us, Alec."

"It's not that simple," he said, using the cane to lever himself out of his chair. "I wish it was. It's not. For one thing, my father's involved. My . . . girls aren't enough for him. He wants a grandson. And you know what he's like when he's set on something. Think it over, Mitch. It'll be better for all concerned if you and I can work something out."

"No chance," I said. "None."

"As you wish. Harvey said you turned him down as a client."

"Should I reconsider that, too?"

"No, you did the right thing. Addison's really just a beach bum with a pedigree. Married my sister for her money. He was satisfied with being a glorified escort until my father's coronary, but now he's on the make, out to impress the old man. It might be best to avoid him and anyone else connected with my father for now."

"I intend to. Especially you."

"I'm not your enemy, Mitch, whether you believe it or not. If you ever want to talk, you can reach me at the house." He limped stiffly to the door. "For what it's worth, I really do regret what happened. All of it."

"I think you know what that's worth."

"Yes"—he nodded, with a trace of a smile—"I'm afraid I do. Take care." He limped back into the lounge, and I could tell by the hunch of his shoulders that walking caused him pain. I should have been glad. But somehow I couldn't manage it. I kept seeing Corey in the color of his eyes, his build, even his smile. I wanted to hate him, needed to. But nothing is ever simple.

The phone on my desk rang. I picked it up.

"Turn around," a voice said. "Look out the window."

I swiveled my chair to face the harbor. The slips were crowded with sailboats and powerboats. People were wandering around the docks, drinks in hand, visiting. I could feel the thump of music booming across the water. The summer party scene was in full swing. But even amid the clutter, Ken Robinette's *Mai Tai* stood out, with twinkling strings of white Christmas lights laced in her stays and up her mast. Rob was standing on her foredeck, a portable phone at his ear. He waved. I waved back.

"I'm hosting a very exclusive dinner tonight," he said. "Can you come?"

"Sorry, I'm working."

"No problem. What time will you be off?"

"Not until two-thirty, but—"

"Perfect. It'll give the wine a chance to breathe."

"What kind of a dinner lasts until two-thirty in the morning?"

"It won't *last* that long; that's when it'll begin. In fact, this dinner is so exclusive that if you can't come, I'll be dining alone."

I hesitated. "I may not be very good company."

"Then I'll try to be cheery enough for two. Would you like to think it over?"

"No," I said. "Save me a seat."

CHAPTER 22

THE *MAI TAI* gave a shiver of anticipation when I stepped aboard her, rocking gently on the ripples in the night breeze. She was glowing like a teenager in a prom frock, scrubbed and shining, Christmas lights twinkling like tethered stars in her lines. A few parties were still in muted swing across the harbor, but on this side, only the *Mai Tai* was awake amid her sleepier sisters along the pier. Alerted by my footsteps, Rob popped his head out of the companionway. He was wearing an apron over a teal sports shirt, white jeans, and deck shoes. An attractive package, and he was probably aware of it.

"Good morning, madam. Welcome aboard me 'umble craft."

"Somehow *'umble* isn't a word I associate with you, Mr. Robinette," I said, following him through to the forward stateroom. "And especially not about this lady. She's exceptionally fine." And she was. Her decks and countertops were lacquered teak, her lockers and cupboards inset with rosewood. Her starboard bulkhead was a burled walnut deck-to-ceiling bookcase. Its top rows were filled with law books, the rest, an eclectic mix of travel and fiction. The galley was exquisite and obviously in use. All four burners glowed under copper-bottomed pots and saucepans. The air was a meld of exotic scents, coriander, ginger, cinnamon. Come wiz me to ze Casbah.

"Whatever you're preparing smells wonderful," I said. "Chinese?"

"Mongolian, actually, via Motown," he said. "I also do dynamite soul food and semi-edible Italian. A glass of wine? Perhaps something a bit stronger?" He opened the lower door of a Dutch locker, revealing a completely stocked bar.

"Very impressive." I nodded. "Courvoisier?"

"Absolutely," he said, deftly pouring two generous dollops into crystal snifters and warming them with his palms. "Dinner will be a few minutes."

"If you could bottle the aroma, you could retire. You're a man of surprising talents," I said, easing down on the settee opposite the galley. "An attorney *and* a five-star chef. What else do you do?"

"I work out a lot," he said, "to compensate for being an outrageously good cook. The local gym is excellent. In fact, its only shortcoming is that I never see you there."

"Is that a hint?"

"Not at all. You look incredibly fit, as I'm sure you're aware. But it's also a good spot to make social contacts."

"The only serious iron pumper I know is Charlie Bauer's deputy, Jackowski, and frankly, I see him too often now."

"Jack's an every-nighter," Rob admitted, smiling, "but he's not the only one. You meet a fair cross section there, from doctors to mechanics. And women as well—your bartender, Big Red, works out twice a week. And your near stepmother, Karen Stepaniak."

"You know Karen?"

"In a town this size, everyone knows everyone."

"It is a small town," I acknowledged, "and a long way from Detroit. How did you end up moored here?"

"The coke trade," he said, eyeing me frankly across the lip of his brandy glass. "Didn't Sheriff Bauer tell you my sad story?"

"No, and to be honest, I asked once. He tactfully changed the subject."

"Did he? Then you're one of the few he didn't tell. The good sheriff isn't a fan of mine, probably because I've beaten him in court once or twice. In any event, I was a rising young attorney who had the dubious good fortune to win a few cases involving dopers, and I found myself with a very lucrative practice and a *very* shady clientele. Do you ever, um, do drugs at all?"

"Never. I need the few brain cells I have."

"Very wise. But you'd be surprised how many apparently respectable types are into it these days. I've represented judges, pilots, athletes. And, of course, a small army of street thugs. The American dream. Better living through chemistry. I prefer defending thugs, actually. They're scum, but at least they aren't hypocrites."

"If business was so good, why did you quit?"

"My health. The downside to a drug-trade legal practice is that when you lose a case, your clients sometimes take it very personally. I lost a few I should have won. Maybe my heart wasn't in it anymore. So I dropped out, moved up here to live a simpler life. Poorer but wiser. Can I refill your glass?"

I glanced down, startled. I'd drained it without noticing.

Déjà vu.

The feeling that had been nagging all night returned, but more clearly now. Déjà vu. A wheel coming around. Terry linked with Andrea again. Alec, battered but still . . . impressive. And my instinctive response? Kill the pain. With brandy.

"I think I'd prefer a soft drink," I said carefully. "And before things go any further, a quick question. Why did you call me tonight? Specifically, I mean."

"If you're asking if anyone retained me to wine you and dine you, the answer is yes and no. Hoffman told me Alec intended to talk to you and that any aid I could offer would be handsomely rewarded. I politely declined."

"No kidding? Why was that?"

"Maybe I'm getting choosier about whom I work for. But since antagonizing clients isn't how young attorneys get ahead, if you want to feel a little grateful, be my guest."

"I am your guest. And if you turned him down, then why the invitation?"

"Naïve though it may sound, I thought you might like dinner

with a friend after a tough night at the office. I also hoped Alec might wear you down enough that I could get past that giant chip on your shoulder. No offense, but that's how it seems sometimes."

"Then why bother?"

"Because I'm naïve enough to hope we can be friends. We've got a lot in common. We've both been around the block, and neither of us really belongs in this backwater."

"Maybe you don't. I'm not so sure about me. I like it here. It can be hard country sometimes, but it grows on you."

"Perhaps. Since you arrived, it's looking better to me all the time. And speaking of improving the way things look," he said, dimming the lights, placing a silver candelabra on the table in the forward stateroom and lighting it, "let there be light. What do you think?"

"It's . . . lovely." I nodded slowly, taking a deep breath. "Look, I apologize for . . . being suspicious. You've gone to a lot of trouble, and I appreciate it, really."

"No offense taken. Suspicion is the first prerequisite of a healthy mind. Especially in my business. Truce?"

"Truce. Neutral subject. Do you actually read all these books, or are they here to impress your dates?"

"No, ma'am, I've read them all. Do you read?"

"Compulsively."

"There are worse addictions, and I speak from experience. I've tried most of them. What do you read?"

"Everything, anything. Romances to Rousseau. But mostly maritime history. Everything in my father's library."

"Your father had a library? He didn't strike me as the bookish type."

"He was, though. He'd been a seaman, and aboard ship there's not much else to do. The habit stayed with him."

"So instead of hanging out at the soda shop, you'd while away your evenings curled up with a good book?"

"Sometimes. And sometimes I'd read in trees."

"Come again?"

"When I was a kid and my father went out on charters, I'd climb my favorite lonesome pine with a good book and a Pepsi and read the day away up there, watching for him to come home."

"That must have been lonely," he said, his eyes meeting mine, holding them for a moment.

"It really wasn't. The view of the lake was incredible, and the tree would rock me in her arms like . . . well, the way the *Mai Tai* rocks you to sleep, I imagine."

"That she does. Well, at least neither of us will be lonely tonight—or hungry, either. Dinner, madame, is served."

It was excellent, Mongolian beef sautéed with chives and peppers. I tried to keep the conversation deliberately neutral, but I gradually thawed. He was a very attractive man, bright, witty, and a good cook to boot. And after dinner, we danced, very properly, to Sinatra on his Bose system. He was going to kiss me soon, I thought, and I was deciding whether it would stop there, when he paused in midstep, jostling me.

"What is it?"

"I'm not sure," he said, moving to the porthole. "Did you leave some kind of a red light on at the Nest?"

I pushed past him. He was right—a faint glow was flickering through the curtains of the French doors. "Call 911," I said. "I'll—" I was cut off by a blinding flash of flame that exploded out from beneath the Nest's new deck.

"Wait a minute; don't go alone!" Rob shouted, but I was already sprinting down the companionway for the door.

CHAPTER 23

I LEAPT FROM THE *Mai Tai*'s afterdeck to the dock and raced down the pier toward the Nest. A billow of greasy smoke roiled from beneath the new back deck, but I couldn't see any fire glow, or even any damage from the blast. Taking a chance, I dashed through the smoke to the French doors, fumbled my key into the lock, and jerked them open. Flames flared up as the air from the door kindled the blaze, but the room beyond appeared dark. . . . I didn't even think; I just jumped through the flames like a damned trained pony. . . .

And landed hard on the floor, shaken, a little scorched, but otherwise in one piece. Blinking rapidly, my eyes watering from the smoke, I quickly scanned the room. It looked all right, no other fires that I could see. Just—newspapers. Someone had piled wadded newspapers against the French doors and set them alight. I charged to the bar, grabbed an ice bucket, filled it with water, and pitched it into the fire.

And all over Ken Robinette as well, catching him waist-high as he vaulted through the doorway over the flames, slamming into me, knocking both of us sprawling away from the blaze.

"What the hell!" he sputtered, scrambling to his knees, knuckling the water from his eyes. "Are you okay?"

"Yes. Did you get the fire department?"

"They're on their way," he said, standing up, scanning the room. "They'll be a few minutes, though. Look, this isn't safe; you'd better grab what you need and get out of here."

"I'm not going anyplace," I said, picking up the bucket. "I can handle this."

"Are you crazy? That was a damned bomb that went off a minute ago. There could be another!"

I hadn't thought that far ahead, and now I was too angry to care. "You go ahead. I'll be right behind you, but I'm putting this thing out first!"

"Don't be a—okay, okay! But let me handle this fire," he said, grabbing the bucket. "Take a quick look, see if there are any more. Then grab what you want and for Pete's sake let's get out of here!"

It made sense. Rob attacked the fire and I quickly reconnoitered the lounge. Nothing. No sign anything had been disturbed. The office door was still locked, but I opened it and glanced in, anyway. Everything looked normal. I was relocking the door when Rob sprinted up.

"That one's out. We'd better go. Can I help?"

"No, everything seems all right. Let's go."

"What about the safe? If there's another blast—"

"It's empty. Red night-deposits the receipts at the bank on her way home."

The room was suddenly filled with the moan of sirens and swept by red and blue lights as a fire truck pulled into the parking lot. I started for the front door, but it burst open before I reached it. Charlie Bauer stormed into the room, followed by two firemen in raincoats and Plexiglas-shielded helmets.

"Mitch?" Charlie said, grasping my shoulders, looking into my eyes. "Are you okay?"

"I'm fine," I said.

"Good, good," he said, glancing around the room, freezing momentarily when he spotted Rob. Then he pointedly let me go. "What's going on here?"

"Arson," I said. "Somebody started a fire over by the door and set off some kind of a bomb out under the deck. We put it out before it had a chance to get going."

"All right." Charlie nodded. "I want everybody out, away from the building. Now." No one argued.

We filed outside and stood silently for twenty minutes or so amid the swirl of the fire truck's flashers, waiting. Suddenly, the Nest lit up and I flinched. But it was only Charlie turning on the lights. He stepped out a moment later, disheveled, his face and uniform smeared with soot. He stalked to his prowl car to use the radio. Rob and I followed.

"Well?"

"Front door was jimmied; that's how whoever it was got in. Other than that, everything seems to be more or less in one piece, Mitch. I'm going to tape the area off for now and take a closer look in the morning with the fire marshal. What happened exactly?"

"I'm afraid I can't tell you much. Rob and I were having dinner on his boat when the blast went off, apparently under my new deck. We called 911, then put out the fire."

"You let her go in there, Robinette?" Charlie snapped at Rob. "Christ, for all you knew there could have been—"

"He didn't *let* me do anything," I interrupted, "I went in on my own. What did you find under the deck?"

"Not much," he admitted, still glowering at Rob. "No structural damage to the building that I could see. We'll be able to judge better in daylight."

"Which will be in a couple of hours," I said, glancing at my watch. "I'll meet you back here at six."

"I'll see you home," Charlie said.

"No need, Sheriff," Rob put in, "since the lady was my guest—"

"Thanks for your concern, gentlemen, but I'm perfectly cabable of finding my own way home," I said curtly, cutting off the debate.

"I didn't mean it that way," Charlie said. "I'm just concerned, is all. This doesn't look like ordinary vandalism to me."

"I agree," I said. "I think it was supposed to intimidate me— which is exactly why it's not going to. I'll see you back here at first light, Charlie."

"Mitch, wait up," Rob called, overtaking me at my pickup.

"Look, I couldn't be sorrier about all this. I hope we'll get a chance to try again."

"Maybe we will, counselor, but not for a while. I'm afraid I'm not going to be very good company until this thing's settled."

"I understand. If there's anything I can do . . ."

"There is one thing. Do you handle homicide cases?"

"I . . . haven't in awhile. Why?"

"Then maybe you'd better do some brushing up. Because if I find out who did this, I may need a good lawyer."

CHAPTER 24

I'D THOUGHT ROB might object, insist that I spend what remained of the night on the *Mai Tai,* or perhaps offer to stay with me at the cottage. He didn't, though—which was a bit disappointing, but probably just as well. Rob was witty, attractive, good company. But I needed some space, some time alone to cool off, and to think.

Most of all to think. The fire: It couldn't have been a serious attempt to burn the Nest. Whoever'd broken in could just as easily have sprinkled gasoline around and . . . *boom.* More likely, it was either meant as a warning of some kind or someone was trying to frighten me off. Habash? Or even Joe Carney, I suppose. He was still eager to buy the Nest, but he couldn't up his initial offer. But most likely, it was Alec. Or perhaps Jason's ex-CIA goon, Hoffman. Showing me they were serious.

And in a way, I was grateful for it. Because until tonight, a part of me retained my childhood awe of Alec and his family. Be reasonable, it said. What they're asking isn't so awful, is it? But the fire had effectively stilled that voice. Burned it out.

I wasn't the green kid who'd run off ten years ago. I'd scuffled and worked and provided for myself and my son. I might choose to leave, but I would not be driven out again. And if they thought a puny little fire . . .

Damn it. There it was again, the fire. There was something about the fire I was missing. . . .

Whatever it was kept dancing around the back of my mind like a moth in the firelight, just out of reach. I kept returning to it on the drive home, but I couldn't quite give it a shape, or a name.

I parked my new pickup in the yard and strode briskly to the house. The front door was unmarked, no sign of tampering. I unlocked it, then reached gingerly around with my fingertips. My grandfather's rifle was leaning against the wall where I'd left it. If it hadn't been, I'd have broken the record for the twenty-yard dash back to my truck.

Instead, I stepped in, picked up the rifle, and checked the magazine. Still loaded. I jacked a round into the chamber, then switched on the lights and quickly searched the cottage, gun in hand. I didn't expect to find anything, and I didn't. Everything was as it should have been.

It was really too late to go to bed, but I was absolutely exhausted. I thought about taking a quick shower to wake up but didn't have the energy. Instead, I double-checked the door locks, put the rifle back in the gun-cabinet rack, and sat down on the living room sofa to try to sort through things. . . .

And promptly fell asleep sitting up. At some point, I toppled over on the sofa and snuggled under my coat.

And I dreamt my way back to the *Mai Tai* . . . and danced with Rob by candlelight. Sinatra was singing . . . and Rob lowered his lips to mine. . . . And suddenly, the blast came from the Crow's Nest.

I snapped awake. Stunned, stupid, I tried to shake off the dream. Then the blast exploded again, shocking me to full awareness. My God, it wasn't a dream; it was real. Gunfire! Somebody was shooting at the house!

I dropped to the floor beside the sofa, huddling against it, trying to melt into the carpet. Another shot. But there was no thump of impact in the house, no crash of breaking glass or splintering wood. Maybe they weren't shooting at me at all. More scare tactics? Gunfire in the night, making me hide in my own living room? I felt my fear start to fade as anger burned it away like a red flame rising. Damn them!

I inched along to the corner of the room and stood up, flattening myself against the wall. Dawn was still a half hour off, but there was enough gray light to see out into the yard and to the low dunes that rolled away along the beach beyond. I suppose an army could have hidden out there, but I'd played in those dunes as a girl and knew every inch of them. No one was there. I was sure of it.

I moved quickly to the gun cabinet, grabbed the Winchester 30-30, and shoved a handful of spare cartridges in my pocket. If whoever was out there liked noise . . .

Keeping close to the walls, I stepped quickly through the kitchen to the front door, reached for it, then froze. An unearthly snarling erupted from the tree line beyond the yard, instantly familiar. Dog was out there. Then a series of rapid shots exploded in the dark. *Wham! Wham!*

"JESUSJESUSJESUS!!!" A man's voice, barely recognizable as human. Then the crack of another shot. A car door slammed; an engine fired up, roared off into the dark. Then nothing. Only my own hammering heartbeat. Silence. I waited at least twenty minutes, until the first light of dawn washed away some of the shadows. Then I eased the door open.

The air was brisk, with a sharp breeze off the lake ruffling the pines that circled the yard. I stood in the open doorway a few minutes, watching the tree line carefully for any movement that seemed out of place. Then I walked quietly down the steps, angling warily toward the trees.

And she stepped out. Dog. Eyeing me with a ferocity I'd never seen before, her eyes alight with murderous intensity. She lowered herself to her belly, almost disappearing in the brush. She crouched. Waiting.

"Dog? Good girl." She gave no sign she heard me. I took a step forward, then another, talking to her softly as I approached, keeping my voice low, and reassuring, I hoped. She let me move roughly ten meters closer, then growled, a deep bass rumble of unmistakable menace. *Stop*, it said. *Right there.*

And I did. We eyed each other for what seemed like a lifetime, twenty yards apart across open ground. And then suddenly, she blinked and cocked her head, listening. A moment later, I heard it, too. The car was coming back.

CHAPTER 25

I BACKED AWAY FROM DOG as rapidly as I could without turning around. I wasn't sure how she'd react if I ran, and I was afraid to find out. I managed to reach the generator shed before the car came into view down the track. I stepped behind it, waited until the car crunched to a halt in the drive and a door opened, then I stepped out with the Winchester leveled. . . .

At Charlie Bauer. He halted halfway out of his prowl car. "Mitch? What the hell's going on?"

"What are you doing out here?" I asked.

"What am I—you said you'd meet me at first light. When you didn't show, I thought I'd better check. Are you all right?"

"I'm fine," I said. "Would you mind taking a few steps away from your car?"

"What?"

"Please, Charlie, humor me, okay? I've had a rough night."

He shrugged and moved from behind the door. He'd shaved and changed uniforms since I'd seen him last. And his uniform was neat as a pin, with no rips or grass stains on it. I lowered the rifle and eased the hammer down.

"What's this all about, Mitch? What happened?"

"Dog attacked somebody out there in the trees beyond the yard just before dawn. Whoever it was fired a couple of shots and yelled a lot. I heard him crashing through the underbrush to his car."

"And you thought it might have been me?"

"I . . . wondered. You got here awfully quick."

"You're damned right I did," he said. "I probably blew half a

144

dozen citizens off the road on the way. Citizens who vote, I might add. You said Dog? You mean that cross-wolf bitch Jud Radowicz had? She's yours now?"

"Not really. She's her own. I feed her sometimes."

"Will she come to you?"

"I don't know. Probably not."

"Then this is going to be tricky," he said, drawing his pistol. "Maybe you'd better go back to the house."

"I'm not going anyplace. And you're not going to shoot that dog."

"Mitch, be reasonable. She's a helluva lot more wolf than dog. You admit she's mostly wild, and if she's just chewed somebody up—"

"She won't attack me," I said with a lot more conviction than I felt. "Now either put your gun away, Charlie or leave. Your choice."

He looked away a moment, then back at me. "You'll be holding that rifle, right? You know how to use it?"

"Probably better than most."

"Fair enough, we'll try it your way," he said, holstering his pistol. "But if she comes at us, Mitch, I'll do what I have to. Where did the shooting come from?"

"Over there, at the tree line. Dog's in the shadows to the left of that big pine."

"Okay. Stay a little behind me, please. Let me get a look at the scene. And watch where you point that gun." I followed Charlie toward the tree line. Dog watched us intently all the way, her eyes locked on us like radar. Charlie moved slowly, scanning the ground with each step. He paused, then knelt carefully, examining a disarranged patch of earth. Dog rose a few inches, growling low in her throat. "Mitch," Charlie said softly, "we've got a problem. I want you to back away . . . slowly. Try to get an angle on her."

"Why? What's—"

"She's been hit, Mitch. Look at her pelt, high, just behind her shoulder. She's wounded. I can't tell how badly, but there's a lot of blood here. And at this point, the only tracks I've found are hers. She's dangerous now, Mitch. I'll have to destroy her. I'm sorry. It's—"

I walked past him, moving directly toward Dog, keeping myself in Charlie's line of fire. "Here, girl, come on," I said, keeping my voice calm, or trying to. "Come on." She let me approach within ten yards or so, then rose to her full height, baring her teeth.

"Mitch," Charlie called from behind me. "For God's sake!" I wanted to stop, to give Dog a chance to get my scent, but Charlie was moving to his left, so I shifted direction slightly to block his view of her—and she bolted. She wheeled and vanished into the brush like smoke on the wind. It happened so fast, I had no chance to bring my gun up. If she'd charged toward me instead of away . . .

"Damn it," Charlie said, "that was probably the stupidest . . . Ah hell. Are you okay?"

"Why shouldn't I be?"

"Because you're shaking, that's why. Or maybe it just seems like it because I am. Jesus, Mitch, that bitch could've had us both."

"I told you she wouldn't attack me. And her name is Dog."

"I'll try to remember that," he said grimly, shaking his head. "They may need it for my obit. Come over here and take a look at this."

Charlie was kneeling at the edge of the tree line. I couldn't see what he was examining at first. And I wasn't supposed to. It was a blind. Someone had carefully interlaced the pine branches and tied them together to conceal a perfectly camouflaged hiding place beneath the tree. It looked almost cozy: a tree bark–patterned sleeping bag, an Aladdin thermos, and a pair of 10x50 binoculars.

"Know anything about this?" Charlie asked.

"No. But I may know who built it."

"Who?"

"Mr. Hoffman, Jason Deveraux's assistant. Or somebody working for him."

"Why would he do that?"

"Alec talked to me last night about"—I swallowed—"about arranging some kind of visitation rights with my son."

"I don't understand."

"I turned him down. And immediately, there's a fire at the Nest. And now this. Coincidence, do you think?"

"What would he hope to gain?"

"To frighten me into cooperating. What else?"

"I suppose that's possible," Charlie said thoughtfully. "The ah . . . bomb you heard at the Nest turned out to be a flash-bang grenade. I found some fragments under the deck after you left."

"A flash what?"

"Flash-bang grenade. They don't do much physical damage, just make noise and light, disorient people if you throw them into a room. Whoever used it didn't intend any real harm."

"My point exactly," I said.

He took a ballpoint pen out of his breast pocket, fished around in the grass a moment, and came up with a gleaming brass cartridge case on the pen's tip. "Nine millimeter," he said. "Automatic. How many shots were fired?"

"At least six, I think."

"All right." He nodded, rising. "I'm going to ask a state police evidence team to examine the area; they've got better equipment. But there could be a problem with that."

"What problem?"

"The blood—they'll need to know where it came from. If they find the dog—"

"Then keep them away."

"No," he said flatly. "This is a crime scene, Mitch, in my county. I have to investigate it. Hell, I want to know what's going on as much as you do. And when they see the blood—"

"Then tell them she's dead."

"What?"

147

"You can say I told you I found her and that I buried her. They won't bother to track her, and you'll be covered. Otherwise, I won't have them here, Charlie, period. Not if there's any chance they'll kill her."

"All right, all right," he said, throwing his hands up. "Judging from the blood she's lost, she may very well *be* dead. But I need to get the evidence team here. Maybe they can get prints off the cartridge cases or the binoculars. Hoffman's ex-CIA, so his prints will be on file."

"You sound doubtful."

"I am. For openers, those binoculars are K Mart cheapos. I think an ex-spook would use better equipment. Besides, he's strictly a REMF type, not a grunt."

"A what?"

"A REMF. Army slang. Means rear echelon mother—well, you get the drift. Anyway, I can't picture him grubbin' around out here in the brush. Might get his suit wrinkled."

"You don't think he's involved, do you?"

"I didn't say that. But I'm wondering. From what I hear, Joe Carney still wants to buy you out. Word is, he even laid some money on your pal Fortier to cuff you around. If he was willing to rough you up, arson wouldn't be much of a stretch."

"Arson might not be, but what about this?" I said, turning over the sleeping bag with my toe. "Somebody planned to keep an eye on me . . . and not just here. That's what's been bothering me about the fire. It wasn't supposed to do any damage; it was strictly for show. But it was set at the back door. They didn't want some passerby to see it. The message was for me, personally. And whoever set it knew where I was. Somebody's watching me, Charlie."

"Looks like it," Bauer said, frowning. "What about Robinette? He knew where you'd be."

"Rob would have no reason to do this."

"No? He's done some legal work for the Deverauxes. Maybe he still is."

"I don't think so. This is hardly the kind of thing they'd hire him for, is it?"

"Maybe it is. He's worked the wrong side of the street before."

"But as an attorney, not a thug. You really dislike him, don't you?"

"He paid for that fancy boat of his with drug money, Mitch. Just because he earned it legally doesn't make it any cleaner. But to be fair, I admit this doesn't seem like his style. What about the people Shan was peddling that load of contraband china to? Could they be trying to muscle you?"

"I don't see why. I haven't anything they want now. The DNR seized it all."

"Maybe they don't know that. Why don't you let me ask 'em?"

"Look, all I know is, Alec talked to me about visitation, and as soon as I said no, all hell breaks loose. Coincidence?"

"I didn't say that, but the bottom line is, if Alec wants to assert his rights or whatever, it'd be a lot simpler to hire an army of lawyers to jack you around until they find a judge who'll roll over for 'em."

"That wouldn't be so easy," I said. "I'd fight it all the way. It could take years. And Alec's never been the patient type."

"True, but he's not a bad guy. Couldn't you work something out?"

"No chance. None."

"Why?"

"It's really none of your business, Charlie."

"Offhand, I'd say the fire and whatever happened here make it my business, Mitch. And I'd like you to tell me anyhow . . . as a friend. What's this all about?"

"Let me ask you one first, Charlie. Has anyone ever been convicted of date rape in this county?"

"Date rape? Not to my knowledge, no. It's tough to prove. Is, um, is that what happened?"

"That's exactly what happened. Alec and I weren't even lovers, Charlie. I thought we were friends. I was dead wrong. Suppose I'd charged him with rape back then? What would have happened?"

"I think you know the answer to that," he said grimly. "Maybe it's not right, but that's how it is."

"And you still think I should work something out?"

"I don't know. You'll have to decide that."

"I already have. Alec's like his father. He won't settle for half of anything. If I give an inch, he'll want it all. And I won't let that happen. Tell him that when you see him. And tell his goon Hoffman, and Carney, and everybody else that the point isn't going to be safe to visit from now on. My shooting's a little rusty, so I'm going to be practicing. A lot. At odd hours."

"My God," he said, shaking his head. "I see you talking, but you know who I hear? Shan. I bet I arrested him a half dozen times over the years, drunk and disorderly, usually after he'd mopped up the floor with two or three guys. He was always a handful. Not just because he was big, I'm bigger. But he'd never quit. It's like he didn't even know how. You're a lot like him, Mitch. Too much, maybe."

"Thank you," I said.

"Damnit, I didn't mean that as a compliment."

"Then what do you advise, Charlie? Should I roll over? Give up? Is that what you'd do?"

"I just hate seeing you out here alone with a gun, that's all. There has to be a better way to handle this."

"If you think of one, let me know. And now I've got a question for you, Charlie. If it comes down to choosing sides, which way will you jump?"

"I hope I'll try to do the right thing, Mitch, whatever it is."

"I hope so, too, Charlie. But meanwhile, I'll keep practicing. Just in case."

CHAPTER 26

OVER THE NEXT FEW WEEKS, I did practice, almost every day. It was the perfect outlet, walking out on the point into the dunes, setting up a few pieces of driftwood, then backing off fifty or sixty paces. And nailing them.

And oddly enough, it brought back an alternate set of memories, like a drawing that had been painted over, memories of my father patiently teaching me his skills, with boats and scuba diving gear. And guns.

He taught me to shoot the first summer I'd joined him, the best summer. Not on a range with paper targets at exact distances. He taught me instinct shooting, on the beach. A gun is only a tool, but it's a dangerous one, like a chain saw, or an acetylene torch. Handle the weapon unloaded, until it feels as natural to hold as a hammer or a hairbrush. Learn to look at the target, not the sights, shoot! In time, you begin to pick up the proper sight picture intuitively, in a split second. If you can see the target clearly, you can hit it.

And after a few days practice, I found I still could—like riding the proverbial bicycle. Still, I continued to shoot, for the satisfaction of reclaiming a lost skill and as a way of blowing off steam. But most of all, for the companionship.

Dog was attracted by the sound of gunfire.

She showed up the second day I practiced. I'd set up a piece of driftwood against a sand dune along the lakeshore and fired a few rounds at it when I realized Dog was watching me intently from a dune about thirty yards to my right. I wasn't sure what to do, so I lowered the rifle and called to her. And she rose and limped stiffly down the dune, but not to me. To the target. She sniffed around a moment, then looked up at me, obviously puzzled. And expectant.

What did she want? Not affection certainly, she'd never displayed the slightest interest in being friends. What then? Food. Of course. Jud must have hunted out here, for both of them. To Dog, the sound of gunfire held no terror. It meant food. Taking a chance, I turned and walked directly back to the cottage. And for the first time, she followed. I'd set out food for her the day before by the generator shed. She trotted right up to the bowl and inhaled it at single gulp.

"Don't wolf your food," I said, opening another can. She backed away as I approached, then sat, waiting expectantly. I emptied the can into her dish. She was a bit more ladylike this time, taking three gulps to swallow the lot instead of one. Then she lowered herself to her belly beside the bowl to rest.

I moved closer, trying to get a look at the wound on her shoulder. It didn't appear to be serious, a deep gash rather than a puncture. She'd apparently cleaned it; there was only a little blood matted in her dark fur. She let me approach to within a few feet. Then she rose, in a single fluid motion, eyeing me warily. But she didn't growl. So I tried another step, then another, until I was close enough to reach out my hand to give her my scent, hoping to God she didn't think it was dessert.

She sniffed my palm, looking me directly in the eye all the while, then turned and trotted stiffly off. I called after her, but she didn't look back. A very independent lady, Dog.

But as the weeks passed, she almost always came to the sound of the rifle, accepted my food, and tolerated my monologues for a while before trotting away on business of her own. She never let me touch her. She'd sniff my hand but showed no interest in being petted, so I never took the liberty.

We didn't exactly become friends, more like blood relatives, distant cousins, say, who have little in common. But sometimes when our eyes met, I think we understood each other. One lone wolf bitch to another.

As a secondary result of improving my relations with Dog, I became a fair shot again, maybe not an Annie Oakley, but better than average. But Charlie was right about the gun. In the end, it made no difference at all.

CHAPTER 27

SOMEONE WAS POUNDING on the door. I blinked half-awake, reaching for the bedside lamp. It wasn't there, which snapped me awake completely. I was in Red's apartment. I'd worked late at the Nest and crashed on Red's sofa rather than drive out to the point.

The living room lights flicked on as Red padded out of her bedroom to the front door. She was wearing panties and an oversized T-shirt and looked as disheveled and groggy as I felt.

"Who is it?"

"Your love machine, babe. The answer to your prayers."

"Jackowski? Jesus, it's four o'clock in the morning."

"Tell me about it. Open up. This is business."

Red glanced at me, shrugged, then picked up the aluminum baseball bat she kept in the corner besided the door. "Just a second." She opened the door a foot or so, keeping the bat out of sight behind it.

"What do you want, Jack?"

"Nothing with you. Is your boss lady here? I gotta talk to her."

"I'm here," I said, wrapping myself in a blanket and stumbling to the door to stand beside Red. Jackowski was in a tan summer uniform, his biceps bulging against the short sleeves. His eyes had an odd glow about them, lighter than the rest of his face, and I realized I'd never seen him without his mirrored shades.

"Mind if I come in?"

"Yeah, I do," Red said bluntly. "We're not dressed, and gee, Jackowski, a hunk like you, we might not be able to restrain ourselves."

"You know, one of these days your smart mouth's gonna buy you more hassle'n you ever dreamed of, dyke lady. Are you two alone here?"

"Up till now," Red said. "What's wrong?"

"There's been more trouble at the Nest—another fire. Your boat's been torched, Mitch."

Damn. I turned away, swallowing hard. Her loss felt like a death in the family. "How bad is she?" I asked, forcing down the ache.

"Gone," he said. "Burned to the waterline. Wooden hull like that, she went like a match." His expression was neutral, but I sensed that delivering bad news was a fringe benefit of his job.

"There's more to this, isn't there?" I said.

"Matter of fact, there is. Witnesses saw the guy who set it."

"And?" Red said impatiently. "Who was it?"

"Ratshit," he said. "It was Jud Radowicz. Looks like you didn't kill the bastard after all, Mitch."

"No," I said, stunned. "It couldn't have been Jud."

"Ain't no doubt about it," Jackowski said impatiently. "A half dozen people saw him, and that ugly puss of his is kinda hard to mistake, you know? It was Rats all right. They said he was limpin' bad, ravin' out of his head. Doused your boat with gas and torched her, then ran off. Kicked in the door of the dive shop, too, but there wasn't any real damage we could see. Charlie went after him, sent me to warn you."

"I don't understand. Why would Jud do a thing like this?"

"How the hell do I know? He was always nuts, and it looks like he's totally unglued now. And since he's obviously got a hard-on for you, Charlie wants you to take precautions. I've got orders to spend the night with you."

"Somehow I don't think Charlie put it quite that way, Jackowski," Red said. "Anyway, Mitch and I can take care of ourselves and then some. If you want to keep an eye on her, do it from the parking lot, okay? Was there anything else?"

"No," Jackowski said, looking me over. "That's it. For now."

"Then thanks for the bad news, and good night." Red closed the door firmly, locked it, then leaned against it, facing me. "Creep. I think I'd rather take my chances with Jud. Are you okay?"

"No," I said. "How could I be? My God."

"Well, at least one problem is cleared up."

"What do you mean?"

"This explains the fire at the Nest and that blind out by your house."

"No," I said slowly, pulling myself together. "I don't think so. It couldn't have been Jud. Dog would never have attacked him."

"Well, maybe not. Jackowski's right about one thing, though. If Rats is ticked off at you, it could mean real trouble. You'd better stay here for a few days."

"Thanks," I said, "but I can't. I've got to go home."

"What are you talking about? You can't be alone out here. God only knows where Jud's been or what his head's like. Hell, the last time you saw him, he went for you with an ax."

"I know," I said, taking a deep breath. "That's why I have to go. My God, Red, it's like getting a second chance. He'll show at the point eventually; it was his home. And I want to be there for him when he does."

"But damnit, Mitch, he just burned your boat!"

"Then he must really hate me. Maybe he thinks I left him to die, I don't know. But I've got to see him, to make things right, whatever it takes. Can you understand that?"

"What I understand is, he's crazy and he always was. Hell, I don't know why I'm arguing with you. If I ever win one, the shock'll probably give me cardiac arrest. But promise me one thing. If he shows, don't take any stupid chances. Be ready to protect yourself."

"I will. Now how do I get past Jackowski? I don't want him

156

following me to the point. If Jud sees a police car, it might scare him off."

"Which'd probably be best for all concerned."

"No, I have to see him. And I'm sure I can handle him."

"Yeah," she said doubtfully. "If anybody can."

CHAPTER 28

IT WAS A WASTED TRIP. I spent what was left of the night at the cottage, but Jud didn't show up, angry or otherwise. At first light, I hiked down the beach to his shack. There was no sign he'd been there either so I spent the next few hours crisscrossing the point, calling to him. The only response I got was from Dog. I saw her at a distance, skulking through the brush. She glanced up long enough to glare at me, obviously annoyed at the racket I was making. I took the hint. If Jud was anywhere near, he would certainly have heard me by now. So I gave up the search and drove into town, to visit the grave of a friend.

The noon sun glistened off the choppy harbor, the breeze off the lake was fresh and clean, and it was all I could do to keep from crying. God. Poor *Sheba*. Her charred hulk looked more like a casket after a cremation than the shell of a boat. A couple of mooring lines under her keel were all that kept her from slipping beneath the harbor's murky waters. I was lost in thought, staring at her, when I felt a gentle touch on my shoulder. I didn't turn. I knew who it was.

"Never did get her mill runnin' as smooth as I wanted," Terry said quietly. "She was trim otherwise, though, especially after all the work you put into her. It's a damned shame. You okay?"

I nodded, not trusting my voice.

"Right. Sure you are. Here, I brought somethin' for you."

He held out an object wrapped in newspaper. I accepted it, glancing up at him for the first time. He looked tired. His shaggy hair was streak-bleached by the sun and his eyes were dark and troubled, a match for my mood. I peeled back the paper. It was a nineteenth-century ship's running light. Its polished brass gleamed as though it had been crafted from sunlight. "It's . . . really lovely," I said.

"Yeah, well, it's also ever so slightly warm," Terry said, glancing around. "I wouldn't show it off if I were you."

"Wait a minute—you mean it's contraband?"

"What it is, is a present," he said evenly. "From a friend who risked his neck to get it. If you want to mail it down to Lansing so some DNR bureaucrat can pack it away in a warehouse, go ahead. Just don't tell 'em where you got it. Anyway, it's the thought that counts, right? And I thought you'd like it."

"I do, very much. I just . . . Never mind. Thank you."

"You're welcome. I hear Rats burned your boat."

"Apparently. He roused half the harbor at three or so, yelling. Half a dozen people saw him. None close up, though, and . . . I don't know. It doesn't feel right here," I said, touching my heart. "I searched the point from one end to the other this morning. There was no trace of him at his shack or anywhere else."

"I don't think he's staying at the point," Terry said.

"Why do you say that?"

"I saw him, Mitch, day before yesterday, walking on the shore, seven, eight miles north of town."

"What? Two days ago? Why didn't you tell me?"

"We were headed up to Cheboygan for a tune-up dive before we try the *Queen*," Terry said. "Addison was trailing me in Jason's cruiser, the *Lady D*. If I'd headed inshore for a closer look, he might've piled her up on the shoals. I just couldn't risk it. It was Rats all right, though. Seventy degrees and he was wearing his old plaid coat. I guess I coulda called you from Cheboygan, but it's not the kinda news you want to pass on long distance, you know? I never guessed he'd try anything like this. I'm sorry."

"Me, too. Why are you back so soon? I thought you were going to dive up there for a week."

"Marine weather says we got a storm comin' in a few days

and Massa Harvey wants to try the *Queen* before it hits. He thinks he's ready for two hundred feet. He's not. At this point, I just want to get the damned plaque off the *Queen* for him and get him out of my life. Money or no money, it's been a charter from hell, Mitch."

"Why?"

"He drinks, he thinks he's Captain Bligh, plus he's been bringing Andrea along because he doesn't trust her out of his sight, I guess. She gets even by sunbathin' on the *Lady D*'s fore-deck, topless. Nothing suggestive, you understand. Girls from the best families shuck their duds on the Riviera, they tell me. Meanwhile, Baggers is droolin' all over my gear."

"Just Baggers?"

"Fine as she is, the lady can't flash much I haven't already seen. What bothers me is the situation. She's got Harvey as jumpy as a bug in a bat cave and he's takin' it out on me."

"Maybe he's been hearing rumors. I've heard a few—about you and Andrea."

"I don't know about rumors, but here's a fact for ya. Addison's a damned puddle diver. Doesn't know squat and won't listen. He's got all high-tech European equipment, but it's not compatible with our backups, so Baggers has to keep runnin' in for tank refills while I take static about how obsolete my gear is."

"Maybe he's right. I'll loan you one of my sets if you like. I guarantee you'll never use anything else."

"I'll stick with American rigs, thanks. Crude suits me, and I can't afford new gear, anyway. There is something you can do for me, though. I want to rent an underwater camera and you with it. I want you to film the dive on the *Queen* for me, Mitch."

"The camera's no problem, but I'm teaching classes every day now. I can't get away, sorry."

"I'll only need you for a few hours. It'll take two dives to get the plaque—one to locate it and unbolt it, another to lug it out. Baggers can film the first dive, but I'll need him for the bull work on the second dive. I doubt Harvey'll be much help in that department."

"Can't you get somebody else?"

"I'd rather have you. How many guys do you trust two hundred feet down, especially with a greenhorn along? Look, it's not like I'm askin' you to do it for nothin'. Hell, you can charge Addison enough for a down payment on a new boat and help out a pal at the same time. What do you say?"

"Well," I said, taking a last look at *Sheba*'s corpse. "I'm definitely going to need another boat. When do you want to do it?"

"Yesterday. But I'll settle for tomorrow."

"I teach a class in the morning."

"No problem. I'll pick up your backup tanks when I get the camera and send Baggers for you in the *Lady D*'s launch around noon. All you'll have to bring is your backpack and a suit. Or just half a suit if you want."

"I'll wear the whole thing. Riviera chic doesn't cut it two hundred feet down."

"True." Terry grinned. "But what a pity."

CHAPTER 29

———◆———

THE REST OF THE DAY blurred past on fast forward. I hurried through my beginner's diving class without drowning anyone and sped back out to the cottage immediately afterward. I paused long enough to give Terry's gift a place of honor on the mantel, then began another search, walking the point, calling Jud's name.

Nothing. No sign of him at his shack, no tracks but mine. I did spot Dog briefly, at a distance. She was stalking something, nose down, shoulders hunched, totally focused on the hunt. Another working girl taking care of business.

And it troubled me—not that she was hunting, but that she was alone. I'd seen her quite often over the past weeks, both at the cottage and on the beach when she came to the sound of the rifle. But if Jud was anywhere in the area, I was fairly sure she would have been with him. They were almost inseparable before . . . that night on the ice.

My own search didn't feel right, either. It was like knocking on the door of an abandoned house. I walked and I called, but after awhile I didn't really expect an answer.

And I didn't get one. That night, I slept fitfully, tossing, waking, listening. I was hoping Jud would come, and afraid he might. And having the rifle near at hand was no comfort at all.

I was up at first light, bleary-eyed and edgy. I dressed and repeated my search, but with even less hope of success.

Afterward, I drove hurriedly in to the Nest, hoping to catch Terry before he left. I was too late. Jeanette said he'd been waiting at the shop when she opened. He'd picked up an underwater camera and two sets of my spare tanks and asked her to remind me Baggers would be in for me around noon.

I should have been champing at the bit. A chance to film a dive on a deep wreck with Terry *and* get paid for it? It was the best thing that had happened since I came back. Yet I couldn't focus on it, couldn't get the image of Jud out of my mind, limping along the shore, raving. Where had he been all this time? And why would he burn my boat? If he meant to harm me, I wasn't all that hard to find. Unless the *Sheba* was only the beginning.

I spent a little extra time with my diving class, trying to atone for my haste the day before. And it helped. For several hours, I was able to forget my problems, and totally concentrate on teaching an eager group of kids how to survive underwater, to appreciate the beauty without being lulled by it, and to be aware of the danger without being paralyzed by it.

After class, I went into the Nest to help with the lunch crowd while I waited for Baggers. I was preparing salads in the kitchen when Red stuck her head through the door.

"You been holding out on me?" she said, arching an eyebrow. "Got a kink in your love life you haven't told me about?"

"Why? What's wrong?"

"There's a gentleman out on the new deck asking for you."

"What gentleman?"

"No one I know," she said, still eyeing me curiously. "But I'll bet you do. He's not a guy you'd be likely to forget. Go ahead. I'll take over here."

"Fine," I said, tossing my apron aside. "Where's he sitting?"

"He's not. He's leaning against the rail in the south corner. Trust me, you can't miss him."

She was right. He was leaning on the rail, looking out over the harbor. An ebon giant, dressed formally in a dark suit, red bow tie, and red skullcap. And even larger than I remembered.

"Mr. Bass," I said, moving up beside him. "You're a long way from home."

"Not so far," he said, his voice an instantly familiar rumble. "A couple hours by car. Less than a minute by phone."

"Is that how you came, by phone?"

"No, ma'am. I rode the bus, and I'll go back the same way. When you look like me, people remember you. I expect most of the clowns sittin' around out here will remember me talkin' to you. So I want the folks on the bus to remember I left afterward. In case anything happens."

"Why should anything happen? What do you want?"

"To talk . . . about life. To make you understand how things are," he said, turning to face me. "You showed some sand back at Johnno's shop. You and that big cracker with the mark on his face. Damn, I thought he was gonna dump Johnno over the rail. Truly did. Man was crazy." His faint smile never reached his eyes.

"It's a little late to get upset about that, isn't it?"

"Maybe so," he nodded, "but Johnno ain't forgot it, either. He never forgets nothin'. You know what a smuggler's auction is?"

"You mean when the state sells off loot they've seized? . . . Is that what this is about, the cargo?"

"There was some contraband china at the last one—Rookwood. Went for a good price—which cost Johnno some serious cash, because he had to smash up the lot he bought from your old man so nobody could connect him to anythin' illegal. And now nobody can. 'Cept you."

"If I'd wanted to burn him, I could have done it at the time."

"Maybe you did." Bass shrugged. "Sometimes the cops take a long time to build cases against people like Mr. Habash. Years. So he's concerned. See, he isn't big like me. And he ain't brave, or even particularly smart. What the man is, is real careful. And he's wonderin' if we should do somethin' about you."

"Like what? Arson? Gunfire maybe?"

"You lost me, lady. What you talkin' about? Arson?"

"I've been having trouble, Mr. Bass, a smoke bomb, a fire,

guns going off near my house. I don't suppose you'd know anything about that?"

"Not offhand. When did all this happen?"

"A few weeks ago. Why?"

"Well, I can't swear on my mama's soul that Johnno didn't arrange somethin'. But I doubt it. Because you're still here tellin' me about it. If Johnno intended anythin' serious, you'd be gone. Besides, we didn't know you'd turned over the rest of your load to the law until it showed up at the auction. Up till then, he was doin' his best to forget he ever saw you, you know? You gave him a bad time."

"Well, if a bad time is what he wants, you're talking to the right lady. Habash isn't the only one with a telephone."

"Yes, ma'am, and that's exactly why I'm here. To ask you not to do anything stupid. Please."

"Please?" I echoed, surprised.

"To be honest, that ain't how Mr. Habash told me to put it. But the way I size you up, I figure the quickest way to make you talk to the law is to warn you not to. So I'm not tellin' you. I'm askin'. You seem like a nice lady, and you got grit. Hurtin' women ain't my thing, but it won't bother Johnno none. You cross the man and things could get nasty."

"Maybe they already have."

"Think what you want. Just so you understand that this is the only warnin' you get. Johnno sends me to reason with folks because I'm a friendly guy. If he sends anybody else, it won't be to talk."

"I see," I said, feeling myself flush, trying to keep my anger in check. "Thanks for laying it out for me, Mr. Bass. And for the record, you can tell your boss I won't cause him any trouble. Not because I'm afraid of him, or you, or smoke bombs. The bottom line is, I can't drop a dime on Johnno without dragging myself and my friends into the sewer with him. My father's dead; the contraband is gone. As far as I'm concerned, we're quits. And I hope it stays that way. I've got troubles enough of my own."

"Yes, ma'am, don't we all? All right, I'll tell him."

"And then what?"

"I truly can't say about that. The man didn't get where he is by bein' predictable. Maybe he'll let it go. You ain't much of a problem for us."

"I'm no problem at all—unless you make me one. But just so we understand each other, I'm on my own ground up here, and I don't scare worth a damn."

"Neither did your old man, way I hear it. And he's gone, ain't he?"

"Are you saying Habash had something to do with that?"

"No, ma'am. I'm just sayin' don't make no waves 'less you want—" He broke off, listening. The moan of a siren filled the air, growing rapidly louder as it approached. There was a screech of rubber out front as the car pulled into the Nest parking lot. Bass eyed me, his expression neutral.

"My boyfriend," I explained, "the local law. He drops by at the darnedest times. Would you like to meet him?"

"I don't think so, no," he said coolly. "In fact, I believe I'll be movin' along. Remember what I told you, lady."

"I'll remember." I nodded. "But if you come back, Mr. Bass, you'd better pack a lunch. You'll be in for a long day."

"I won't be back," he said. "Not personally. But you talk to the wrong people, somebody'll be along to settle up. Maybe even somebody you know. Take care now, hear?" He sauntered down the steps and strolled off down the pier. Just another tourist taking in the sights.

I watched him for a moment, trying to assess what he'd said. Then I hurried back inside to see what the excitement was about.

CHAPTER 30

I PUSHED THROUGH the French doors just as Charlie Bauer and Jackowski stalked in through the front door looking extremely unhappy. Charlie motioned me back to my office. Jackowski followed us in and closed the door behind us.

"Sorry to bust in on you like this, Mitch," Charlie said, "but I've got an emergency. I need you to get me a diver who can work deep, ASAP."

"Why? What's wrong?"

"We've got a report of a body down. Off the *Kidd.*"

My heart froze, dead stop. "Who?" I managed.

"Addison, his name is; Harvey Addison. Andrea Deveraux's husband."

"Sweet Jesus," I said softly, turning away so he couldn't read my eyes. "What happened?"

"I'm not sure; things are pretty confused out there. Bottom line is, Addison, Terry Fortier, and Baggers Gant were diving on the wreck of the *Queen of Lorraine.* Baggers was videotaping the dive from outside the hulk. Terry and Addison went in; Terry came out, but Addison didn't. I want you to find me someone who can go down and recover the body."

"What about the state police divers?"

"No time. They're both down on Saginaw Bay after a light plane, and marine weather says we've got a three-day blow on the way. I need somebody right now."

I glanced out my office window. The sky was darkening on the horizon and Lake Huron already looked rough, a rising wind clipping off the tops of three- to four-foot seas. "Then I guess I'm elected. My tanks are already out there. I'll get my suit and—"

"You gotta be kiddin'," Jackowski said. "Hell, if there ain't anybody else, I'll do it myself."

"You?" I said. "I know you're a certified diver, but have you ever worked that deep?"

"Not exactly," Jackowski admitted. "I've done sixty, seventy feet, though. I know what I'm doin'."

"You're a weight lifter right?" I asked. "How much can you pick up?"

"I can bench four hundred plus," he said, puzzled. "Why? You think you can lift more?"

"That's not the point. If you'd tried to bench four hundred your first day in the gym, it would have broken you in half, right? Deep water's like that. The *Queen*'s at two hundred feet. If you try to go from sixty to two hundred in one shot, I'll still have to go down. For two bodies instead of one."

"She's right, Jack," Charlie said. "I don't know doodly about diving, but I know that much. But I don't want you doing it, Mitch. Get me somebody else."

"Not many people can work that deep, Charlie. I've put in more time at two hundred feet than anyone I know up here, and there's no time. It has to be me."

"Bullshit," Jackowski snapped. "If you can do it, I can."

"Be my guest," I said. "But notify your next of kin first. Addison's been training for weeks to try it."

"Yeah, but he went down with his competition. I won't be makin' that mistake."

"What the hell is that supposed to mean?"

"Come on, lady," Jackowski said with unconcealed contempt. "You work in a damn saloon. You must've heard the talk about Fortier boffin' Andrea one more time for auld lang syne—"

"Put a lid on it, Jack," Charlie snapped. "Damn it, Mitch, there must be somebody else who can do it."

"Absolutely," I said. "Both Terry and Baggers can, and they're already out there."

"No," Charlie said, avoiding my glance, "I don't want either of them going back down. In fact, I've ordered them to stay out of the water. It was probably an accident, but Terry and Addison went down together and Addison didn't come back. And like it or not, Jack's right. There's been talk."

"That's garbage and you know it, Charlie," I snapped. "Look, the storm'll be here before dark. Unless you want to wait for it to blow over, we've got to go now. Straight up, if something suspicious happened down there, do you think I'd cover it up? Is that it?"

He hesitated. "No, of course not."

"Then what's the problem? Don't you think I'm up to it?"

"It's not that, either."

"Then what?"

"It's too dangerous, Mitch," Charlie said, meeting my eyes at last. And there was a lot more to read in them than honest concern. "One man's dead already. I just . . . don't want you going down there."

"I'll be damned," I said, smiling a little in spite of myself. "I don't know whether to be flattered or annoyed. Maybe we can sort it out it over a beer sometime, but it'll have to wait. Have you got a boat?"

"Patrol boat's already at the pier."

"Fine, I'll grab my gear and meet you there in ten minutes."

"Yeah." He sighed. "Okay."

"You're making a mistake, Charlie," Jackowski said.

"Maybe." Charlie nodded, "I make 'em all the time. Sometimes I think hiring you on is one of the biggest I ever made. Let's go."

CHAPTER 31

CHARLIE WAS ABOARD the sheriff's patrol launch when I parked beside his prowl car at the south end of the pier. He already had her fired up, motor grumbling, gray exhaust fumes hacking astern. The launch was butt-ugly, black-and-white markings, numbers instead of a name on her transom. Her running gear was rude, crude, and built for abuse, which was just as well, considering the look of the bay.

"Just caught the latest weather report," he said, vaulting onto the dock. "Storm's picking up speed. They're saying it'll hit by late afternoon now. Is that enough time?"

"It'll have to be."

"Too bad. I hate bein' on the big lake in rough weather. I can swim well enough, but I'm a lot happier with both feet on solid ground. I suppose that seems silly to somebody in your line of work."

"Nope. Respecting deep water isn't paranoid, Charlie, it's intelligent. Your buddy Jackowski ought to take a page from your notebook. Where is he, anyway?"

"I sent him back to the office. Somebody's gotta hold the fort, and if you're going down, I want to be there. Do you mind?"

"Not a bit. We'll have enough to worry about out there without a Neanderthal underfoot."

"Sorry about that. He wasn't always a jerk. Since he started tryin' to turn himself into the Schwarzenegger of the north woods, he can be a major pain sometimes."

"He didn't say anything I haven't heard before. About a thousand times."

"No, I guess not. Okay, it's your show. What do you want me to do?"

"Grab my jacket and tanks out of my truck. I've already rigged 'em. I'll suit up on the way out. I'll want to dive as soon as we get there."

"You just bringing one set of tanks?"

"My backup tanks are already on the *Kidd*. The way the weather looks, I'll have time for only one dive, anyway."

I tossed my duffel bag aboard the launch and Charlie followed with my backpack, handling the 125-pound rig with ease. He ran through a quick check of the launch's gauges and radio while I did the same with my gear.

"We're gassed and everything reads normal," he said. "You ready?"

"No, but let's do it, anyway." I cast off the mooring lines and Charlie goosed the launch away from the pier. As soon as we cleared the harbor mouth, he opened the throttle and she barreled out into the bay, bucking her way through the choppy five-foot seas, waves that could be thirty feet high in a few hours. Ship killers. They'd hammered countless major vessels to pieces and swallowed them down. *Tashmoo, Cedarville,* the *Lucia A. Simpson.* I'd memorized the names of hundreds of them. It wasn't a comforting thought.

"Do you know where they're diving exactly?" Charlie shouted over the engine's roar.

"The *Queen's* about six miles out to the northeast. You should be able to spot them when we clear the point. I'll get my gear on."

I moved cautiously to the stern, unzipped my duffel bag, and stripped down to my swimsuit. I hauled my "woolly bears" out of the bag and slipped them on. The fluffy long underwear suit looked ludicrous for a summer afternoon, but where I was going, it's always deep in dark December.

The full-body Viking dry suit was next, a bulky, bulgy neoprene outfit that makes you look like a pregnant walrus. I felt Charlie cut the throttle and slow the launch as I finished strapping on my tank harness.

Terry's twenty-seven-foot white Bayliner, the *William Kidd*, was fifty yards or so off our port bow, bobbing like a kite in the choppy waves. The much larger motor yacht, *Lady D*, was just beyond. Andrea was clutching the rail, watching us, her eyes invisible behind her sunglasses. She was wearing a deck-length golden beach robe. I wondered if she was wearing a top beneath it.

Charlie eased the launch alongside the *Kidd*. Baggers Gant, the towheaded Hoosier Terry used as a gofer and safety diver, tossed us a line. We tethered the boats together, ten feet apart. Terry was still in his gleaming black dry suit, barefoot, his hair a tangle, eyes fierce and wild. In a killing rage.

"What happened?" I shouted.

"I don't know," Terry yelled back. "We got into the main salon okay, found the damn plaque Addison wanted, and got about half the bolts out. I knew we'd need another dive to finish, so I signaled Harvey time's up and made my way out. It's so damn silted up in the corridor that I didn't realize he wasn't behind me until I was halfway down it, and by then I didn't have enough air to go back. Baggers was filming us from the porthole, but Harvey apparently roiled things up in there. We couldn't see squat anymore and had to come up."

"Why didn't he follow you out when you signaled?"

"How the hell do I know?" Terry shouted angrily. "Maybe he wanted to be sure he was on film poppin' the last of the bolts by himself. I just don't know. He wasn't much on following orders, though, I can tell you that."

"What's it like down there?"

"Ugly," Terry yelled. "The reef tipped her when she struck. She's upside down, and the weight of the cargo in her holds is gradually crushing her superstructure. The passageway and the main salon were tarted up with a lot of gingerbread and all that crap's popping loose because the bulkheads are buckling. There's at least two inches of silt on everything and it clouds up if you look at it crossways. It's as mean as I've ever seen, Mitch."

"How do I get into the passageway?"

"The safety cable's moored to the railing beside the main deck entrance. We ran a lifeline in from there."

"All right." I nodded, pulling on my neoprene diving cap and slipping the elastic band of my helmet lamp over my forehead. "I'm going down. You gonna back me up?"

"Damn straight,," Terry said. "Lemme get my tanks—"

"No," Bauer said, "Baggers can do it."

"Now look, Charlie—" Terry began.

"Sort it out on your own time," I snapped. "Just make sure somebody's there with a line when I come out. If we get caught out here in a blow, we'll all wind up swimming home." I pulled down my face mask to end the debate, stepped over the gunwale onto the stern ladder, and let myself fall.

CHAPTER 32

THE DARK WATER of Thunder Bay closed over me in a soft green explosion. The weight of the tank harness disappeared into neutral buoyancy, and I felt only the mild drag of the weight belt as I safety-checked my regulator, then found the half-inch nylon mooring line that trailed from the *Kidd* down to emerald infinity below.

I began swimming slowly down the line, gliding gently through the murky green haze, pausing every fifteen feet or so to swallow hard and pinch the bridge of my nose above the mask to adjust my ears to the pressure change. Visibility was especially poor because of the rough weather above, and after the first fifty feet, I couldn't see the boats overhead anymore, or anything below, only the nylon line, faint as a thread, leading down into the gloom. A few fish passed near me now and again, indistinct glints of silver darting through the mist, most of them moving downward with me, a sure sign of a serious storm coming on the surface.

A hundred feet down, I paused at the deflated inner tube Terry'd snubbed into the line as a shock absorber. I cleared my ears, then did a quick double check of my equipment, for safety and to remind myself that I was in an alien, hostile environment now, no matter how enchanting it was. It's a game all divers play. Deep water, like the Lady of the Lake and the sirens of old, can lure you down in a thousand ways, lull you into making that minuscule mental error that will let you stay on in the icewater halls. But there's only one way you can ever truly belong here: the *Queen*'s way. And now Harvey's.

I left the inner tube and continued down. At this depth, the temperature had already dropped to ten degrees centigrade and was still falling. My Viking suit, so bulky on the surface, was sleek as a second skin now, form-fitted by the pressure. A wet suit would compress to the thickness of a plastic garbage bag at this depth, and be just about as useful. Suddenly, I instinctively grabbed the line, startled by a dark shape looming out of the murk below, huge and formless, stretching away beneath me as far as I could see. A great fish glimpsed from above: the keel of the *Queen of Lorraine*.

She was upside down, her stern buried in the ooze of the bottom. Her forward hull, supported by her crushed stacks, towered above the lakebed like a mountain. Patches of moss clung to her metal skin, giving her a scrofulus, unhealthy look, but other than that, I could see no rust, no deterioration. She was frozen in time, unchanged since that terrible November night when she'd been mortally wounded by the bow of the *Halmstad* and plunged to the bottom, only minutes from the sanctuary of the north bay shore.

I switched on my helmet lamp and the huge vessel instantly disappeared as the light haloed in the turbid water around me, limiting visibility to three or four meters. The *Queen* reappeared moments later as I followed the line down past the gash in her side. It hardly seemed big enough to have killed such a giant ship, no more than fifteen inches across at its widest point, but the angle of collision was such that when her captain swung her into that last desperate dash for the beach, her own speed forced water through the gap in a torrent. And she'd rolled. And died. And yet she seemed so untouched by time that she might have lurched to the lake bottom only hours ago, not decades.

I found Harvey Addison's swim fins tied neatly to the main deck rail a few feet from the grappling hook at the end of the *Kidd's* mooring line. A second, even more slender line led from the railing across the deck and disappeared through an open bulkhead door. It was an odd feeling to look *down* from the main deck at the bridge and the wheelhouse below. The *Queen*'s masts were buried in the muck and her stacks had collapsed, but her superstructure had survived with little visible damage thus far, still suspended five or six meters above the lakebed.

A flicker of movement below caught my eye. The wheelhouse door was swinging gently to and fro in the current. The area around the door latch was dented and the scratches on the metal were still bright. Those marks hadn't been made years before. They were new.

I slipped my flippers off and tied them to the rail beside Harvey's, a cave-diving technique that would tell anyone who followed me down that I was inside the ship. The fins would be useless in there, anyway. You have to move very slowly in a wreck. A snagged hose or a bang on the head can finish you, and flippers only roil up the silt, making visibilty worse.

I tied the end of my own lifeline next to Terry's. It would unwind automatically from the safety reel on my belt. I would follow Terry's line in, but I didn't know what was on the other end. And apparently, it hadn't helped Harvey much.

Keeping one hand on the slender line, I swam cautiously toward the open bulkhead doorway. The weight of the great ship and her cargo of steel looming above me made me even more aware of the pressure at this depth. Every seam of my clothing, every wrinkle, would leave a welt on my skin that wouldn't fade for hours. Even sound is compressed in deep water. The rumble of a passing freighter would whine like a buzz saw down here, and the normally comforting burble of your breathing regulator is strangled to a squeak. Or a scream.

The doorway was alive with motion. Dogfish. Dozens of the ugly monsters, three to four feet long, their tentacled heads too large for their slimy leather-skinned bodies. With a storm coming, the wreck would be infested with them. They're harmless; their rows of needlelike teeth are dangerous only to crayfish, but they trail you through the murk like clumsy submarine zombies, inhaling the silt in your wake. The gutter rats of the deep wrecks. I hate the damned things.

A rush of anger surged through me like an electric current, anger at Charlie for letting me talk him into this, at Harvey for getting himself killed down here, and at the captain of the Swede freighter for ramming the *Queen* in the first place.

I pushed through the doorway, ignoring the bumps and brushes of the dogfish as they lumbered awkwardly out of my way. I'd entered some sort of anteroom. Metal stairways led up—or rather, down now to the bridge and to the engine room and cargo holds above. I followed the lifeline through a second bulkhead doorway. And froze.

Sweet Jesus. What a god-awful shambles.

I was in the ship's central passageway, a long, narrow hall that ran its full length. The *Queen* was the flagship of the Deveraux line, a freighter with lavish accommodations for company officers and their guests, though fortunately she had no passengers aboard the night she sank. Her steel bulkheads had been paneled in lacquered hardwood, with ornate brass sconces every five meters or so, but the weight of her cargo bearing down from above had buckled the walls enough to tear everything loose.

Light fixtures dangled from the walls like grappling hooks. Jagged panels and firring strips stuck out at odd angles like a tangle of jackstraws, each with its own row of protruding nails. Most of the cabin doors had either popped from their hinges or splintered in half. Overhead, long strips of hardwood flooring had given way, hanging down like spiked tentacles. And through the maze swam the dogfish, their greedy mouths sucking in the muck Terry and Harvey had churned up earlier.

Terry was dead right. This was as ugly as I'd seen. And if Addison hadn't been somewhere forward near the end of that lifeline, I wouldn't have gone another inch. But he was. And bad as it looked, Terry'd made it out in one piece. And if he could . . .

I checked the time. Ten minutes left on my first tank, a full fifteen on the other. Plenty of time. No excuse there. Cursing silently, I began to move down the hall, following Terry's line, promising myself that if I lived through this, I was going to find a new line of work. Skydiving. Or lion taming. Something sane.

The hallway wasn't quite as bad as it looked. The obstacles, vicious as they were, were farther apart than they appeared from the doorway. As long as I moved slowly and carefully, I was able to thread my way through them with no real difficulty. But then everything began to disappear.

There was a dark cloud of roiled silt at what I assumed must be the end of the passageway. Dogfish were moving through it, feeding, and Terry's lifeline led into it, so there had to be something beyond, probably the salon. But I couldn't see anything through the haze. Nothing.

I slowed my progress to a crawl, inching my way along the line into the cloud. Visibility diminished rapidly until I could see no farther than the length of my arm, then less. I could see only a few inches of the lifeline, an occasional firring strip or floorboard, and the damned dogfish as they blundered into me out of the murk. And then I reached the end of the lifeline.

It was tied around a doorknob at the end of the passageway, holding the door open. I felt a surprising flood of relief, both at finding the door at last and finding it open. Maybe Charlie's suspicions were contagious. I'd been half-afraid I'd find it closed.

The interior of the salon was even more turbid than the passageway had been, if that was possible. I couldn't see a thing. It was beginning to look like Harvey'd made a basic puddle diver's mistake: He'd lost the door. My problem was that the main salon was a large room and several smaller suites opened into it. He could be anywhere in there.

First things first. They'd been working on the dedication plaque, and it was directly opposite the door. I snubbed a loop of my own lifeline over Terry's on the doorknob to take up the slack and started slowly in.

The room was a nightmare, furniture, flooring, bookshelves, all upended and smashed on the ceiling below me, the whole jumble covered with a fine layer of gray-green sediment that roiled and swirled around me as I swam slowly above it. A shattered crystal chandelier glittered crazily below for a moment, fracturing and reflecting the light from my helmet lamp like a pool of diamonds.

When I finally reached it, I had to admit the plaque was impressive, a three-foot square of hammered brass listing the company's officers, ships' captains of the Deveraux fleet, and with a bas-relief of the *Queen* herself. It must have cost a bundle even in 1926. It had been secured to the bulkhead with a dozen brass bolts. Eight of them had been removed and placed neatly in a bag on the ceiling below. A ninth bolt was halfway out.

But no Harvey. Not a sign of him. I checked my time again. It had taken four minutes to get down to the *Queen,* four more to thread through the passageway, sixteen minutes total transit time, then, minimum, on thirty minutes of air. Not much leeway. I'd have to find him quickly or go back without him.

I tried to concentrate, not an easy thing floating in the belly of a wreck halfway to the center of the earth. Still, I did my best to put myself in his place. I've lost my way to the door; I'm running out of air; I'm—

His lamp. His air would be long since gone, but his helmet lamp should still be working. I reeled in a few feet of lifeline, tugging myself back to the chandelier in the center of the room. Then I turned off my helmet lamp. And waited. A lifetime.

After a thousand heartbeats or so, the walls began to glow faintly, gradually resolving into the pallid green eyes of the portholes, four on each side of the room. And off to my right, a brighter, yellowish gleam. I took a bearing on it as best I could, switched my own lamp back on, and swam cautiously toward the light. And found Harvey.

He was kneeling against the outer wall, his mask pressed against the porthole glass. Maybe he'd been trying to get it open, though it was too small to get through, even without his tanks. Or maybe he'd watched Terry's and Bagger's lights gliding away up the mooring line, leaving him behind, or . . .

It didn't matter now. I tugged him gently around. He stared at me sightlessly through his mask, but there was no life in his eyes, no expression. A blind stare. I felt a flicker of panic but forced it down. He was dead. His life force, whatever it is, was gone. To an afterlife? To oblivion? I don't know. I knew there was nothing to fear from the body he'd left behind. And yet, down deep, I did fear it a little. I couldn't help it.

I tried to picture him as he was the night we met in my office—smooth, amiable, a carnally attractive hunk. A lady-killer. But this time, he'd tangled with the wrong lady.

I checked over his equipment: air regulator, timer, pressure gauge, tank harness. Everything seemed to be in good order, no signs of violence or tampering. I didn't expect any, but I knew Charlie would ask, so . . .

No.

Something was out of place. I wasn't sure what, but there was something. . . . I checked the time. In three minutes, I'd be cutting into my safety margin.

Damn. I ran through the equipment check again. Nothing obvious. Even when I was looking at it, it seemed so normal that it almost didn't register. It was my name, stenciled neatly on the side of his air tanks. They were my tanks. Harvey was wearing one of my backup sets, the tanks Terry'd picked up earlier.

There was nothing sinister in that; divers borrow tanks all the time. But it was chilling to see my tanks on his corpse. And for a moment, a part of me was afraid that if I looked into his mask now, I'd see my own face. It was time to get out. Before the death that had taken him came back. For me.

CHAPTER 33

—◆—

I TWEAKED THE VALVE on Harvey's flotation vest, allowing just enough inflation to make him buoyant, then unwound a length of lifeline from his reel, the line he hadn't bothered to use, and tethered his body to my weight belt. I tried to get a fix on the door, but the water was just too cloudy; I couldn't see more than a few feet. I unhooked my lifeline and began to reel it in, following it out toward the door.

It was slow going. Addison's body dragged behind me like a sea anchor, blundering into the debris, yanking me off course at unexpected moments. Deadweight. Twice his suit was impaled by rusty nails in the flooring strips dangling from overhead. I managed to pull him free both times by tugging gently on the line. But as we neared the door, his regulator hose snagged in a tangle of wiring and I had to stop to work it loose, wasting precious time and slicing my right palm open in the process.

Cursing my luck and Harvey and this damned death trap of a ship, I started moving toward the door again—and suddenly, I was staring into a dead face straight out of hell!

His skin was bloated and gray, his blind eyes milk white, teeth bared in a grimace of agony. His uniform jacket was nearly torn away, revealing a terrible wound, clotted with gore and splinters of protruding bone.

And I panicked. And ran. Or tried to.

I scrambled backward, a scream strangling in my mask. Shoving Harvey aside, I clawed my way mindlessly through the wreckage on the ceiling, so shattered by horror I even forgot to swim. I might have gotten away, but Harvey's corpse hooked on the wiring again, jerking me sidelong into a jumble of furniture. A searing blaze of pain exploded above my heart as something ripped through my suit and deep into my chest. Bone-deep.

Instantly, instinctively, I stopped thrashing, frozen in place by pain and fear. I was badly hurt. Maybe mortally. Icy water surged through the puncture, spreading beneath my suit, squeezing what little breath I had out of me like an iron hand. My consciousness was out of control, skittering about like a cockroach on a hot griddle. *Trapped!* it was screaming. *It's dead; it's dead! Run! Get away!*

But I couldn't run. I was impaled, pinned like a butterfly on a board. I gathered the dregs of my strength, grasped the lance in my chest with both hands, and pulled it out.

A table leg. A splintered table leg. I stared at it with no comprehension at all as blood began pumping through the rip in my suit, clouding the filthy water. I'd crashed into a broken table and speared myself. On a goddamn table leg. And I was going to die. I'd seen a body. And panicked. A body. Nothing more. He was dead. Like Harvey. And dead is dead. And now he'd killed me, too.

No. I'd killed me. I'd panicked. And wounded myself. And torn my suit. But even worse, I'd dropped my lifeline. I was going to die down here. Like Harvey. Like . . . that other one. Because I'd lost my nerve. And lost the door. Like an amateur. Like a goddamn puddle diver. I came down after Harvey, and now somebody would have to come down after me. Maybe even Jackowski. It should have made me angry, but somehow nothing seemed very important. What little I could see of the salon was beginning to flicker and fade as the blood oozed from my chest and my awareness dimmed. And I began to fall, drifting down and down into December. . . .

Someone tapped me on the shoulder.

A jolt of pure horror shot through me, snapping me back to consciousness as I tried to thrust myself away—but it wasn't *him*. It was a dogfish. Only a dogfish. And I wasn't dead yet. Almost, though. Almost.

The wound in my chest was less painful, chilled to numbness by the icy water. I could hardly feel it anymore, and I was glad of that. Maybe dying wouldn't be so bad, only . . .

I didn't want to die in here. In this terrible place that killed Harvey, with the clouds of silt and the dogfish and that *thing*. Out in the hall would be better. They'd know I tried if I could just make it out into the hall. I came down to get Harvey out of here. I should at least do that much.

I started to untie Harvey's lifeline from my belt, then hesitated. I knew I'd be able to swim better without him, but if I was afraid to die in this place, he must have been, too. It would be wrong to leave him behind. Cowardly. No. We'd go together. Or we'd stay. Together. I couldn't leave him now. And he seemed to be trying to help. He'd floated free of the wiring all by himself.

I checked my timer, but I couldn't make sense of the numbers. It didn't matter. We were lost, anyway. Somehow I had to find the door. Maybe I could find a wall and follow it around, but I wasn't sure how big the room was, and there were other doors. If we swam into another room . . .

Maybe I should just find a porthole for one last look at the world the way Harvey had. The portholes. That seemed to make sense. If I could find the portholes . . .

Switching off my helmet lamp was very hard, maybe the hardest thing I've ever done in my life. But I did it. And we waited in the dark. And after awhile, I could see the pale glow of the portholes again. I shifted around until four of them were to my right and the other four to my left. And directly ahead, a dark area in between.

I fixed the dark area in my mind, switched my helmet lamp back on, and swam slowly forward, with Harvey trailing patiently behind. And we found the plaque. And the plaque was directly opposite the door.

I tried to explain the situation to Harvey. We had to swim

straight to the doorway. I was losing consciousness, fading in and out. My chest hurt terribly and my right arm was nearly useless. So he had to help me. And if we met that thing again, we couldn't panic this time. It can't hurt us now. It's dead, that's all. And dead is dead. But we have to swim straight. If we miss the door, we'll never find it again. And we'll have to stay here. We have to swim straight.

We placed our feet against the plaque and pushed off, swimming for the door. And we met the thing again—a couple of times, I think. Only he didn't seem as horrible now. He just seemed . . . so terribly sad. And he asked us to wait. He didn't like it in here, either. He didn't belong in here. Take me with you, he said. But I couldn't. I'm sorry. I'll come back for you. I promise. But we can't stop now. We have to swim straight out.

And we did—or Harvey did, anyway. I banged into a bulkhead frame and got confused, but Harvey drifted past me, tugging me through the doorway and out into the passage.

The hallway was much worse than before. Harvey kept stopping, snagging the shattered woodwork, getting hung up on nails. I told him to stop it. He wouldn't listen. So I just had to yank him free and drag him along like a dog on a leash.

And we were too slow. My regulator was already choking off when we made it to the anteroom. I tried to retard my breathing, to stretch it out another few seconds. But it was too late. Too late.

I yelled at Harvey that we were out of air. We had to go up now. And as soon as we cleared the outer door, I hugged him close to me and twisted the valve of his flotation vest wide open, and he began to rise, surging upward toward the surface, carrying me with him toward the light. Faster and faster toward the light . . .

CHAPTER 34

TERRY WAS THERE. He had his back to me, but I knew him. I'd know him anywhere. He was wearing a leather bombardier's jacket, his hair shaggy and loose over the collar. He was staring out the window into the night. I started to ask him if Harvey was all right, but my chest was bandaged so tightly I couldn't seem to get enough breath. . . .

And then it was afternoon. And a nurse was there, plump, silver-haired, somebody's grandmother. She asked me how I felt. My mouth was too dry to answer, so she gave me sip of water. She took my pulse, then asked me how I felt.

"Like I've been eaten by a bear and crapped over a cliff," I said in someone else's voice. She smiled and faded away. And in a little while, Charlie Bauer came in. He looked haggard, exhausted, but the concern in his chiseled face made him seem gentler than I'd seen him before. He cared, and it showed. He wore it well.

"Hey, Mitch," he said, easing awkwardly onto the plastic chair by the side of the bed, "how are you doing? Gonna live?"

"I'm not sure," I said honestly. "What happened?"

"What happened? You scared me out of ten years' growth, is what. You came busting up out of the water with Addison's body like some kinda guided missle, bleedin' like . . ." He ran a freckled paw through his hair. "Mitch, what the hell went on down there? For God sake, they needed more'n two dozen stitches to sew you up; you had the bends from coming up too fast. . . . You damned near died. What happened?"

"It was . . . a real mess in there," I said slowly. "Terry told me it was, but . . . It was really bad. I managed to find Harvey, but then I . . . got hurt. I speared myself. On a table leg, I think. And I lost the door. Stupid. Really stupid . . ." I trailed off. There was something else. Something important. "Tanks," I said. "Addison was wearing my tanks."

"Yeah." Charlie nodded. "He was. Fortier said Addison got his tanks refilled up in Cheboygan. Apparently, they didn't do it right. Pressure was low or something."

"If they fill them too fast, the tanks heat up and expand," I said, trying to focus, to collect myself. "When they cool off, the pressure drops. It happens sometimes."

"That's probably how it was. Anyway, Addison's tanks came up low, so he borrowed a pair of yours. And, um, he had an accident. One that was meant for you."

"What do you mean? What happened to him?"

"I had the crime lab run a spectrographic check on your tanks. It's standard procedure in diving accidents. But this was no accident, Mitch. The air in the set Addison was wearing was contaminated, laced with carbon dioxide. The lab technician said it must have happened when they were filled last. Mitch, does Jud Radowicz know how to run the compressor in your dive shop?"

"I think so. He gofered for my father sometimes. Do you think Jud did this?"

"Who else? The night he burned your boat, he broke into the dive shop, but he didn't take anything or do any damage. It didn't make sense, until now."

"But damn it, Charlie, if he means me harm, why not just come after me? He knows I live alone."

"Mitch, don't ask me to explain how Jud's mind works. Maybe he wanted you to die in the water, the way he almost did. Or maybe he didn't mean to kill you at all. Addison apparently was able to function for most of the dive before the carbon dioxide built up enough to put him under. But whether Jud intended to kill you or not, he definitely meant you harm. And that makes Addison's death murder."

"No," I said numbly. "I can't believe it."

"I understand why you wouldn't want to." Charlie nodded. "But it had to be Jud. The lab technician said you can't contaminate tanks when they're filled, because they're under pressure. It has to be done when they're empty. Jud must've emptied one of your tanks, gave it a shot of carbon dioxide from a life-raft cartridge maybe, then topped off the tank with air and put it back in the rack. You know any other way it could've happened?"

"No," I said reluctantly. "The tech's right. It would have to be done while the tank was empty."

"I did consider other possibilities, especially because of the trouble between your pal Fortier and Addison. It occurred to me that Jud and Fortier might have arranged somethin' together. But according to the girl in the shop, there were four sets of tanks with your name on 'em and she picked the ones Fortier took; he didn't. And he took 'em straight to his boat."

"You're barking up the wrong tree there, Charlie. For openers, Terry's not the type. But if he did want Addison dead, killing somebody two hundred feet down is no problem. Turn a valve on his tank, puncture a line, or even close a door behind you. Harvey's gear was okay. I checked all that, and . . ." I blinked, trying to force back a memory that was surging up from my subconscious.

"What is it?"

"There was someone else down there," I said.

"What do you mean?"

"Someone else. Another . . . body."

"In the ambulance, you kept saying there was a guy down there," Charlie said. "That we had to get him out. But you were hurt pretty bad, Mitch. Are you sure he was real?"

"He was real," I said. "He was one of the crew from the *Queen*. No, not crew. An officer."

"An officer?"

"He was in uniform," I said wonderingly. "He was—oh God, Charlie. He was wounded so horribly!" And suddenly, I was crying. And I couldn't stop. I just couldn't stop. And Charlie was holding me. And I realized that he was shaking, too. And the idea of Charlie coming unglued seemed so incredible, I made myself stop somehow, pulled the strings of my broken puppet back together.

"I'm all right," I said quietly. "Let me go, please."

"Of course," he said, releasing me, looking away, swallowing. "It was my fault. I should never have let you go. I—"

"You didn't *let* me go," I said carefully. "It was my idea, and my responsibility. And I have to go back."

"You can't."

"I have to. There's something I need to see again, something important. And I promised I would."

"You were mumbling about a promise in the ambulance. But you also said the guy down there talked to you."

"Did I? Well, maybe he did. Anyway, after the storm passes, we can . . ." I trailed off, confused, staring at the window. It was late afternoon. And the sun was shining. Charlie was watching me intently. "How, um, how long have I been out?" I asked.

"Three days. You lost a lot of blood, and you were in the decompression chamber for over twenty hours. Christ, Mitch, you nearly bought the farm. The storm blew out yesterday. I sent a team from the Coast Guard Auxiliary down to the *Queen* this morning. Didn't Terry tell you?"

"I didn't talk to him. I mean, he was here, but . . ."

"He stayed with you almost the whole time," Charlie said, a trifle grudgingly. "He was about half-crazy. He said if you died, he was going to kill me for sending you down there. He meant it, too. Hell, even Jackowski was angry about it. You've got a bigger fan club than you realize."

"Did Jackowski try diving the wreck with the Coast Guard divers?"

"No, what happened to you gave him second thoughts. Just as well. There was nothing to see, anyway. The storm finished off the *Queen*. Her cargo shifted and smashed down through her decks. There's nothing down there now but the shell of her hull and twenty thousand tons of rolled steel buried in the bottom."

"No," I said, confused. "That's not right. I told him I'd get him out. He didn't belong there."

"You ah, you better get some rest," Charlie said, rising, towering over my bed like an oak. "I just want you to know that I'm sorry as hell about . . . everything. If I'd had any idea . . . Anyway, I owe you one, Mitch. A big one. I won't forget it."

"I won't, either," I said. "I can't. I promised."

Terry came in a little while after Charlie left. He hugged me gently and misted up. Said he was glad I was all right. Told me he had to go away for a few days, something to do with Harvey. It didn't make much sense to me. I was sliding back into the darkness and nothing was making much sense.

And later that evening, I thought I saw Alec leaning on his cane, watching me silently from the doorway. Or perhaps it was only a dream.

CHAPTER 35

GERALD HOFFMAN was no dream. The next morning, I was up and about, bumbling around my room in one of those ridiculous hospital gowns, wobbly as an easel with rubber legs, but mobile. And ready to go home. I'd had enough of hospital rooms. Maybe even enough of the north country.

. I was collecting my things, tossing my toothbrush and makeup into the little travel kit Red had dropped off. And when I glanced up, Gerald Hoffman was in the room, as though he'd materialized, like a bat. He was wearing a khaki tweed sport coat with patch elbows and a taupe western-style shirt and leather string tie, but the rough-and-ready look only accentuated his indoor pallor and watery eyes. He looked more like a patient than I did.

"Up and about already," he said in that faintly patrician southern accent. "Good. Glad to see it."

"I'm dressing. Get out of here."

"I'll only be a moment. I've brought you a present."

"Keep it. I don't want anything from you."

"It's not a bomb, miss. I picked it up in the gift shop downstairs. Here, I'll open it for you; you look a bit unsteady." He stripped off the red wrapping and opened the box. It contained a laquered wooden plaque: THINK. He laid it carefully it on the unmade bed.

"Think? About what?"

"About your future, and your son's future. And how easily both could be guaranteed if you'd simply honor the arrangement you and your father made with the Deveraux Institute."

"I didn't agree to any arrangement. And there sure as hell wasn't any honor involved."

"No? Personally, I think you were part of it all along, but that's irrelevant now. Things have changed."

"What things?"

"Someone's trying to kill you, miss. An illegitimate half brother, they tell me. So far, he's managed to evade the local-yokel law, which doesn't surprise me. You need me. I can offer you protection."

"Protection? I'd be safer dancing *Swan Lake* in a buffalo stampede."

"I wouldn't be too hasty. This last incident nearly killed you. It was only luck that Addison went in your place. Think about that. You seem to be a very accident-prone young woman. Your father was, too, as I recall. Perhaps you'll follow in his footsteps."

"Is that supposed to be a threat?"

"Not at all. Threats are for amateurs, and I'm a professional. And it's my professional advice that you and I come to terms. I've been told to resolve this situation, and I intend to. I can make you a rich woman, Miss Mitchell. The money your father cheated the old man out of was small change. He's willing to pay—"

"You sleazy lowlife! Shan didn't cheat you out of a dime and I wouldn't take water from you if I was on fire! You don't frighten me. Ex-CIA or not, on the best day of your life you couldn't have handled my father. Fires and window peeping are more your speed. You've made your little speech. No sale. Now get out of here. And take your present with you." I tossed the plaque at him. It glanced off his shoulder and landed on the bed.

There was a rap on the door, and Ken Robinette stuck his head in. "Mitch, are you okay? What's all the noise?"

"It's all right," I said. "Mr. Hoffman was just leaving. Unless you'd like to run that part about my father's footsteps past me again?"

"I'm sure a bright girl like you can remember it." Hoffman smiled tautly. "Are you ambulance chasing these days, Robinette?"

"No, sir, just visiting a friend," Rob said, adjusting his tie. He was wearing a dark three-piece suit and looked sleek, competent, in control. And I was very glad to see him.

"A friend?" Hoffman said, glancing at me, then back to Rob. "A poor business practice, changing sides."

"I'm always on the same side," Rob said easily. "My own. And as for business, you'd do a deal with Hitler if your boss wanted a tattooed lamp shade. You'll need me again sometime."

"I doubt it. I'm going to close the books on this very soon. Within legal limits, of course. Perhaps you should advise Miss Mitchell just how flimsy legal contraints can be."

"She doesn't need my advice. A second-year law student could beat you on this one. The way things are, you've got no case, Hoffman, none. And you know it."

"If I want a legal opinion, I'll consult a legitimate firm, not a small-town shyster who lives on a boat. I hope she does retain you. It'll make my job easier."

"It might at that," Rob said blandly, opening the door and waving Hoffman through it. "Stay in touch, Mr. Hoffman. Sir."

Hoffman gave him a last hard look and stalked out. Rob watched him go, then carefully closed the door.

"What was that all about?" he asked.

"Mind games," I said. "Hoffman tried to spook me. Maybe last week, he could have. Not anymore." I tossed his plaque in the wastebasket.

"He wanted you to go through with the original arrangement, didn't he? Are you going to?"

"Not a chance."

"Glad to hear it," he said, taking me in his arms.

"Why should you be?"

"Because if you did, you wouldn't need a lawyer anymore,

and I want you to need one. I'm sorry I'm so late to the fair; I was out of town on business. I only just heard. Let me look at you." He held my shoulders gently, meeting my eyes, reading them. His eyes were glittering, angry. At Hoffman? I couldn't be sure. He kissed me—coolly and effectively. Hello.

"You look a little drawn," he said.

"I feel drawn. By an artist with a broken arm."

"I think I prefer you this way, delightfully ravaged. It'll give me an excuse to fatten you up. Has, um, has Alec talked to you? Since your accident?"

"Alec? No. I think he was here, but I was still groggy. We didn't talk. Why?"

"Because he came by my office this morning and asked me to see you. It seems the old man has turned you over to Hoffman as a . . . problem to be solved, Michelle, no questions asked. Alec wanted me to talk you into working out some kind of a compromise before anything else happens."

"I see," I said coldly. "Well, Hoffman made his pitch, counselor. Go ahead and make yours. I'm all ears."

"Michelle, what are you talking about?" Rob said, genuinely puzzled. "I said he asked me. I didn't say I agreed. I turned him down. Had to. Conflict of interest."

"I don't understand. What conflict?"

"Interest, ma'am," he said slowly, as if explaining to a child. "I'm interested in you. I'm interested in our being friends. Good friends, I hope. Which means I had to choose sides. And I have. Yours."

"What about Hoffman?"

"The hell with him. If he goes after you legally, he'll hire an army of lawyers from New York, anyway. They only used me because they thought I was shady enough to play along and keep my mouth shut."

"You're taking quite a risk, businesswise."

"I'll chance it," he said briskly. "They said at the desk that you were being released. So, since I'm temporarily at liberty, where can I take you? Home? The Nest? Or maybe you'd like to stay on board the *Mai Tai* for a few days? Strictly as a matter of convenience, you understand."

"Thanks, but I'd better pass. For now, anyway. You can give me a lift, though, to the Deveraux Institute."

"The Institute? Now? What on earth for?"

"I'm not sure myself. Something Hoffman said about . . . accidents."

"Did he threaten you?"

"He tried, but that's not what bothers me. It's something else. I'm not sure what. But I have to find out."

"How? By asking at the library information desk?"

"As a matter of fact, that's exactly what I'm going to do," I said, managing a smile.

"Are you sure you're ready for the world?" Rob said, eyeing me thoughtfully. "You don't seem . . . altogether yourself."

"I'm myself all right," I said quietly. "But I can't remember ever feeling less together. I can be changed in a minute. Can you wait?"

"For a minute? Of course. Or a lot longer."

CHAPTER 36

WE BICKERED ALL THE WAY to the Deveraux Institute. Rob thought I should go straight home to rest and recuperate. He was right. We both knew it. But I didn't care. I said I'd call a cab when I finished, but he said he'd wait, and I was too low on energy to argue.

Still, once I was in the building, I felt my spirits lift. I've always loved the Institute, spent every spare moment I could here as a girl. It's a combination research library and nautical museum that occupies most of a city block in downtown Huron Harbor on land Jason's father had donated.

The building is over fifty years old but still looks ultramodern, patterned on a Frank Lloyd Wright design, cantilevered roofs, glass walls, and beautifully finished oaken counters and shelves inside.

The museum section is so densely filled with artifacts that you could wander through it for days and not see everything. Even the library section has elaborate displays above the bookshelves, a panorama of Great Lakes shipping, everything from hand-carved Anishnabeg canoe paddles to a cross section of the *Edmund Fitzgerald*'s turbine.

I left Rob to wander through the museum and went directly to the library's data terminal. I spent ten minutes scanning, taking notes, then took my short list to the desk.

The woman on duty was a fresh-faced young professional in a gray business suit that should have muted her eager-to-please appeal but somehow set it off instead. Even a mouthful of braces didn't dim her smile. Her name tag said CANDY BEARSS. I think we were of an age, but she made me feel like my own grandmother. She winced at my list.

"I'm afraid some of these books are restricted access," she said apologetically. "Are you a historian? Accredited with the Institute, I mean."

"My name's Mitchell," I said. "I'm . . . involved in some recovery work for the Deveraux family."

"Oh," she said, brightening, "then I'm sure it'll be all right. I think I can get most of these. . . ." She disappeared briskly into the stacks, still talking over her shoulder at me. I didn't try to follow what she was saying.

Instead, I glanced around the room, waiting, remembering. I'd been here many times, of course, but they changed the displays often. Funny, but it had never occurred to me how *many* artifacts they had on hand.

"Here you are, Miss Mitchell," she said, placing a small stack of books on the counter. "Since most of these are restricted, I'm afraid you'll have to study them here."

"No problem. I wonder if you could help me with something else, though? If the Institute acquired a new artifact—say a large bronze dedication plaque, roughly three feet square—where would it be displayed?"

"Oh, if it was an interesting piece, I'm sure we'd fit it into the display rotation eventually," she said. "It might take awhile, though. We have several large storerooms in the basement filled with pieces we haven't room to display now."

"I see," I said, picking up the books.

"They still acquire things all the time, though," she added helpfully. "The family's quite wealthy, you know."

"Yes," I said. "I've heard that."

His name was Stanley Joseph Maychek. I found a picture of him, posing stiffly with a group of company officers at the Soo Locks in the late sixties. He couldn't have been much more than a boy then. So young. And so much more alive than when I'd seen him last. He was the second mate on the *Queen of Lor-*

raine, signed aboard her in '67. He had a wife and two children in Saginaw, and his parents were still living. Or at least they were the year the *Queen* went down. His picture on the page blurred and swam before my eyes for a moment.

"I'm sorry," I said softly. "I'm so sorry."

Candy, the librarian, was eyeing me with obvious concern. Then she looked away. It didn't matter. His name was Stanley Joseph Maychek. And he'd told me the truth.

CHAPTER 37

ROB DROPPED ME OFF at the cottage at dusk. He said it was crazy for me to be alone on the point with Jud on the loose. He offered to stay, as a bodyguard, chef, whatever. I passed with minimal grace. I said I needed rest and he was a distraction, and he was. But the whole truth was, I wanted to be alone. To rest, and think. But most of all to wait. For Jud.

In spite of what had happened, I wanted to see him. I needed to. If he hated me enough to try to kill me, then eventually he'd come after me here. I'd failed him once because I didn't believe him. I needed this last chance to set things right.

Dog had cleaned out the food I'd left, so I refilled her bowl. Then I wandered into the living room, sat in the chair facing the beach, and watched the rose-tinted light bleed from the horizon into the lake. And I dozed.

And dreamed of my father, the way he was that first year, the year I came to live with him. Tanned and fit and hard.

My God, he was so young. I'd never thought of him that way, but he was. He probably wasn't much older than I am now. As young as Stanley Maychek will always be.

"Careful, Mitch," he said, looking up at me from the beach. "That old pine reaches halfway to heaven. Don't fall."

"I'm all right," I said. But it wasn't true. I was afraid. Terrified of falling. But I couldn't let him see it. So I kept climbing higher. Up into the fragrant pine boughs, swaying in the breeze. Then up through hazy green water, swimming hard, away from the shattered, murky passenger salon on the *Queen*. Up toward the emerald glow of sunlight. Toward . . .

Dawn. The sun warming my face woke me gently. But it didn't dispel the dream. It clung to me like a cobweb, brushing against my memory at odd moments.

"Careful," my father'd said. "Don't fall." But I had fallen. Into a clouded room where everything was upside down. And people died. Maybe Rob was right, I shouldn't have stayed out here alone.

I went out to the beach in front of the cottage, spread a blanket on a dune, and tried to relax. I basked in the sun, listening to the song of the surf, feeling my strength seeping slowly back.

But lake sounds had lost their comfort. There was anxiety in the thump of the waves and the cries of the gulls. I was wounded and spent but afraid to doze. Afraid to dream. So I willed myself to rest, and to think.

And gradually, my head cleared and my nerves steadied. I began to assemble the fragments of the past months into a mosaic of sorts, to see a pattern or two and to make a little sense of it.

The clipping. My god, it all began with that. Corey'd saved his friend and I'd sent a newspaper clipping home to my father. And he was so proud, he passed it on to the local paper, which ran the story.

Jason or Alec must have seen Corey's picture. And apparently decided to buy him from my father. Like a puppy or a used car.

Why did they think it would be so easy? Because they'd done it before. They'd paid him off all those years ago to force me to have an abortion. And when I ran away, they thought they'd succeeded in buying the death of my child.

But times changed. Andrea has no children and Alec has girls. Not good enough for a dinosaur like Jason. Easily resolved. Just toss a few bucks to the peasantry and buy Alec's woods' colt. The arrogance of it . . .

But they'd misjudged my father. He was in love. And he and Jud had found a wreck worth serious cash. Chump change by Alec's standards, but enough for Shan, because he wasn't looking to get rich, only to get out, to run off to Baja with Karen and bask in the sun and dive in warm water. And he decided to trick Jason into paying for the trip.

He had Karen forge my name on a couple of letters and tried a con, but Hoffman was suspicious and wouldn't pay off. And then . . . something happened. And my father died, alone, in the dark. In the swamp, only a few yards from safety.

Was he murdered? I was almost sure of it. I didn't know why or how, but too much had happened since. His death was no coincidence. And whatever had pulled him down was still out there. Someone had set a fire at the Nest. As a warning? A threat? Again, I didn't know. And the same person had built a blind to watch the cottage.

Bass? If Habash had wanted the rest of the cargo, Bass might have wanted to spy on me, hoping I'd lead him to it. But why start a fire at the Nest? Besides, when he asked me, politely, to keep my mouth shut about his frog of a boss, he could have used the fire to underscore his threat. "Next time it'll be worse," something like that. But he didn't. Because he didn't know about it.

No question, Bass was a formidable man, a man my father might have feared—in an alley or on a rooftop. But in the swamp? I tried to picture Bass skulking through the brush in his black suit.

No, no way. He was an urban warrior. He couldn't have handled my father in the swamp. And I was almost certain he'd had nothing to do with the fire or the blind.

Carney? He wanted to buy me out, and the fire might have been meant to frighten me. But the fire and the blind had to be connected, and Carney had no reason to stake out the cottage. Besides, he'd hired Terry to rough me around. He'd never have dared tangling with my father in the swamp or anywhere else.

Hoffman? Not a physical type, but probably twice as dangerous as Carney and Bass together. No soul. A genuinely evil bastard. He was definitely capable of a little arson to spook me into going along with the despicable arrangement Jason and my father had cooked up. But he wouldn't have done it on his own, and according to Rob, and to Hoffman himself, Jason hadn't turned him loose on me until after . . . Addison's death.

The *Queen*. That terrible room. It was hard even to think of it. But I had to. Because Harvey had died there, in my place. Wearing my tanks. I'd failed Jud, and now he hated me enough commit murder. . . .

And yet something about that didn't feel right. It must have been Jud. He'd been seen at the harbor the night he burned my boat. And Terry'd seen him a day or two before. He'd come back and he meant to kill me. But a stubborn corner of my heart refused to believe he could hate me that much. Maybe I didn't want to believe it.

And last, Stanley Joseph Maychek, the corpse in the *Queen*. I'd promised to get him out. And I couldn't. He was gone now. Crushed into the lakebed by countless tons of steel. And yet it wasn't finished. Not yet. The salon was still intact in my memory. And it still held unresolved business for me.

Because of something Stanley said? No. That made no sense. I'd been hallucinating. I couldn't have promised him anything, nor could he have spoken to me.

And yet he had. He'd told me . . . something. I didn't altogether understand. Perhaps something I didn't want to face. But it was true. That much I knew. Hallucination or not, what Stanley had told me, or that I sensed subconsciously, was validated by his photograph at the Institute. And if it was true, perhaps in time I would understand it.

I did understand that it was a warning. From beyond the grave? Nonsense. I've never been superstitious or particularly religious. I'm a practical woman working at a trade where trusting anything you haven't double-checked can get you killed. I believe in air regulators and depth tables and decompression limits. In technology, and my own skill. Not ghosts, or goblins, or dreams. And yet. And yet . . .

I watched the sun die, watched the very air over the lake turn aquamarine, then cobalt blue. And still I stayed, until the light died altogether, swallowed by the water. And some part of me, a small candle of hope that I'd nourished all these years, died with it.

Later that evening, I drove into Huron Harbor, stopped at the first pay phone I came to, and called Karen Stepaniak.

"Hi, I'm leaving, going back to Texas as soon as I can make arrangements. I want you to sell the Crow's Nest and the cottage for me. How soon can you manage it?"

"Well, with the profits you've been showing, it should sell fairly easily, Mitch. But this is very sudden. Are you sure it's what you want to do?"

"Yes," I said. "Very sure."

CHAPTER 38

I WENT BACK TO WORK two days later. I had no choice really, the Fourth of July weekend was upon us, the biggest holiday of the boating season, and Red needed all the help she could get.

Working was absolutely the right thing to do. The Nest was busy all day, a steady stream of boaters, divers, fishermen, and tourists, buying everything from box lunches to bait. Charlie Bauer stopped by to see how I was. He said Jud had been seen twice, at opposite ends of the county, unconfirmed. And the hunt continued.

Rob popped by, too, and Karen Stepaniak. Rob, I dismissed out of hand, saying I was fine and too busy to talk. Karen took one look at the crush of business in the Nest and promptly volunteered to serve as temporary cashier during the lunchhour rush. "The better the books look, the easier the sell."

I hid out in the office, burying myself in the profit-and-loss ledgers, bringing the accounts up to date one last time, and avoiding people. But even in the bustle of the Nest, I couldn't seem to shake the feeling of disorientation. "Careful," my father had said. "Don't fall." So when Alec Deveraux limped in with his wife and daughters in tow, for a moment I thought it might be just another illusion, a vision of a road not taken.

But they were real enough, dressed for boating, Alec in white duck trousers, a navy pullover shirt, and canvas jacket. His wife wasn't at all the fashion plate I'd pictured. She was an effervescent little butterball of a woman with a timeless moon face that belonged on a cameo brooch. She had sparkling eyes and mousy brown hair worn in a pageboy bob styled with lawn shears. Her clothes were just as casual, sloppy slacks and a Yale sweatshirt. She wore happiness like a comfy bathrobe, fussing over Alec and the girls, chatting cheerily with Red as she seated them at a corner table.

The girls were an even bigger surprise. They were exquisite—honey-skinned, sloe-eyed Eurasian beauties of nine and eleven or so, in matching white sailor suits. And as much as I despised Alec, I had to admit they were a lovely little crew. And I wondered why, knowing how I felt about him, he'd brought them here and risked a potentially ugly confrontation.

I didn't have to wait long to find out. Leaving his wife to order, Alec excused himself and made his way back to my office.

"Hi," he said cautiously. "Do you have a minute?"

"Not really. What do you want, Alec?"

"For openers, to see how you were. You look remarkably well for someone who's been through what you have been. Are you all right?"

"I'll survive. I've had a lot of practice. Was that all?"

"No. I understand you're leaving. I need to talk to you. May I sit down? I've been out on the boat all morning and this damn leg of mine's acting up."

"Look, Alec, I'm really not in the mood—"

"It won't take long, I promise. And it's important." He winced as he lowered himself to the chair, using his cane as a brace.

"Don't tell me," I said; "let me guess. You've brought your wife and children by to show me what a terrific family you have and how grateful Corey should be for a chance to join your little clan, right?"

"As a matter of fact, I do think they're a terrific bunch," he said, unoffended, "but that's not why I brought them."

"No? Then why are they here? As character witnesses?"

"In a way." He nodded. "Look, I know what you think of me,

so I'll come to the point. Do you recall the last time that we spoke? I warned you about Addison?"

"I remember. Considering the way things turned out, maybe you should have warned him."

"I wish to God I had," he said, looking away. "If I'd realized how serious that situation was . . ."

"What situation?"

"An old flame with new ambitions," he said bluntly. "But that's not why I'm here. I want to talk to you about my father. And Jerry Hoffman."

"What about them?"

"Since his surgery last fall, my father's become . . . obsessed with maintaining all he's built. I'm afraid it's affecting his judgment."

"And you're worried he might leave something to Corey in his will? Is that it?"

"No. It may surprise you, but I don't care about his money. I have more than enough of my own. I'm more worried about you. And my father's . . . soul, I suppose."

"You're not making much sense."

"I know. This isn't easy for me. I love my father, but I'm not blind to his faults. And it's not some distant future I'm worried about. It's what's happened already. You see, he feels so much stronger since his bypass, he thinks he's been given a new lease on life. He's trying to begin again, to get it right this time."

"Get what right?"

"To mold his . . . heir properly. In his own image. Like God."

"Even if that's true, it shouldn't worry you. If I get struck by lightning tomorrow, you could probably win custody of Corey. You'd still be in control. Seems to me that I have more to fear from you than from your father."

"You're wrong on both counts. You have nothing to fear from me. Nothing. Except the truth. And the truth is, I wouldn't get custody of your son. My father would."

"I don't understand. What are you saying?"

"Look at my wife, Mitch, at how she is with our girls. If ever a woman was born to be a mother, she was. Don't you think if we could have had children of our own, we would have? But we can't. *I* can't. Killing that horse when I was fourteen smashed up more than my leg, Mitch. I wish I was Corey's father, but I'm not. I'll never be anyone's *biological* father."

"You're lying," I said slowly. "My God, look at him. Look at his picture. Corey looks enough like you to—"

"To be my brother," he finished softly. "So he does, Mitch. So he does. I'm sorry."

And it was true. I could read it in his face. I didn't want to believe it. But it was true. And God, I couldn't bear it. I rose slowly and walked past him, out of the office, pushing through the crowd in the Nest but not seeing them. I heard Alec call after me, but I didn't slow. I hurried out the door and around the building, instinctively heading toward water, toward the lake. For a moment, I thought about walking into it, but I didn't. I ran instead. Away from Alec, the Nest, everything— sprinting blindly down the beach as though my soul was in flames.

CHAPTER 39

I DON'T KNOW how long I ran. Not long. Ten minutes perhaps. And then my pace slowed to a lope, then a walk. I reeled down the beach on rubber legs, wobbly as a wounded doe. But there was no running from the truth. And Alec had told me the truth. I'd sensed it in his eyes, the pain they showed. Or at least the truth as he understood it. Which wasn't necessarily all of it. Or even any of it.

Gradually, I became aware of my surroundings. I must've run a mile or more. I was on private beach now, plodding unsteadily past lakefront homes with manicured lawns and signs that said NO TRESPASSING. I turned and faced the lake, letting the shore breeze nuzzle my cheek, dry my eyes, and blow away some of the hurt and confusion. I stood there awhile, listening to the murmur of the waves. Then I turned and trudged slowly back to the Nest, lost in thought all the way.

A lone figure was sitting on the sand as I approached. He levered himself painfully upright with his cane. And in the afternoon sun, with the lake breeze tousling his hair, he looked very different to me: not the drunken, arrogant monster I'd hated all these years. More like the adopted big brother I'd depended on once, a long time ago. He wasn't, of course. Maybe he'd never been either of those things. I wasn't sure what I felt about him now.

"I'm sorry," he said quietly. "I guess I didn't handle that very well. Are you okay?"

"No. But I'll live. Go away, Alec. You've done your duty. Now leave me alone."

"Of course." He nodded, looking away. "Look, I don't know what I can say now. I didn't realize what must have happened until a few months ago when I saw your son's picture, saw the resemblance. And to be honest, my first instinct was to protect my family, and my father. I hope you can understand that. But believe me, I never meant you harm, never. We were friends once, Mitch. And like it or not, we're . . . connected now. We shouldn't be enemies."

"I don't know," I said dully, shaking my head like a zombie. "Too much has happened, Alec. Too fast. I need time to sort it out."

"I understand. But what you have to understand is that running away won't end this. Returning every cent of the money wouldn't end it. My father doesn't care about the money; he never did. All he wants is . . . his son. He's given Hoffman free rein to get it done, and Hoffman's a dangerous man, Mitch."

"Damn," I said. "Nice try, Alec. For a moment there, I almost bought your story. Except for the money. My father never got a dime from his little scam. I happen to know Hoffman refused to pay without verifying my signature."

Alec hesitated. "I don't know where you got that idea, Mitch, but the money *was* paid, or at least your father's share was. You don't have to take my word for it; they filmed the whole transaction."

"What do you mean, they filmed it?"

"Hoffman videotaped the meeting. He's a fanatic about having irrefutable records. Probably a holdover from his CIA days."

"Are you taking Hoffman's word for this or have you actually seen the tape?"

"I've seen it. I'll get you a copy if you want."

"Yeah," I said slowly, "maybe you'd better. Tell me, was, um, was Robinette there when all this took place?"

"Of course. He drew up the agreement and witnessed your father's signature. He even verified the money count. Surely he told you about it. I thought you two were friends."

"I thought so, too, but . . . Rob's a lawyer, and a very discreet one. How much money are we talking about?"

"A lot. A quarter of a million as a deposit, the balance to be paid on delivery. I thought you were aware of all this."

"I knew about the arrangement," I said, swallowing. "But I was told the money hadn't actually been paid."

"But we assumed you had it all along. The renovations to your business, your new pickup—"

"All paid for out of my savings, Alec. Money I earned. If my father actually collected his . . . deposit, I don't know what happened to it. Maybe he was killed for it."

"My God," he said softly. "I had no idea things could have . . . gone this far. What do you want me to do, Mitch? Should we go to the police?"

"I don't know. I need to think. It's too much, Alec. It's just—" I turned and walked slowly toward the Nest. If I stayed a second longer, I was going to shatter. And I couldn't do that, not yet. People were counting on me. My son. Perhaps even my father.

"Listen, I'll be at the house if you need me," Alec called after me. "And please, remember to be careful. Don't underestimate Hoffman, Mitch. Or my father."

"I won't," I said, turning back a moment. "In my business, careful comes with the territory, Alec. But thanks for warning me. I know it cost you."

"The warning stands, Mitch. I wish it didn't, but it does."

"I'll remember," I said.

⟐ "My God," Karen said, bustling from behind the cashier's counter, taking my arm. "Mitch, what happened? You went charging out of here like the place was on fire, scared me half to death. Are you all right?"

"Yeah," I said numbly. "I'm fine."

"No you're not. You look like you've been hit by a train. Come on, girl, I'm taking you home."

"No, really, I'm—"

"Don't argue. The lunch rush is over; I can come back and help Red out at dinner if she needs me. I don't get many chances to mother anybody, so humor me, okay?"

I hesitated, then shrugged. "Maybe you're right," I said. "I am a bit bushed. And maybe it's time we had a talk, anyway. Just us girls."

CHAPTER 40

KAREN DROVE ME OUT to the cottage in blessed silence. She tried a couple of conversational gambits, openly curious about what Alec and I had talked about, but she didn't press when I let it pass. I didn't want to talk. Not yet. I needed to think first, to make sense of it all.

It was odd making the trip home with someone else driving. Rob had dropped me off a few days before, but I'd been too groggy to pay much attention to my surroundings then. Even the road to the point looked different to me somehow, birch and aspen glowing in the afternoon sun, branches praying to the light, leaves arustle.

The riverbank near Silver Creek Bridge where my father died was completely overgrown with grass and weeds now. No marks to tell of what happened. Still, in my mind's eye, I could see the scars he'd left on the ice, ugly gray gouges in the river's frozen skin. And only ten feet from the bank. But he hadn't made it to shore. He'd gone the other way instead. Into the dark . . .

Running away. From what? What could have made him afraid? In my dreams of the past few nights, he was young again, the way he'd been that first summer I'd come to live with him. I could picture him that way and the way he was that last terrible weekend five years later when he'd driven me out, drunk and ranting, crazed and aged by booze. But I couldn't imagine him afraid—of anything.

"Home sweet home," Karen said, parking her car in front of

the house, startling me out of the haze. "Come on. I'll fix us a nice cup of tea, and no arguments."

"Who's arguing?" I asked, trailing her into the cottage, slumping gratefully into a chair at the kitchen table. "I really appreciate this, Karen. You've been a lifesaver, from the beginning."

"Right," she said, flushing a bit, "I'm a veritable prize." She busied herself over the stove, and I watched her: a brisk, blond, professional woman who'd been my father's lover. And his partner in crime. And I wondered what else she was.

"Here you go, one hot cuppa. In the only unchipped cup I could find, I might add."

"Thank you," I said, sipping the tea. It was dark and bitter. And matched my mood. She'd given me the Rookwood cup, the same one I'd given her that first morning. And she was right—it was the only decent piece in the cupboard. Probably shouldn't be using it at all. It should be on display on the mantel with his other . . . artifacts.

I blinked at the cup, trying to bring the delicate tracery into focus. "What a bastard he was," I said slowly.

"Who was?"

"Shan. My ever-lovin' dad. Your lover and friend. You, um, you don't know what this cup is, do you?"

"What do you mean?"

"I mean you don't recognize it. That first morning, when I gave you coffee in it, you thought it was mine. Said something about my . . . civilizing this place."

"Are you all right, Mitch? You're not making much sense."

"Maybe not to you, but I'm starting to make sense to me. This cup is from the wreck my dad and Rats were raiding. He'd already sold part of the load to a buyer in Saginaw. But you didn't know about that, did you?"

"No," Karen admitted, easing down across from me. "Your father wasn't an open book, Mitch. Most men aren't." She placed a Virginia Slim carefully between her lips, lighted it in slow motion, the flame glittering in her eyes.

"Still, it's funny, since you were lovers, that he never showed you the cup . . . or told you he'd scored a quarter of a million dollars in your little scam."

"Is that's what Alec told you? He's lying, of course."

"Is he? He offered to give me a videotape of the whole thing. Must make quite a pile, a quarter mil."

"I wouldn't know. I've never seen it."

"So you said. And maybe it's true, since my father didn't show you the cup, either. But I wonder why he didn't? I had a lover once. I told him . . . everything I could."

"And how did it work out, all that honesty?"

"The relationship didn't work in the long run. But while we were involved, honesty made it . . . more fun. More dangerous. Same thing, sometimes—danger and fun. Like . . . skydiving— but with no parachute, no clothes. You have to trust somebody to catch you when you fall. Isn't that what love is?"

"Maybe for you. Not for me, or your father." She blew two narrow plumes of smoke downward from her pert little nose.

"But if he really trusted you, and he must have, since you were helping him con Jas—" I choked, gagging on the name, and the images it conjured up in my mind: Jason finding me in the guest room, unconcious, helpless, dead drunk. I wondered if he'd removed all of my clothing, or just enough to . . . No. He would have taken off every stitch. Would have savored every . . . God.

Karen was watching me, oddly distant. Not really concerned, just curious. "Are you all right, Mitch? You're sweating."

"I'm okay," I said, nodding. I felt like my head was barely attached, that it might fall, dribble across the room. I liked the idea of leaving my body somehow, finding another one. Andrea's maybe. Terry liked Andrea's.

Karen glossed over the silence by babbling on about some minor real estate deal that her boss had blown, about what a tightwad he was, making her walk his damned dogs, stiffing her on commissions. I couldn't follow much of it.

I wanted to bring the conversation back to the money and my father, and most of all, Rob. But I couldn't quite manage it. I was tired, and it was so very pleasant just to sit and relax, soothed by the sound of a woman's voice, restful as the waves on the beach. . . .

Karen was a good person. I'd had doubts about her when I guessed she'd written the letters. But she'd done it for Shan. Women were always doing things for him, even me. And I was just a kid. "Careful," he'd said, smiling up at me from the beach as I climbed my lonesome pine. "Don't fall."

"I'm not afraid," I said.

"What?" Karen asked.

"Oh," I said, blinking myself awake. "Sorry. I must've been dozing."

"How do you feel now? Better?"

"I do. A lot better," I said, deliciously relaxed. "Best I've felt in . . . Heck, I don't know. Long time. Could I have some more tea?"

"Of course," she said, filling my cup from the small kettle.

"You're not having any?" I asked. "You should. It's really good."

"I'm sure it is." She smiled. "But I've always been more of a coffee person. You'd better let it cool a minute before you—"

But it was too late. I burned my fingers and dropped it, shattering the cup on the table. "Damn!" I said, staring stupidly at the brown pool spreading out from the Rookwood shards. Karen watched it a moment, then calmly rose, unrolled a paper towel, and mopped up the mess. I couldn't seem to focus on her. When she moved, it was as if we were underwater, her image wavering and shifting. Some of the tea dripped over the edge of the table onto my lap. It felt warm, wet. It didn't matter.

A car pulled up outside, a police car. I hoped it was Charlie. But it wasn't. Jackowski climbed out. And Rob was with him.

CHAPTER 41

THEY ENTERED WITHOUT KNOCKING, looking the cottage over like landlords on rent day. They wandered casually into the kitchen. Rob glanced a question at Karen, who nodded. She rose, taking her cigarette with her, and he slid into her chair directly across from me. Jackowski leaned against the counter, watching, his muscular weight lifter's arms folded, his eyes invisible behind his mirrored sunglasses. Robocop.

Karen stood beside him, smoking thoughtfully. They both seemed to be shimmering, rippling, as though I was looking at them through a waterfall. Maybe I was underwater, still in the passenger salon of the *Queen*. With Stanley. "To sleep—perchance to dream . . ."

"Hi, Mitch," Rob said warily, "how are you doing?"

I blinked, couldn't think of an answer.

"She's out of it," Karen said dryly. "Stoned to the bone."

"Did you get all of it down her?" Jackowski asked.

"Most of it. She spilled some in her lap."

"Probably won't matter," Rob said. "Mitch, honey, didn't you tell me once you didn't do dope? Never even tried it?"

"No," I said slowly, as though I'd just wakened from a twenty-year sleep. "Never. Not once."

"Good for you." He nodded. "Nasty stuff, drugs. Unless your clients are in the business. In which case, dope can be very lucrative. And very effective—especially the first time you cop a buzz. You're gonna be a cheap date, Mitch. No resistance at all. Look, I need to ask you few things. And I want you to tell me the truth."

215

"What's happening, Rob?" I asked. "I don't understand."

"You don't have to understand, babe. You just relax and trust me. Everything's fine as wine. You feel good, don't you?"

"I feel . . . funny. Everything's moving. Karen . . . put something in my tea, didn't she?"

"Just a little buzzer to help you loosen up, Mitch. You've been under a lot of strain. What are friends for if they don't try to cheer you up when you're down? Now, we're gonna have a little chat, and you're gonna tell me what I want to know. No fibbing, now. Because we're friends, right?"

"No," I said. "We're not friends."

"Sure we are. I'll prove it to you. Last winter, your dad told me where he stashed the money he got from Jason. So I could give it to you and your boy—what's his name, Corey?"

"Corey"—I nodded—"he's my . . . son."

"Right. You see, Shan said the money was in the Crow's Nest, but we looked very hard for it and we couldn't find it. Do you know where it is?"

"No," I said. "I don't know. In the Crow's Nest?"

"He didn't just say in the Crow's Nest," Karen put in. "He said *up* in the Crow's Nest."

"Bullshit," Jackowski said, "I crawled over every fucking beam in that rat hole. There was nothin' up there."

"Maybe if you hadn't been so sure that's where it was, he would have told us more," Karen said acidly.

"Don't give me that," Jackowski flared. "We all thought—"

"Quiet down, damn it," Rob snapped. "Don't get her confused. She's only operating on half a brain cell as it is. Okay, Mitch, suppose your old man did say it was . . . up in the Crow's Nest. Would that make any difference?"

"Up?" I said slowly, trying to think. "Don't fall," my father said.

"That's right, up," Karen said impatiently. "You know what *up* means. You're not that wrecked."

"I don't know," I said. "Can't think."

"I think she's scammin' you, Robinette," Jackowski said softly, leaning on the table, staring intently at me. My face looked tiny and distorted reflected in his glasses. "She knows something. Maybe not where it is exactly, but somethin'. It was there in her eyes for a second. Didn't you catch it?"

"You're dead wrong, as usual," Rob said. "The junk she's on is a mix of ludes and Pentothal. I got it from a client who used it to turn out teenybop hookers. I've seen it work myself, close up and personal. Believe me, if she knows, she'll give it up."

"Like her old man did?"

"Karen's right—we didn't give it enough time. And you were the one who was all hot to crawl around the rafters looking for it."

"If this stuff is so foolproof, how did Shan manage to punch out your lights and get away?"

"Because he was a lot tougher than any of us realized," Rob said coolly, "you included. He was an old hard-line alky with ninety-proof blood. No wonder it didn't work right on him. Even so, he didn't get far, did he? Cracked up his truck and crawled off to die like a dog. The junk's working just fine on her. She really doesn't know where the cash is, that's all."

"Give me two minutes alone with her and I'll find out if she knows or not. Guaranteed."

"Hey, if you want to shake it out of her afterward, be my guest. But it'll have to be afterward. No need to settle for a quarter of the money when we can have all of it. But we have to be careful; Hoffman won't pay off for anything that looks coerced. So no rough stuff yet. The lady's going to need all of her teeth to smile pretty for the camera."

"Camera?" I said.

"Exactly." Rob nodded. "A video cam. Mitch, honey, you're about to star in your very own beach movie. I've got a client who can distribute it nationally damn near overnight. With your face in half the low-rent porn shops in the country, the old man won't have any trouble winning custody if he draws the right judge. You're about to become an unfit mother for reasons of moral turpitude, lady. The title's a bit long for a marquee, but it'll play just fine in a judge's chambers. And Hoffman will buy it. Oh, he'll whine and hold his nose, but he'll pay. For every single frame. Come on, babe. It's show time."

CHAPTER 42

WE WERE WALKING UNDERWATER. I couldn't shake the feeling. Everything was shimmering, shifting. My limbs were leaden, as though I'd been working deep too long. Jackowski took my arm and led me out, and I had no strength to fight him, only broken fragments of a will to resist.

Rob took a video camera out of the backseat of the prowl car, checked it, then stalked down to the shore to a spot he'd already picked out, a flat sandy arena shielded from the house and the road by cedar scrubs and a low, gorse-crested dune. And I knew I was in terrible trouble, and I was more afraid than I'd ever been in my life, yet the fear seemed so deeply submerged, so deadened that I could barely comprehend why I was afraid at all.

Jackowski spread out a blanket he'd brought from the cottage and began stripping off his uniform shirt, watching me all the while. I was paralyzed, a bird watching a snake. His weight lifter's muscles seemed alive, rippling, flexing, writhing like worms beneath his sunlamp tan.

"Come on, Karen," Rob said, "get peeled. Let's get this little show under way."

"Look, I don't know about this," Karen said, swallowing. "Can't Jack just—"

"Damn it, it has to look like an honest-to-God orgy, funky enough so that any judge who sees it will award custody of the kid to Deveraux. No offense, lady, but you're a little past the age where anybody'd pay you a quarter mil for a straight fuck. For this kind of money, you're gonna have to get it on and make it look real. And do my eyes deceive me, or are your nipples comin' to attention even as we speak? C'mon, who are you kidding? You're gonna love every minute of this."

"What if she fights?" Karen said, stepping out of her shoes, unbuttoning her blouse. "Won't that blow the picture on film?"

"She won't give us any trouble. Christ, look at her. She barely knows her damn name. Besides, about thirty seconds into the game, her hormones'll kick into overdrive and she'll be ready to fuck a Shetland pony if we bring it on. The last time I used this stuff, the chick was only thirteen, but she wound up takin' half a dozen guys in both ends and begging for reinforcements."

Rob was unbuttoning my shirt as he spoke, talking past me as though I was a mannequin. And I was. A body, nothing more. I fumbled at his wrist, trying to stop him, but he brushed my hand away like a butterfly. I had no strength at all, none. He tossed my shirt aside and unsnapped my bra. I covered my breasts with my hands. It didn't matter. Karen was nude now except for her red lace panties. Her breasts were small, almost girlish, with pale rose aureoles, nipples erect.

She helped Rob unsnap my jeans and slide them down over my hips. She told me to raise my foot. I didn't, but she lifted it easily and slid my tennis shoe off, then my jeans, and I couldn't seem to stop her. And then I was naked on a deserted beach, surrounded by these . . . strangers. I tried to walk away, but Jackowski took my arm, holding me casually, easily, like a child.

The wind off the lake caressed my skin, giving me goose bumps, and I felt my nipples hardening and I couldn't stop them, or any of it. . . . God. And I was so afraid Rob was right, that I was going to lose myself somehow and let this thing happen.

Rob led me over to the blanket and Jackowski pulled me down to it.

"We'll start with a straight-on shot," Rob said, coolly checking the light meter on the camera. "Get Mitch on her hands and knees, facing me. You take her in the ass while Karen suckles her breasts from underneath. That'll give us a clear shot of Mitch's face with Karen's snatch in front of it but still keep Karen's face out of the picture. Spread your knees wide, babe, and shake your moneymaker. Make it look good."

"That all we'll need?" Jackowski asked. "Just the one shot?"

"I want that one for openers. Depending on the judge, it might be all Deveraux's lawyers'll need. But we'll have to shoot enough footage so nobody can claim she wasn't a willing participant. Take it easy on her at first, get her hot, and she'll get with the program, believe me."

And suddenly it was happening, too fast, too fast. Jackowski seized my hips and pulled me down, pressing me against his waist, shifting me around like a sack of flour, and I tried to keep from falling, and I was on my hands and knees, and Karen slithered beneath me, her breasts brushing mine, her hands on my rib cage, holding me as she spread her knees and began to writhe. I felt Jackowski slide himself between my thighs, not entering me yet, but thrusting against my abdomen, and my heart was hammering and I couldn't breathe. The dunes seemed to flow and ripple like a whirlpool around our island blanket, and Rob seemed to be swaying as well, back and forth, hypnotic as a cobra, his head monstrous behind the mechanical eye of the camera.

"God," I gasped. "No. Please . . ." And I closed my eyes and tried to grimace, to ruin the picture, but I could feel my bones melting, turning fluid, losing myself in the heat of their bodies, the wonderful warmth of Karen's skin. . . .

"NOOOOO!" The howl came from so deep within me that it sounded like someone else, a dying cry from the shattered fragments of my soul. And everyone froze for a moment, startled. And then a patch of ground seemed to erupt from behind Rob, snarling an answer, and she exploded into motion, a blur, hurtling at him from behind.

Dog.

She hit him full force between the shoulder blades, a hundred and forty pounds of fangs and sinew, smashing him down, savaging him, ripping his thigh open. And he was screaming, trying to crawl away, and she tore at his shoulder and then at his throat, and he went down, gagging, twitching, drowning in his own blood.

Karen was screaming, trying to untangle herself from beneath me. Jackowski threw me aside, scrambling on hands and knees toward the pile of his clothing—and his gun. I grabbed his ankle, hanging on with the dregs of my strength. He slapped me hard, and my head exploded with pain and white light. And rage.

I held on somehow and sank my teeth into his calf, biting deep into the muscle with everything I had. And he screamed and hammered me with his fists, stunning me, knocking me aside, and then Dog was on him, seizing his bloodied leg in her jaws, tearing him away from me, the two of them rolling down the dune. And Jackowski went limp, closing his eyes, forcing himself to lie still. To play dead.

Dog stood over him a moment, teeth bared, snarling, but then Karen ran, naked, screaming over the dunes. And Dog released Jackowski, leaving fallen prey for the chase.

Karen sprinted to the top of the next dune, then stumbled, tumbling down through the underbrush, wailing like a child all the way. Dog watched her fall, making no move to pursue. . . .

She was still watching when Jackowski shot her. He scrabbled to the pile of his clothing the moment she let him go, jerked his weapon free, set himself in a two-hand hold, and fired, once, twice, and again, the bullets slamming into Dog atop the bluff, spinning her around, tumbling her back down the dune. He limped toward her, still firing. And I felt each bullet tear into my heart as it struck her. And I couldn't stop it. She was already dying, crumpled into a fetal crouch in the sand, huddling against the shock of the bullets.

And I left her, crawling away on my hands and knees to Rob. He was dead, staring blindly into the sun, his throat ripped open. And it meant nothing to me. The hell with him! With all of them! I pulled the camera out of his grasp and staggered across the dune after Jackowski.

He was standing atop the bluff a few yards above Dog's twitching body, still firing, coldly choosing his shots to maim rather than to finish her outright, so rapt in his sadism that he never saw me—until I smashed the camera into the terrible gash she'd ripped in his thigh. He screamed and fell, rolling down the dune toward Dog. He managed to right himself, to push himself away from her. But he'd dropped his damned gun halfway down.

We both scrambled after it, but I got there first and snatched it up, barely able to hold it, and I fired, more to drive him away from us than to hit him. The slug tore out a gout of earth several meters beyond him. He rolled away, spinning like a cat, pitching a double fistful of sand toward me, blinding me. And then he came at me again, charging up the dune, teeth bared in fury and pain.

I fired at his blurred shape, then fired again. And he turned and fled, staggering through the sand like a smashed insect, disappearing over the crest toward the lake.

I knelt a moment, blinded, my eyes streaming, too numb to cry, too enraged. Dog was wheezing softly, like a child with a cold. And I reached out and touched her, the first time she'd ever let me. But she never knew. She was already dead.

I don't know how long I knelt there. Not long, I think. And then I shook my head hard, like a boxer waiting out the count, and staggered to my feet. I wrapped myself in the blanket, then forced myself to stumble up and over the dune after Jackowski.

He hadn't covered much ground. He was only forty or fifty meters ahead of me on the beach, limping badly, unable to put much weight on the leg Dog had savaged, slowed and tattered by the thorny underbrush that grew down to the water's edge.

He glanced up, saw me coming, scanned the tangled terrain around him, then quickly turned and waded out into the lake, plunging into the water, swimming strongly away from shore.

He churned through the sunlit chop like a racer, his powerful arms compensating for his wounded leg. By the time I reeled down to the beach, he was at least seventy-five meters offshore. He slowed, then turned to face me, treading water easily, and even at that distance I could feel his hatred, glaring at me like a torch.

"Go ahead, bitch! Shoot! Take your time! Because you're dead meat! Anyway you look at it! Know what happens next? You'll have to keep me out here, and you're gonna nod out! Your adrenaline'll wear off, and you'll sit down to watch me. And then you'll go under. And I'm gonna come for you! Or maybe Karen'll bring help. Know what they'll find? You, waving a gun at an officer of the law! I'll tell 'em we were having a beach party and you and your dog freaked and killed Rob and tried to kill me, and who do you think they're gonna believe? By then you'll be lucky if you can remember your damn name! Karen's the only witness, and she'll back my story. I'll still sell Deveraux that tape, and with a couple of affidavits from me and Karen, that's all they'll need! So go ahead, shoot! You couldn't hit a fuckin' battleship at this distance. But it's the only chance you got!"

He was right. Dazed and stunned as I was, I knew that much. I could already feel the drug beginning to take effect again, blurring my vision. And I was so tired. I just wanted to rest, to sit down and . . .

No. Jackowski was right. I'd pass out. And I couldn't, not yet. He'd kill me. He was still shouting at me to shoot. And I wanted to. I wanted him dead more than anything I've ever wanted. For my father. And for Dog. And for me. I raised the pistol in a two-hand hold. . . .

The slide was back, locked open. The gun was already empty. Jackowski realized it at the same instant I did. His face split in a brutal leer and he slowly began to swim in, eyeing me as he came.

I stared stupidly at the useless pound of metal, then took a deep breath and dropped it. And I let the blanket slip away, too. Then I waded slowly out into the water. Jackowski stopped swimming, watching me warily, then his grin returned.

"Come on, bitch! Hurry it up! Water's fine!"

But it wasn't. It seemed much colder than it should have. Still, it was my element, my lake. If I was going to die, let it be here. In deep water.

I plunged in. The shock of submerging cleared my head a little, and when I broke the surface again, my motor functions took over. I swam steadily through the choppy waves my body on autopilot, doing what it knew it had to do.

Jackowski kept ranting, cursing me, pumping himself up like a mad dog, working himself into a killing fury. And I was enraged, too, but my anger was cold. As cold as lake ice in moonlight. As cold as the salon in the *Queen.* As cold as the Lady herself.

A dozen meters from Jackowski, I slowed, breathing deeply, saturating my lungs with oxygen.

"Come on, bitch!" Jackowski roared, lunging toward me. I dove deep, swimming hard for the bottom, the water flowing over me like a cool caress, tempting me on, whispering. . . .

I shut it out and jackknifed, coming up at Jackowski on an angle, zeroing in on his injured leg. He submerged, too, looking for me, and saw me coming. And I could see death in his eyes and in the massive iron-trained muscles of his arms. But it didn't matter in the end. He shouldn't have done so much shouting. He'd wasted most of his air. . . .

CHAPTER 43

SOMEHOW I KEPT WALKING. One foot in front of the other: step, step, step. Five paces, turn right at the sofa, eight more paces, right again at the television set. I wasn't sure how many circuits of the waiting room I'd made. Quite a few. When I'd begun, the room would dissolve every few paces, the walls turning liquid, the curtains shimmering, bursting into flame in the red sunset light. The light was gone now, faded into dusk, leaving the room in near darkness. It didn't matter. I knew the route. And the room was a little more stable now. I could make almost a complete circuit sometimes before . . .

Charlie Bauer was watching me from the doorway. Not saying anything. Just watching. I wasn't sure how long he'd been standing there. He was holding a plastic garment bag draped over his shoulder. His dry cleaning? It didn't make much sense. But nothing else did, either. So I kept on walking. Maybe he wasn't real. I'd seen things that weren't real on the drive into town. My father had waved to me from the water below the Silver Creek Bridge; Stanley Joseph Maychek, in full uniform, had stood like a sentry by the emergency room entrance when I'd brought Karen in, battered and bleeding from her fall. I knew Stanley wasn't real. He couldn't be. He was dead. Like my father and . . . the others. Maybe Charlie wasn't real, either. Maybe he wasn't there at all.

"Hi, Mitch," he said quietly. "How are you?"

"I'm okay." My voice seemed to be coming from a radio in another room. "A little groggy."

226

"Maybe you should lie down—"

"No!" I said sharply. "I'll be all right. Let me alone, Charlie. Please."

"I'm afraid I can't do that, Mitch. I'm sorry. But with a man dead and another missing, and you and Karen banged up—"

"I'm not banged up. I'm all right."

"No you're not, damn it. My God, you look like a zombie, Mitch. Talk to me, please. What happened out there?"

I stopped, closing my eyes, trying to think about it. And I was swimming, down and down into emerald water . . . dragging something behind me. Something horrible. . . . I opened my eyes. Charlie was still there, watching. "Sorry," I said. "What did you say?"

"I asked you what happened, Mitch."

"What does Karen say happened?"

"She's talking her head off, saying Jackowski and Robinette were responsible for Shan's death and the fire at the Nest. She's not making much sense, Mitch."

"Isn't she? I guess that's natural. She's been through a . . . bad time."

"What kind of bad time? What happened?"

"She told me the dog attacked them," I said, keeping my voice level, dispassionate. "Jackowski wounded it, then ran into the water to get away. I heard the shooting, but when I got there, it was too late."

"I see. What were they doing out there?"

"Looking for money, I guess. At least, that's what Karen told me. Is that what she told you?"

"Something like that," he admitted. "She said your father and Jason Deveraux had some kind of a deal going. Robinette did the legal work and knew a lot of cash was involved. He got Karen to drug your father by promising her a share."

"But she and my father were lovers."

"They were. She and Rob were also lovers. She's a prize, Karen, uses men like some people pop pills. She doped Shan, but apparently he got free, tried to drive back to town. But he didn't make it. They thought they'd blown their chance, so they decided to lay low. Then you showed up and they tried again. The fire at the Nest was to bluff you into checking on the money. But it didn't work, did it?"

"It couldn't. I didn't have it. Rob and Karen told me my father never got it, and I believed them. But when I bought my truck and remodeled the Nest . . . they thought I'd found it."

"But you knew about the deal, didn't you? Because Deveraux tried to cut the same deal with you that he made with Shan. Only you turned him down. Why didn't you tell me about it, Mitch? Didn't you trust me?"

"No," I said simply, "I'm sorry, but I didn't. It's nothing to do with you. It's me. I don't . . . trust people easily."

"I see." He nodded. "Well, maybe you were right not to. Hell, Jackowski was going bad right under my nose, bulking up on steroids he got from Robinette, the two of them thick as thieves. I watched it happening but looked the other way, hoping he'd get past it. I didn't realize how far over the line he'd gone. I should have seen it. I blew this thing, Mitch. It's as much my fault as anyone's." He looked away a moment and shifted the garment bag he was holding to ease its weight on his shoulder. I still couldn't think why he'd brought it. But it didn't really matter. So I kept walking.

"There are still things I don't understand, Mitch."

"Like what?"

"Karen said Jackowski ran into the water to get away from the dog and drowned. But he was a diver, Mitch. An expert swimmer."

"The currents are tricky off the point," I said carefully. "And maybe Jackowski wasn't quite as good as he thought."

Charlie stared at me without speaking for what seemed like a year. "You're really not going to tell me about it, are you?" he said at last.

"I am telling you, Charlie. Everything I can. Am I under arrest or anything?"

"You? Of course not. I suppose Karen could be, for criminal

228

trespass or conspiracy. Or something. But somehow I don't think you'll be interested in pressing charges. Will you."

It wasn't a question.

"No," I said, turning away, resuming my unsteady march. "I suppose she's as guilty as the others, but somehow it doesn't matter much now. She got roughed up pretty badly, came out of it with nothing, and she'll have to live with what happened for the rest of her miserable life. For a woman like her, that's punishment enough. Let her go, Charlie. As far as I'm concerned, she's paid her dues."

"Yeah." He nodded. "I suppose she has. Funny, though, what she said about you."

I hesitated, then made myself continue walking: step, step, step. "What did she say?"

"Nothing," Charlie said, watching me carefully. "Absolutely nothing. Whenever I asked her anything about you, she'd suddenly get the shakes and develop amnesia. Said I'd have to ask you, and whatever you told me would be the truth. She seems terrified of you, Mitch. Scared to death. Why? Why should Karen be afraid of you?"

For a moment, I was under the water again, blacking out, my lungs bursting, lunging upward toward the light. . . . Breaking through, gasping, choking, breathing again, sweet, sweet air. Then looking frantically around for Jackowski, thinking he might have made it up, too. . . . But he hadn't. The bay was empty to the horizon, its surface broken only by the waves. He was still down there, tumbling gently in the deep currents, in the dark. Like Stanley. I turned to swim for shore. And realized Karen was watching me, huddled on the bluff, still naked, her arms wrapped around her knees for comfort, shivering, staring. Watching me swim in. Alone.

"I don't know why she should . . . feel that way," I said, forcing myself to meet Charlie's eyes. "She has nothing to fear from me. She's been through a lot. Maybe she's hysterical."

"Yeah." He nodded slowly, unconvinced. But let it pass. "Maybe she is. But you're not. Are you?"

"No. I'm . . . fine."

"Good. Then maybe you can help me out with one last thing." He swung the garment bag off his shoulder and draped it across a chair. He hesitated, then unzipped it. And some aspect of his stance gave me a subliminal warning, like a footstep on my grave. Something's coming.

Carefully, almost gently, he raised the hanger and held it up for me. It was a coat. A tattered red-and-black-checked wool winter coat. It seemed out of place and out of season in the antiseptic waiting room.

I glanced up at Charlie, but for once his face told me nothing. I ran my finger over the frayed collar. And when I touched it, I felt an icy chill dance up my wrist, a faint shock of recognition. And for just a moment, Jud was there, wearing this coat, his birthmark a dark stain in the moonlight. And then he was gone.

"It's Jud's," I said.

"Are you sure?"

"Yes. He, um, he was wearing it the last time I saw him. Hell, it's the only thing I ever saw him wear. Where did you find it?"

"One of the state police divers hooked it while they were looking for Jackowski. It was in sixty feet of water—about a half mile off the point."

"In the lake?" I said, frowning. But I knew it was true. It was soaked, and streamers of soft green algae hung from its seams like angel hair. "I don't understand," I said. "The people who saw Jud at the harbor said he was wearing this coat. But he couldn't have been, not this coat. Algae like this doesn't grow in a week, or even a month. This has been in the water a long time."

"That's what I thought, too," Charlie said, carefully replacing the coat in the bag. "But it's nice to have my judgment confirmed. Do you know if Jud had another coat? Maybe one like this?"

"I don't know. I really didn't know him very well."

"Yeah, well, no one else did, either," Charlie said, straightening, sliding the bag over his shoulder. "I've got to get back to the point to see if they've recovered Jack's body. Oh, I, um, I buried your dog. Hope you don't mind."

And suddenly, my eyes were stinging. I couldn't see, couldn't breathe. But I kept walking. I had to. "Where?" I managed at last.

"On a bluff near where I found her. I marked it."

"Thank you. That was . . . a nice thing to do."

"The state boys took a blood sample, to test for rabies, but—"

"She wasn't rabid," I said, flaring. "She was just defending . . . her territory. Our territory."

"Thought it must be something like that. I suppose she was justified in a way. It was Jackowski who wounded her when she caught him in the blind the night of the fire. Karen said he was spying on you, hoping you'd check on the money and show them where it was. This money Karen's talking about, do you know where it is now?"

"The money? I think so, yes. It's up in the Crow's Nest."

"Really? From what Karen said, Jackowski and Robinette had already searched every inch of the bar and the shop, too."

"Not that Crow's Nest," I said, with a ghost of a smile. "The other one. The first one."

231

CHAPTER 44

I WAITED AT THE HOSPITAL until ten, when they let me see Karen for a moment. She was groggy, sedated. A little battered from her fall, the nurse said, but otherwise all right. With the nurse hovering nearby, I couldn't say anything to Karen. But I didn't have to. I could read it in her eyes. No more trouble. She'd had enough.

And then I drove out to the cottage. I was afraid to go there alone. I was afraid they might come for me in my dreams—Jackowski, or Rob, or even my father. But they didn't. I fell asleep in my chair, listening to the waves. And I didn't dream. Or at least I didn't remember.

It was nearly noon when I woke, to a pallid ashen sun. The lake was a glittering pool of molten brass, the color of ancient armor. I felt terrible: My shoulder ached, my throat was raw, and I had an ugly bruise on my temple from Jackowski's fist. But my mind was clear, more or less. Perhaps clearer than it had been since I'd gone down to the *Queen of Lorraine*.

I knew I should probably stay in bed, but I couldn't. I was too edgy, energized by fear and anger, fight-or-flight syndrome. My mind knew the immediate danger was past, but my subconscious didn't quite believe it. And maybe it was right.

I got up, took a week-long shower, scrubbing until I thought my skin might come off. And it helped. A little.

I put on clean jeans and a sweatshirt. And then I took a walk.

The beach looked as though an army had marched across it in the night, trampled by the police and their diving crew. And

232

it seemed proper that the sand was scarred, considering all that had happened here.

I'd been groggy the day before, but I had no trouble finding the place where they'd dragged me. I circled it warily, the way you would a quicksand pit. And a little beyond, I found what I'd come to see.

It was atop a bluff, facing the water. Two sticks lashed together. The rude cross that marked Dog's grave. I wondered why Charlie'd made a cross. I doubt Dog was a Christian.

Still, it was a decent thing to do. And he'd chosen a good site, high and clean, with a fine view of the lake. I could almost see her sitting there, staring out over the water. Waiting for Jud.

But of course, she wasn't. Not anymore. If there's any justice in this universe, they were together. She'd thrown her life away defending mine. Wherever her soul had gone, in whatever shadowy land she hunted now, Jud was with her. And he'd been there all along.

She'd known it from the first. It was the only reason she'd befriended me. She knew he wasn't coming back. And in my heart, so had I. Seeing his coat only confirmed a truth I'd known but hadn't wanted to believe—because of what it meant.

It meant the trouble wasn't over yet. My life had been smashed and people had died, and yet nothing was truly settled.

It was time for a reckoning. Time to add up what was owed and pay it. One way or another.

CHAPTER 45

THE AFTERNOON SUN had an alchemist's touch, gilding the oaken shelves and the artifacts of the Deveraux Institute's library, transmuting the air into golden haze. I wandered aimlessly through the stacks, brushing the spines of books with my fingertips, glancing at the titles but not seeing them. The aisle darkened. Alec was standing at the end of it, leaning on his cane. He was wearing a dark suit and an expression to match.

"He's here, Mitch," he said. "You'd better get things under way."

"Any trouble?" I asked, falling into step beside him.

"No, I told him you wanted a meeting and he agreed to come," Alec said. "When he saw the newspeople, Hoffman wanted him to back out. I convinced him to stay, but he won't wait long. And just to be absolutely sure we understand each other, I agreed to arrange this, but don't ask me to choose sides. I won't."

"Understood," I said. "Thanks for doing what you could."

"I owe you this. Or my family does. Besides, it's almost worth it just to see you looking so . . . businesslike—a dress, briefcase, the works. So, shall we do some business?"

The main room was abustle with people, local merchants, a few reporters, students who'd wandered out of the stacks to see what the fuss was about. A cameraman from KNHH, the local TV station, was panning the room with a minicam, shooting background footage.

The center of attraction was a long oak table draped in blue velvet. A half dozen ship's artifacts were displayed on it: a magnificent brass compass, a burled walnut ship's wheel, pieces my father'd spent half his life collecting. It seemed strange to see them anywhere but the cottage. But it couldn't be helped.

Jason Deveraux was seated at a table in the corner of the room, holding court. There was no other word for it. He was dressed casually, a tweed sportcoat over a dark turtleneck, canvas slacks, and deck shoes. His beard needed a trim. Just a benign old paterfamilias chatting up a couple of press people. No one bowed to him or tugged on their forelocks, and yet there was no doubt where the epicenter of authority in the room was. That old man radiated power like a sun.

Alec moved off to join his wife near the door, leaving me alone in the center of the room. Jason broke off his conversation as I approached, watching me come. He had no idea what I would say, probably expected an ugly scene, yet he seemed genuinely pleased to see me. He rose courteously and smiled. He was a monster, responsible for untold agony in my life. If I'd been armed, I might have shot him. But somehow I couldn't hate him. We were beyond that. In uncharted waters.

The room gradually fell silent as newspeople and spectators shifted their attention toward us expectantly.

"Mitch," Jason said easily, "you know Jerry Hoffman, of course. Have you met Mr. Kessler and Mrs. Grebe of the *News?*"

"Hello." I nodded, swallowing, steeling myself. "Look, I'm not used to this kind of thing," I said, raising my voice, "so I'll be brief. Mr. Deveraux, ladies and gentlemen, on behalf of my late father, Shannon Mitchell, I'd like to present the Deveraux Institute with his collection of maritime artifacts, with an appraised value of some thirty thousand dollars."

Polite applause interrupted me. While I waited it out, I placed my briefcase on a corner of the table and popped the lid. "In addition," I continued, "I'd like to take this opportunity to return the fee for a salvage commission my father accepted from the Institute shortly before his death, in the amount of two hundred and fifty thousand dollars."

There was a moment of breathless silence. Jason didn't

move, didn't react. Then Alec began clapping, triggering a round of applause from everyone but the cameramen shooting the event. In the end, even Jason joined in, but his eyes never left my face. He let the applause continue a few moments, then waved it to a halt.

"Miss Mitchell, as chairman of the board of directors of the Institute, I'd like to thank you. Such generosity on the part of a young businesswoman like yourself shames us; it truly does. In fact, it makes me feel so personally inspired that I'm going to match your donation—in your late father's name, of course. Why don't the two of us adjourn to the library office, put our heads together, and see if we can't come up with a clever way to spend all this cash? If any of you folks have any questions, I'm sure my son, Alec, can field 'em."

Jason offered me his arm. I ignored it and walked briskly behind the checkout desk to the librarian's office. Hoffman rose to follow, but Jason waved him off. He followed me in, closed the door behind us, and leaned against it, eyeing me in silence.

"I don't understand," Jason said at last. "What do you think you've accomplished by this little gambit? I don't care about the money. I told you that."

"I know." I nodded. "I believe you. It's what makes you so damned dangerous. Three people are dead because you don't care about money. You throw it around like so much bloody bait and then act surprised when sharks show up. Well, if there are any more sharks out there, I want to be certain they know I don't have it anymore."

"I see. And that's all there is to it?"

"Not quite," I said. "Robinette said you planned to hire a small army of lawyers to try to win custody of my son. True?"

"Alec has certain rights—"

"You can stop hiding behind Alec, you bastard. This is between you and me. It always has been."

He hesitated a moment, scanning my face, making an instant evaluation. "All right"—he nodded—"between us, then. What do you want, Mitch?"

"To be free of you. I want your signature on an agreement giving up all claims on my son. In return, I agree to forego any claims or criminal charges against you. Here," I said, taking it out of my jacket and passing it to him. "It's a consent decree. You don't admit to anything, but it covers the situation."

He laid it carefully on the desk without reading it. "Criminal charges? You must be joking."

"There's nothing funny about rape. And juries are a lot more sympathetic than they used to be."

"But a rape complaint filed ten years after the fact? Against me? It would never stand up in court."

"Sure it would. It'll be ugly, but easy. Corey is the living proof that it happened. DNA tests can establish paternity—yours, not Alec's. Your defense would have to be that I consented, but since I was only a teenager at the time and you were—what, fifty-five?—I doubt a jury would buy that."

"It would still come down to my word against yours. And since my word does carry a certain weight—"

"Wrong," I said, cutting him off. "There was a witness, one who was there and can verify my story every step of the way."

"What witness?"

"Alec," I said.

"An empty threat, Mitch. Alec would never testify against me."

"Maybe not," I conceded. "To be honest, I'm not sure what he'd do. But let's say it does come to a trial and Alec's subpoenaed. Are you absolutely sure he'll lie under oath to protect you? Especially since, by telling the truth and helping to convict you, he'll probably get control of everything you have? Position, power, all of it."

Jason said nothing. His eyes were locked on mine.

"Think about it," I said. "Alec's a lot like you. In his place, which would you do? Perjure yourself? Or do the right and honorable thing and tell the truth?"

"Yes," he said slowly, "you have a point." He picked up the paper and scanned it. His hands were trembling. Suddenly, he looked every minute of his age, and more. "Who drew this up? Was it Alec?"

I didn't answer.

"All right." He nodded. "You win—for now." He placed the agreement on the desk, signed both copies, and passed me one. "Anything else?"

"Yeah. Do us both a favor. Fire Jerry Hoffman. He's dangerous."

"He's also incompetent," Jason said bitterly. "I gave him a task and all I got was a body count. I fully intend to . . . reassign him, after a prudent interval, of course."

There was more I wanted to say. I wanted to tell him what I really . . .

It wouldn't matter. He wouldn't care. I turned and stalked to the door.

"Mitch," he called after me. "You may think you've won, but you haven't really. In a few years, the boy will be legally an adult. I can offer him far more than you'll ever be able to. If he chooses to join me, you won't be able to prevent it."

"I won't have to," I said, turning to face him. "By the time Corey comes into his own, you won't want him anymore."

"Really? And why not?"

"Because you'll be past it," I said evenly. "You're already losing your edge. I doubt my father could have conned you out of a quarter million a few years ago with a couple of phony letters. You hired a shyster like Robinette without realizing flashing money at him was like dropping a baby in a gator pit. You're slipping, Jason. In a few years, the last thing you'll want is to bring a young wolf into your fold. You'll be scrambling just to hold on. I don't have to fight you to win. I only have to wait."

His smile was a trifle too quick, trying to camouflage a wince. Some part of what I'd said struck home. It was true and he knew it. It wasn't much of a victory after what he'd put me through. But it was something.

In the main room, the crowd had thinned a bit. Charlie Bauer was standing by the display table, waiting for me.

"I delivered your briefcase to the bank," he said. "Quite a little show you put on."

"It's not quite over yet," I said. "There's more."

"What do you mean?"

"Why don't you to come to the point tonight for supper and maybe I'll tell you the rest of it."

"Maybe?" he echoed.

"I need to think about it, Charlie. All I can promise you is a meal. Will you come?"

"I'll be there," he said. "Is this a business dinner, or pleasure?"

"I don't know," I said. "We'll see."

CHAPTER 46

I WENT BACK TO WORK the next day, but it was impossible. Everyone wanted to talk about the donation and the . . . incident on the beach. I finally gave it up, told Red to tell people I'd gone home, dropped the blinds on my office door, and tried to lose myself in paperwork. It worked, sort of. Sometimes I'd get so lost in the figures, I'd forget Rob and . . . everything. For two or three minutes at a time.

The evening with Charlie had been a disaster. We were both on edge, as though a bomb was ticking away beneath the dinner table. And in a sense, one was. In the end, I gave him what he came for. Then wondered if I'd made the biggest mistake of my life.

I stayed late at the Nest, working straight through. Around ten, there was a rap on the door. "Mitch? You in there?" Terry.

He looked changed, more . . . adult. He'd gotten his hair trimmed and he was wearing a dark suit. Even a tie.

"I heard about your trouble," he said. "How you makin' it?"

"I'll get by. Why the suit? Is it prom night?"

"Worse. A funeral." He groaned, slumping into one of the captain's chairs, loosening the tie. "Just flew in from Miami. Jason asked me to accompany Addison's body home, talk to his folks."

"You? Not Andrea?"

"Yeah, well, Andy's not very good at that kinda thing. I'm not crazy about funerals either, but ol' Jason could talk a bear into a broccoli diet."

"Jason? Are you two on a first-name basis now?"

"Um, yeah, I suppose we are," he said, trying not to look smug. "I've been helping out a little. Andrea's been pretty shaken up by this whole thing."

"I can imagine."

"In fact, that's one reason I stopped by. She wants to fly down to Acapulco this weekend, get away from it all. She asked me to tag along." He tossed a key ring on the desk. "Do me a favor and see the *Kidd* gets beached and stored for me? I'd appreciate it."

"It's a little early in the season to pack it in, isn't it? What about your other charters?"

"I canceled 'em all and cut Baggers loose. I expect I'm going to be pretty busy for a while."

"With Andrea," I said.

"Looks like it." He nodded. "No hard feelings, I hope?"

"None at all," I said, meaning it. "In fact, I think we should have a drink on it. You want to do the honors?"

"Absolutely." He grinned, relieved. He crossed to the liquor cabinet and poured two snifters of Courvoisier. "I'm really glad you're taking it well, Mitch. To tell you the truth, I was a little worried. Well, anyway . . ." He handed me the glass. "You're all right, Mitch. You always were."

I rose, reading his face, his very special face. I raised my glass. "A toast. To Stanley Joseph Maychek. God rest his soul."

"To . . ." Terry paused, his snifter halfway to his lips. "To who? Who the hell's Stanley—whatever?"

"You don't recognize the name? You should. He's a friend of yours, a good friend. He's the one who helped you kill Addison."

He paled, as though he'd been struck. "What are you talking about?"

"I'm talking about Stanley Maychek, the second officer of the *Queen of Lorraine*. The guy I met in the salon. You should have warned me, Terry. I might've been okay if you'd warned me."

"You were raving about a body when we pulled you out," he said warily, "but I didn't see one. Christ, the way the room was silted up, there could have been an army in there and I wouldn't have seen 'em."

"But you knew Maychek was there," I said. "You put him there to scare Harvey away from the door. And it worked. But he didn't belong in there, Terry. He told me."

"He told . . ." Terry echoed, eyeing me oddly.

"It doesn't matter." I shrugged. "I would have figured it out, anyway. He was the second mate, and there'd been a collision. I don't know where he was when she rolled, checking damage in the hold, or maybe aft warning the crew, but the one place he wouldn't have been was all the way forward in the passenger salon. The room's a dead end and there weren't any passengers. My guess is that he was on duty in the pilothouse. I noticed the door'd been pried open. Is that where you found him?"

"I don't know what you're talking about, Mitch. No stiff killed Addison; Rats did. He contaminated a set of your tanks the night he burned your boat."

"No. Jud didn't burn anything, Terry. He couldn't. He's dead. Has been since that night on the ice. What people saw the night *Sheba* burned was a guy with a mark on his face, wearing a plaid coat. Sounds like Jud all right, but they were summer people. None of them actually knew him."

"But I know him, and I sure as hell saw him."

"That's right, and it's the one thing I'll never forgive you for—letting me hope that Jud had survived. But he didn't. They found his coat, Terry, when they were diving—off the point. It's been in the water for months. He's dead. But you said you saw him, and you couldn't have been mistaken. So you lied."

"Mitch, you're not makin' much sense."

"Sure I am, and we both know it. You want me to lay it out for you? You've always had a thing for Andrea, and seeing her, all of her, this summer set if off again. You wanted Addison gone. No problem. It's easy to off somebody in deep water, turn a valve, puncture a hose, nothing to it. The trouble was that people knew about you and Andrea. So if the lady's husband had an accident, you'd be the prime suspect. You needed somebody to pin it on. And lucky you. You had a friend who was in a lot of trouble. Suppose somebody tried to kill her and got Harvey by mistake?"

"Mitch—"

"Let me finish, Terry. I spent a lot of time working this out. You had to make Harvey's death look like it was meant for me. So you brought Jud back. You dressed like him, smeared on a fake birthmark. Then you pried open the door of the Nest, set the *Sheba* afire, and made enough noise to be sure you'd be seen—or rather, that Jud would."

I waited for him to argue with me, to deny it. But he didn't. He just stared into his brandy glass, avoiding my eyes.

"The rest was a snap. You asked me to film the dive on the *Queen*, knowing I'd do it. Because we were *friends*. And since I didn't have a boat anymore, you did me the favor of toting my tanks out to the dive site on the *Kidd*. Then you drained enough air out of Harvey's tanks to make 'em read low. So he had to borrow mine, the only set that matched his."

"The way I hear it, only one of your sets was poisoned," Terry said carefully. "I didn't tell the chick that works in the shop which set to give me. She chose 'em."

"I wondered about that. You couldn't have contaminated the tanks while they were under pressure, and the odds were against Harvey getting the only bad set. In fact, I'd already used a set that morning teaching my class. But it didn't matter which set he borrowed. There was nothing wrong with any of them."

"No? Charlie had the air in the tanks analyzed. The set Harvey used was laced with carbon dioxide."

"Right, and Harvey's blood had high levels of carbon dioxide. But it didn't come from my tanks. He just ran out of oxygen down there. You set it up beautifully, Terry. You deliberately worked into your safety margin. Harvey was so hot to get that plaque that he probably never noticed. Then you slipped away in the murk and shoved Stanley in to guard the door on your way out. And when Harvey realized you'd gone and tried to follow, he ran into Stanley—and panicked. He hyperventilated just like I did, used up most of his remaining air in just a few seconds. . . ." I sipped my brandy, trying to wash down the faint taste of bile in the back of my throat. It didn't help.

"And right then he was a dead man," I continued quietly. "Even if he'd found the door, he'd never have made it down that god-awful corridor. But he didn't. He ran out of air in the salon and died there. The only hitch you ran into was me."

"It wasn't my idea to send you down there, Mitch. You know that."

"I know. You'd probably expected to go back down after Harvey yourself, with Baggers as a witness, or maybe even a cop. And at some point in the murk, you'd slip Harvey's *empty* tanks a quick shot of carbon dioxide from a life-vest cartridge. And everybody'd think Jud killed him trying to get at me. Hell, I thought so myself—until I saw that coat. And even then . . ."

"What?"

"I didn't want to believe it, Terry. I still don't. So why don't you tell me I'm wrong. Show me where I screwed up."

He didn't answer. He just sat there eyeing me like a stranger. "What the hell," he said at last. "I never could win an argument with you, Mitch. You're smarter'n me, and we both know it. So I'm not gonna try to talk you out of anything. Believe what you want. It doesn't matter."

"What do you mean, it doesn't matter? Of course it does."

"No, it really doesn't," he said. "Not anymore. There's nothing left of the *Queen*. And I helped Addison's folks scatter his ashes over the Gulf myself. So even if what you said is true— and I'm not saying it is—there's no way to . . . prove anything. Is there?"

"No," I said, taking a deep breath. "I guess not."

"So. Have you talked to anyone about this?"

"I'm talking to somebody about it now," I said. "The truth is, I'm worried about you, Terry. You were always a hardcase, but this is different. I don't think you can handle it."

"I'll handle it. Damn it, Mitch, the guy was a fourteen-karat phony. Mr. Bigbucks, with Andrea's money. And after he found out we'd had a . . . thing, he really stuck it to me—especially when she was around. He'd snuffle after her like a goddamn lapdog and then expect me to kiss his ass. Christ, he wasn't man enough to polish my gear. He was nothin' but a puddle diver, and a lousy one at that."

"And so you killed him? Because he was a puddle diver?"

"I didn't kill him at all! He killed himself, because he panicked when he saw a stiff. He could have made it out. You did. Look, I'm sorry as hell about what happened to you down there. You know that. But I didn't ask you to go down there; Bauer did. It wasn't my fault."

"Maybe not altogether, but you could have warned me about the body, Terry. I would have warned you."

"What could I say with Bauer standing there? Sorry, Mitch, but if you're gonna play a man's game, you take your chances like everybody else. Far as I'm concerned, you and Harvey both had bad luck in deep water. I'm glad you made it. Too bad for him."

"I'm sorry you're going to play it this way." I sighed. "I hoped . . . Well, I guess it doesn't matter." I picked up his key ring and tossed it back to him. "You'd better have someone else look after the *Kidd* for you. Ask a friend."

"Fair enough," he said evenly. "I'll do that. But if I were you, I wouldn't talk to anyone else about what you think happened down there."

"It's a little late for that," I said. "Too many people know about it already."

"What do you mean? Who knows about it?"

"Stanley Maychek, me, and Harvey. And most of all, you."

"You really have flipped out, you know that?"

"Probably," I conceded, "but I know you, Terry. Better than anyone, I think. This thing will destroy you eventually. And you won't make much of a lapdog, either."

"That's really the bottom line here, isn't it?" he said, his eyes hard and feverish. "It's Andrea. That's what's really eating you. You're jealous. You were so jealous the last time, you fucked up your whole life. Well, I've got a second chance and I'm gonna take it—Andrea, everything. You think I killed Addison? Fine. Keep it in mind. And from now on, stay the hell out of my way!"

"Terry!" I called after him as he stalked out. "Don't go to your boat!"

"What?" he said, hesitating in the doorway.

"Don't go to your boat, or your house. The DNR raided your place last night and found enough artifacts to buy you a twenty-year stretch. They're looking for you."

"They raided my house?" he said, incredulous. "But why . . . My God. You incredible bitch! You burned me, didn't you?"

"Not exactly. Charlie Bauer was at my place last night. He saw the piece you gave me after you torched the *Sheba*. He asked me where I got it. And I couldn't think of a good reason to lie to him. Not for you. Not anymore. As you said, you play the game, you take your chances."

He stormed out, slamming the door behind him. I watched him through the glass as he shouldered his way angrily through the crowd. For a man who had everything, he didn't look very happy.

Or maybe he's right. Maybe I'm just jealous. But I don't think so. In spite of everything, I don't hate him. In fact, I almost hope he makes it to Acapulco with Andrea. He's earned it.

And he deserves it.

But it won't be enough. The girl he really wants is a mirage, a dream from a long-lost summer. First loves are like that: hard to let go. The danger is that if you hold on to dreams too long, and your luck's really bad . . . sometimes they come true.

⚓ I have dreams of my own now, new and bright. I want to bring my son . . . home to this country. And we'll run in the hills together and sail in the bay. And I'll teach him to dive in deep water and to live in the world.

For good or ill, that godforsaken point is my home now, the

place my soul belongs. I knew every inch of it as a girl, and I'm learning it again.

Sometimes on warm afternoons, I take a good book and walk out to that old lonesome pine near the water's edge. And I climb up to its second fork and nestle down in its boughs and read the day away, swaying high above the dunes and the surf, halfway to heaven. Up in the first Crow's Nest.

And sometimes I drift and dream, and the lake breeze tousles my hair, and it's my father, saying good night the way he used to all those years ago.

But more often, it's her—the Lady of the Lake. The only mother I've ever known. Cradling me in the sky. Rocking me to sleep.

And sometimes, just at dusk, when the sun is lowering and the air is still, I swear I can hear her singing softly, down and down, in the deep green halls of her icewater mansions.

Build yourself a library of paperback mysteries to die for—DEAD LETTER

NINE LIVES TO MURDER by Marian Babson
When actor Winstanley Fortescue takes a nasty fall—or
was he pushed?—he finds himself trapped in the body of
Monty, the backstage cat.
_____ 95580-4 ($4.99 U.S.)

THE BRIDLED GROOM by J. S. Borthwick
While planning their wedding, Sarah and Alex—a Nick
and Nora Charles of the 90's—must solve a mystery at
the High Hope horse farm.
_____ 95505-7 ($4.99 U.S./$5.99 Can.)

THE FAMOUS DAR MURDER MYSTERY
by Graham Landrum
The search for the grave of a Revolutionary War soldier
takes a bizarre turn when the ladies of the DAR stumble
on a modern-day corpse.
_____ 95568-5 ($4.50 U.S./$5.50 Can.)

COYOTE WIND by Peter Bowen
Gabriel Du Pré, a French-Indian fiddle player and part-
time deputy, investigates a murder in the state of mind
called Montana.
_____ 95601-0 ($4.50 U.S./$5.50 Can.)